THE UNFORTUNATE DECISIONS OF DAHLIA MOSS

A NOVEL
(IRL)

MAX WIRESTONE

REDHOOK

www.redhookbooks.com

Copyright © 2015 by Max Wirestone

Redhook Books/Orbit
Hachette Book Group
1290 Avenue of the Americas
New York, NY 10104
www.HachetteBookGroup.com

Printed in the United States of America

RRD-C

First edition: October 2015

10 9 8 7 6 5 4 3 2 1

Redhook is an imprint of Orbit, a division of Hachette Book Group.
The Redhook name and logo are trademarks of Hachette Book Group, Inc.

The Hachette Speakers Bureau provides a wide range of authors for speaking events. To find out more, go to www.hachettespeakersbureau.com or call (866) 376-6591.

The publisher is not responsible for websites (or their content) that are not owned by the publisher.

Library of Congress Cataloging-in-Publication Data

Wirestone, Max.
    The unfortunate decisions of Dahlia Moss / Max Wirestone.
        pages cm
    Summary: "Meet Dahlia Moss, the reigning queen of unfortunate decision-making in the Saint Louis area. Unemployed, broke, and on her last bowl of ramen, she's not living her best life. But that's all about to change. Before Dahlia can make her life any messier on her own, she's offered a job. A job that she's woefully underqualified for. A job that will lead her to a murder, an MMORPG, and possibly a fella (or two?). Turns out unfortunate decisions abound, and she's just the girl to deal with them"—Provided by publisher.
        ISBN 978-0-316-38597-8 (hardback)—ISBN 978-0-316-38599-2 (ebook)—ISBN 978-1-4789-0675-9 (audio book [downloadable]) 1. Single women—Fiction. 2. Murder—Investigation—Fiction. I. Title.
    PS3623.I74U54 2015
    813'.6—dc23
                                                                    2015013856

For Clay, who's checking, and Baxter, who isn't.

THE
UNFORTUNATE
DECISIONS OF
DAHLIA
MOSS

CHAPTER ONE

The only time I ever met Jonah Long he was wearing a fake beard, a blue pin-striped captain's outfit, and a toy pipe that blew soap bubbles. He did not seem like someone who was about to change my life.

"I have a proposition for you," he told me. Admittedly, that does sound like the kind of thing a life-changing person might say. It's right up there with "It's dangerous to go alone—take this!" and "You are the chosen one." But a plastic bubble pipe really takes the edge off this sort of thing.

It was a nautical-themed party, which partly explained his ridiculous outfit. I thought he was hitting on me. "I'm in a non-dating phase," I told him. Not entirely true, but I repeat: bubble pipe.

"A financial proposition, Dahlia."

I had no idea who he was. I was irked that he knew my name, but it was clear from the way Charice was hovering over him that my roommate was involved. She was wearing an over-sized mermaid's outfit that made her look faintly seal-like—especially with her mugging at me as Jonah spoke. Eh? Eh? I felt like I should throw a fish at her.

But really, what could I do? I had seventeen dollars and

1

twenty-three cents in my bank account at the time of this exchange, with less in savings. I could only use ATMs that dispensed tens. Despite my correct sense that Jonah was (1) ridiculous and (2) trouble, at the phrase "financial proposition," he had my undivided attention.

"Come into my office," I told him.

I didn't have an office, to be clear. Actually, this is a good time to come clean on all the things I didn't have, just to get them taken care of, right up front.

Things Dahlia Moss Did Not Have:

- a job
- an internship
- cheerful prospects of finding a job
- a reliable car
- a boyfriend
- supportive family members
- rent
- any skill or experience as a detective

Honestly, that's just hitting the highlights, but I feel they look less depressing as bullet points. Still with me? If you are, you can't say I didn't warn you.

Anyway, no office. What I did have was a room—or more technically, Charice's room, which she let me sleep in for free.

"Quite a place you've got here," said Jonah.

He was referring to the fact that there were no decorations of any kind, just cheap, misshapen furniture and blank beige walls. This is what happens when garage sales keep you financially afloat.

"What's your financial proposition?" I asked, gesturing for

Jonah to sit in a sagging director's chair while taking the luxury of the folding bed for myself. At business meetings, I had read, it was best to take the position of power, although I doubt a folding bed is what *Forbes* had in mind.

I could tell that Jonah was getting serious, because he took off his beard.

"I want you to recover the Bejeweled Spear of Infinite Piercing."

This is the kind of statement that makes one pause, and it is especially the kind of statement that makes one pause when it immediately follows a debearding. First, the debearding: It was like one of those teen movies where the ugly girl takes off her glasses and is revealed to be a bombshell. Except that here we were moving from community theater sea captain to J.Crew model, which I would argue is a greater distance.

"The Bejeweled Spear of what?"

"Infinite Piercing," said Jonah solemnly.

"How can something be infinitely pierced?"

Jonah was not interested in this sad and overly literal question. "It's been stolen from me, and I want you to recover it."

"Maybe an earlobe shaped like a Klein bottle?"

But earlobe-based math puzzles were not why Jonah was here. "Don't get lost in the weeds," he said. "The important thing is that the spear was mine, and I want you to recover it from the thief who stole it away from me."

And here Jonah looked deeply satisfied and proceeded to blow bubbles from that damned plastic pipe. The noise was appealing, but it looked ridiculous.

It bears mentioning that this was not the first ridiculous boy that Charice had funneled through our apartment. Charice specialized in ridiculous, and so I got guests not unlike Jonah with relative frequency. They didn't usually have quests for me, but I've seen lots of strange birds pass through. Charice favors odd theme parties that just sort of happen, like flash mobs. Literally, I've gone to the bathroom for a span of time and come back to find three people dressed like vampires in our sitting room. My general strategy for dealing with Charice's parade of guests was to treat them as a sort of living theater. Occasionally, they were.

"All right, fine. Tell me more about the spear," I told him, only half holding back a sigh.

"It's an item from the Kingdoms of Zoth," said Jonah.

Ah. Now I saw where we were going. It still didn't make sense, but I could at least recognize the general destination. I waited for an explanation from Jonah, not because I didn't know what the Kingdoms of Zoth were, but because I had hoped that he would imagine I was the sort of person who didn't know what the Kingdoms of Zoth were. He didn't. Ah well.

Zoth is an MMORPG. That's Massively Multiplayer Online Role-Playing Game. One of those computer games with a million people playing at once. In this case, imaginary avatars dressing up in knights' armor and parapets and killing griffins—that sort of thing.

The truth is, I knew quite a bit more about it than that. *Zoth* was a niche game—there are other, bigger games you've probably heard about. *World of Warcraft*, or *EverQuest*, or *The Lord of the Rings Online*. Those were games that had commercials on Hulu. Inviting, easy-to-learn. *Zoth* was a game for the hard-core. There weren't commercials, because they didn't want everyone playing. This game was for the serious, for the connoisseur. For the type of detail-oriented guy who would put together an elaborate and expensive sea captain's costume, complete with bubble pipe.

"You want me to find a stolen item from an imaginary world?"

"Not imaginary, Dahlia. Digital. These are entirely separate things."

The conversation had gotten weird, even given my usually high standards. To recap: A man dressed as a sea captain had sneaked away from one of Charice's nautical-themed parties and wanted to hire me for detective work in a video game. There were countless reasons to question this proposal. And even blinded by the prospects of an ATMable sum of money, I found a couple of them myself.

"Why hire me for this? Surely you can find someone more qualified."

Jonah clearly had been anticipating this question, because he answered in a smooth and curiously rehearsed way. "Oh, I think you'll do. I've heard that you've played *Zoth* yourself. And that you have some experience working for a detective agency."

That last bit was very carefully phrased. I wondered who had fed him the line and had to assume it was Charice. "Some experience working for a detective agency" is technically true if we understand that "some" means two days and "experience" means answering the phone as a temp. I explained this to Jonah, who did not seem to regard my confession as a revelation.

"It's immaterial," Jonah told me, "because I've already got everything all worked out. I already know who took the spear."

My grandmother used to say that there was nothing worse than trust-fund kids with plans, and I find myself thinking of her now as I type this account. Jonah had both in spades, although at the time I understood neither the depth of his wealth nor his designs on me. I just thought I was being presented with a suspiciously well-wrapped package. Emphasis on "suspiciously." But who were we kidding; I was a pauper, and I needed the package.

"What is it, exactly, that you would like for me to do?" I asked with a glimmering notion that this was the sort of question a drug mule might pose.

"I want you to meet up with the thief and shake him down."

I was looking at Jonah, and he was clearly making the sort of face that Satan makes when he's on the cusp of adding a new soul to his collection. There I was, watching the mischievous gleam in his eye and thinking this was surely some kind of trap, but I couldn't escape the gravitational pull of money. Jonah could sense it too, because he volunteered details on payment without my even asking.

"One thousand dollars, right now. Another thousand after you've met with the thief. That's my offer; take it or leave it."

One thousand dollars buys a lot of ramen. Things had gotten so rough for me in the past few weeks that I had to walk to job interviews because I could not afford the bus. There was no choice here, not really.

"Well, Jonah. You just bought yourself a detective."

———————◆———————

Jonah handed me an envelope.

"Open it," he said with a twinkle in his eye. The kind of sparkle you'd find on Santa's face. Or a mental patient's.

I opened it. It was brimming with twenties. One thousand dollars in twenty-dollar bills. Hundreds would have been more sensible, but the weight of the twenties made me feel rich, and I suddenly couldn't stop smiling. I don't know if it was Jonah's intent, but nothing quells skepticism like money.

"There's a note as well," said Jonah.

And so there was. When I got over my euphoria, I discovered a small sheet of paper folded into thirds. I unfolded it and read the message.

To: KRISTO
From: REVENGE
What comes around goes around.

I recognized the font, a serif that screamed high fantasy while only whispering legibility, as being from *Zoth*, and so I asked:

"You're Kristo?"

"I am," said Jonah. "Level-sixty human thief at your service."

"Someone sent this to you after the spear was burgled from your account?"

"Exactly," said Jonah. "I can see that you are just the person for this sort of thing."

There was something patronizing in his tone of voice that I frankly should have wondered about, but I had made one thousand dollars in five minutes, and for that price I would take the patronage. Instead, I found myself wondering who would steal a spear and then leave a snarky note. It could only increase the risk of getting caught, and for what? A punch line?

"So you want me to figure out who Revenge is?"

"I know who Revenge is. His name is Kurt Campbell. I think you'll like him; he's very charming."

This was kind of a non sequitur, but I let it slide.

"How do you know that he stole your spear?"

This was a question Jonah had wanted me to ask, because his answer was another of his prepared speeches.

"Up until three weeks ago, he was my roommate and classmate, but through a series of *entanglements*"—and here Jonah put particular emphasis on the word—"Kurt lost his place in our graduate program. Following that, he lost his job, his income, and from there it was a short trip until I asked him to move out. He did not take it well."

I was more than a few months behind in rent, and I hoped Jonah did not know that I was living on Charice's largess.

"You aren't hurting for money," I said, gesturing to my envelope of twenties. "You don't need a roommate to contribute to rent. Why kick him out?"

"Oh," said Jonah, bored. "The principle of the thing."

"We're not talking drug addiction or something ugly here?"

"Ho, ho, ho," said Jonah, which was an incongruous laugh for someone in a sea captain's costume. Even beardless, one expected some sort of *yarr*. "No, Kurt's not that sort of guy."

"How did he lose his job and his spot in school in one fell swoop?"

"Entanglements," said Jonah.

I had somehow known that's what he was going to say.

When I was a second-grader, my older brother, Alden, was deeply into *Dungeons & Dragons*, and talking to Jonah suddenly reminded me of Alden's stories. He would design these elaborate adventures and was so desperate to have someone play with him that he would occasionally try to make me fit the bill. I loved playing—I always idolized Alden, plus the game had horses—but I never seemed to go where Alden wanted me to. He'd present me with a quest, and rather than killing the dragon, I would linger about the princess's castle. He'd always get all clammy on the details whenever I was somewhere he hadn't planned on me being. What's the throne room look like, Alden? *I don't know . . . gray?* Is there a banner? *I guess.* What does the banner look like? *It's also gray.* Are there pictures of flowers on it? *No.* But when you went to where Alden wanted you to be, you were drowning in description.

The roommate losing his job was a gray banner in a gray room. So I did what I had done with my brother. I tried to figure out where he wanted me to go.

"So," I said. "You ousted your roommate, and you think that he stole some bauble from you in *Zoth* as retaliation. Was anything else stolen?"

"No," said Jonah. "Just the spear."

"Did you play *Zoth* with Kurt?" Surely yes. I had played *Zoth* only a little, and the idea of breaking into someone's account and stealing something of value seemed daunting. How would you know what had value? Oh, the Bejeweled Spear of Infinite Piercing sounded impressive enough, but *Zoth* was one of those games in which everything sounded impressive. You'd load Truesilver Arrows of Unerring Path into your Wildwood Bow of Goblin Striking while sipping on Improved Plumberry Tea of Mana Replenishment. This was at level two.

"We played together, yes. He was part of my guild, the Event Horizons."

"A very techie name for *Zoth*, isn't it?"

"The guild migrated over from *Martian Chron*—"

"Who else is in your guild?"

And Jonah suddenly got rather sharp with me. At the time I assumed that it was because I had interrupted him. "The guild is not important," he said, his voice suddenly loud. And then he returned, just as suddenly, to his previous cherubic mood. "What I mean to say is that you do not need to trouble yourself with the rest of the Horizons. It's Kurt you should be interested in."

Given that Jonah had just given me one thousand dollars, it seemed wise to stay off topics that made him raise his voice.

"Kurt knew that the spear was important to you."

"Well, yes," said Jonah, pleased that we were back on track. "But everyone would have known that. *Zoth* has more than a half million players, and there is a single spear. Think about that."

I did think about it, and it did not impress me very much. But I was not a *Zoth* person.

"How did Kurt steal it from you?"

"He took it from my computer," said Jonah hastily. "The machine remembers my password, so if you have access to it, you have access to my account. But that's not important either."

And again, the effect was like being shuttled through one of Alden's games. Look at that, not this. Nothing down that hall, silly girl. Investigate the dragon.

"How about you tell me what's important."

"The important thing is dinner."

Dinner was never the answer in Alden's games, that's for sure.

"As in, what comes after lunch?"

"Yes. The dinner that you're going to tomorrow. I've arranged for you to meet Kurt tomorrow at a nice restaurant. He thinks that he's meeting me. But he won't. He will meet you."

"And I will...?"

"You will tell him that I know that he took the spear. You will inform him that I have hired you as a private detective to ensure its recovery. And he will fold on the spot. Then I'll give you the second thousand dollars, and it will be the easiest money you ever made."

It all seemed impossibly dumb to me, but I was reminded of another of Grandma's sayings: A fool and his money are a golden opportunity. If Jonah was handing out cash for purposes as silly as this, I might as well benefit.

But he was wrong about it being the easiest two grand I ever made. For one, Jonah hadn't known about the Modern Wood-men of America scholarship, which was an easy two grand indeed, if a little hard to reproduce.

For another, he would never live long enough to give me the second thousand dollars.

———————◆———————

After Jonah left, I took a moment to count the twenties and inspect that it really was American currency and not some sort of gummy candy money. Something had to be off—money doesn't just fall out of the sky like that—but I couldn't put my finger on anything that was actually a problem. On the face of it, Jonah was some rich kid who'd been fed a line about my detective skills and was caught up in the romance of having his own private eye. But even as I failed to rub the ink off the money he'd given me, I couldn't shake the feeling that some-thing greater was happening.

I took the bills and placed them inside my copy of *Northanger Abbey*. If I was going to be stolen from, I could at least take consolation from knowing that the thief liked Jane Austen. And then I crept back into the party.

I generally avoided Charice's parties, despite living among them. I was never one for parties, and I was especially against them since I had entered my long, dark era of unemployment. My parents, whom I would describe as sharklike real estate peo-ple, encouraged the idea, suggesting that Charice's gatherings were a good place to "network," but I could never stomach the "What do you do for a living?" questions, which are hard to take after thirteen months of failed job interviews.

I ventured out now. Guests in sailor suits danced while a woman pecked out the theme to *The Love Boat* on the marimba—which is to say that things were just getting started. Charice was making drinks for a boy who, from the looks of it, had dressed as flotsam. Even if my parents had been right about my needing to get my name out there, it's hard to know what you'll gain by networking with flotsam.

I passed by the driftwood and headed straight to Charice. I didn't turn any heads, which is good, because I felt under-dressed. This is a Dahlia Moss superpower. With my "quiet girl at the library" look, I am genetically suited to not being noticed at parties. In my best moments, I think I look like Carmen Sandi-ego, with long wavy brown hair and sunglasses and a fedora. Setting aside the fact that I don't wear a lot of fedoras. In my worst moments, I think I look like Roz from *Monsters, Inc.*, but maybe everyone thinks that.

"Did you put Jonah Long up to that?"

"No," said Charice. "Put him up to what?"

The question must have taken her by surprise, because it was not in Charice's nature to deny involvement with anything. Most of the time, this was simply because she *was* involved, but even in the rare case that she wasn't, it wasn't like her to just say no. More often you would get a raised eyebrow and Mona Lisa smile, suggesting that she was possibly involved, even if she didn't know precisely what you were talking about.

Charice was the head-turner at parties, by the way. I like to think of Charice as a *jolie laide*, which is my way saying that I don't really understand why men constantly throw them-selves at her. She's not really—a *jolie laide* is supposed to have a "flaw" that somehow makes her more beautiful, like a big nose that's somehow entrancing and perfect. Or snaggle teeth. Or alopecia, although you see that one a lot less. But I couldn't tell you what Charice's flaw was. She looks like Peppermint Patty, but grown up and with 0 percent body fat.

I parried her question for now, but I knew that I would have to answer her eventually. "How well do you know him?"

Charice poured a sludgy red substance into a pink plastic cup and slid it over to me. "Drink this. It's my special mix."

Despite some long dark nights of the soul caused by Charice's special mixes, I gave the sludge a swig. It was just the sort of terrifying combination of fruitiness and liquor that I expected.

"How well do you know Jonah?" I asked again.

"Not well. He came to my Seed Time party a few months back. Great fun, but I never saw him again. A shame, because he's a good person to have around at parties. A gentleman of leisure."

I remembered that party. Charice had been inspired by *Harold and Maude* and sent people in teams to plant saplings all over the city. I remembered two biologists getting into a fistfight over a cactus, but I couldn't recall Jonah at all.

"What you mean by 'gentleman of leisure'? He's rich? What do his parents do?"

"His parents *don't* do. They *own*. A pharmaceutical, I think. Anyway, he called me last week and asked me if I had any parties coming up. I told him about this one, and he showed up in that fantastic outfit. I thought we were in for a grand time."

"But?"

"He only wanted to speak to you, Dahlia. He was barely here before he went into your room, and when he came out he bailed on me altogether. What did you do, punch him?"

"He gave me one thousand dollars."

Charice considered this. "I didn't realize you would turn out to be such a high-class hooker."

13

I noticed that flotsam boy was taking quite an interest in our conversation, and I brought my voice down to a whisper. "Charice, he hired me to be a detective. You didn't feed him lines about how I worked for an agency last year?"

"No," said Charice, her face practically splitting in half with delight. "A detective? That's the best thing I've ever heard."

CHAPTER TWO

I often ask myself why I've gone so long without finding work. Real work—not census taking or working a part, part-time job at a frozen-yogurt place. It's not a question I have a definitive answer for, aside from not interviewing well and, of course, my hideous facial scarring. (I'm kidding about the scarring. But not the interviewing. Jesus God, not the interviewing.) Probably I'm too contrarian for my own good. I don't know where it comes from. I was never one of those rebellious girls in high school. I didn't wear the super-short skirts my parents forbade. I never dated a "bad boy" or wore heaps of black eyeliner. I looked and acted boring. I always have. My destiny probably involves me knitting tea cozies.

And yet, I've got a certain rebelliousness I just can't shake. What was the one thing that Jonah asked me not to do? Talk to his guild mates. And what was I doing? I was logging in to *Zoth*, for the first time in two years, looking for a member of the Horizons to talk with. This is not the behavior of someone who aces interviews.

It wasn't hard work. Most of the trouble was loading the hours' worth of patches to the game since I had played last. I knew the name of Jonah's guild, so I just looked them up online. It's not like there was any secrecy. They had their own webpage. Once I figured out who I was looking for, it was just a matter of typing in names in a /whereis routine until I found someone in a zone nearby.

I had hit the Random button on character creation until I entered the world as a male elven archer with a blue pompadour. That might sound interesting to you, but in *Zoth*, this was the equivalent of wallpaper paste. I would blend in anywhere.

After a couple of false starts, I eventually learned that some-one named "Tambras" was afk—away from keyboard—in a pub not too far from where I entered the world.

A few minutes later, I entered the Pirate's Mead Tavern. As digital bars go, it was jolly. There were parrots, the sounds of loud, boisterous laughter and drinking—even though there weren't too many people around—and a tall, bald man playing an accordion. It's the kind of place that would be utterly aggra-vating to visit in real life, but translated to a computer moni-tor, it seemed cozy and fun. In real life, that bald guy would be looking at my breasts and would eventually expect a tip.

I found Tambras leaning against a wall, tossing knives into the air. He looked like a smooth operator. He was a high-level character, decked out in patterned nubuck leather, and looked like he could have been the front man for a medieval rock band. He had an interesting face—not one of the defaults. He'd put some time into it. And his hair—it was thin white stuff that was not your classic fantasy trope. Even the knife routine was cool, some sort of custom idle animation that I assumed he had paid extra for. I knew this was the guy I was looking for, not just because he looked like a Tambras but because the game told me that was his name, in a big serif font floating above his head. Even I couldn't mess that up.

Tambras was still away from keyboard and so, just like on the cop shows, I went to get food. I suppose the classic food-stuff for a stakeout is greasy takeout, but I had a Fresca and some Saltines. No self-respecting private eye would imbibe this combination, but then neither would they be piloting a pom-padoured elf in a half-empty pirate bar. A half box of Saltines later, Tambras packed away his knives and was on the move.

"Oh, hey there, Tambras!" I typed.

Tambras turned around. His eyes were different colors, I noticed, now that he was looking dead at me. One blue, one purple. Someone was a Bowie fan?

"Do I know you?" he said.

"Well," I said. "A friend of mine is trying to get me to join your guild. Do you have a second?"

"Who?" said Tambras. "What friend?"

It's important to point out here that this is all just typing—there's no actual *conversation*. But I felt as though I could hear the skepticism in Tambras's voice. Who would invite *you*?

"His real-life name is Jonah Long," I told him.

Tambras frowned at me. Literally, the character frowned—and he had to type six extra characters to express the emotion.

"Why did I have to ask?"

"Oh, I'm sorry," I told him. "Do you not get along with Jonah?" This was the wrong question, I instantly realized. The most important thing was to get Tambras talking to me. It's not like real life, where people have an obligation to communicate. One wrong word and our knife thrower would be on his merry way, especially this early in the conversation, when I was just another generic elf. But despite my wincing, he stuck around.

"That wasn't what I meant, but now that you mention it, no. I don't. Jonah is not my favorite guy."

17

"Oh. Sorry."

There was a pause, at which point I felt sure that Tambras was going to leave. But it didn't happen, and so I asked:

"What did you mean, then?"

"Jonah just invites everyone into the guild. Almost everyone knows him personally. "

"Do you know him personally?"

"Well, no, not *me*. Just all the new folks. And maybe Orchardary. But it's like a disease. Eventually his mother will be playing with us."

"rotfl," I typed, even though this wasn't particularly funny. Mrs. Dalloway I wasn't, but Tambras kept looking at me. "He's really more of an acquaintance anyway." I told him. "But he was telling me something about some kind of theft?"

"Hrmph."

Who types "hrmph"?

"I don't want to join a guild where you might get stolen from by your own teammates," I said to Tambras. "Does that kind of thing happen all the time?"

"I don't know, he's your friend."

"Acquaintance," I repeated, because it seemed to me that if I wanted to keep talking to Tambras, acquaintance was the way to go. And it was true, anyway, not that it mattered.

"What was he doing, bragging?" typed Tambras.

I stopped for a second, because it seemed like the conversation had made a turn that I didn't follow. It's like when you're talking to your aunt about the new Spider-Man movie, and everyone is suddenly saying that it tastes like blueberries. A beat has been missed.

"Bragging about being my acquaintance?" I asked, though I knew this couldn't be right.

Tambras /scoffed at me. He had quite the glossary of emoticons.

"No, you nitwit," he said. "About the theft."

Yes, this was all tasting like blueberries. Nothing to do but soldier forward, though.

"He seemed really bummed about it. He couldn't believe that someone would steal the spear."

Tambras looked at me blankly. "Jonah stole the spear."

"What?!"

"What."

"He told me it was stolen from him."

"I don't know anything about that," said Tambras. "Maybe you should talk more to your *acquaintance* about it." And, yes, he actually put the italics there. The boy was a wordsmith. But then he took off.

I went to bed troubled. The warm glow of having money for rent and food didn't last nearly as long as I had hoped.

———◆———

I woke at eight and began the laborious process of putting myself together for a job interview. At this point I regarded job interviews less as a means to get a job and more as a ritualistic process of destroying the ego, the way some religions believe suffering brings you closer to God.

I had a particular outfit I used for these sorts of thing—my navy blue dress suit, which barely showed ketchup stains at all, and which Charice described as "thready." And also, lately, a pair of black high heels, because my mother insisted that interviewers like to see women in high heels, and at this point I would try anything. The heels were a recent addition to my arsenal, and I didn't really have the knack for them.

So I was teetering around the apartment when there was a

knock at my door. The shock of a visitor in the pre-noon hours nearly knocked me over, although my acumen with heels was low enough that I might have just fallen over anyway.

It was a courier with a package from Jonah Long.

I thanked the guy profusely, being unable to tip him, and waited until he left to open the package. I don't know what I had expected to find—I suppose something detective-y. Maybe a clue. But instead there was clothing.

Jonah had bought me clothes. I read the card:

Dahlia:

Just noticed you were looking a little worn, and so I picked up a few things to help you look the part.

Jonah

I can't honestly remember if there was a period of shock before I became angry. There must have been, but I have no memory of it. I just remember thinking, *That arrogant little prick. I'm going to break his face.*

And the clothes—please don't imagine this as some kind of *Cinderella / Pretty Woman* moment. They just seemed to be a random collection, as though Jonah had stopped by a high-class Salvation Army on the way home. There was something called a "casino tux" jacket, a black-and-white number that looked like something a stylish croupier might wear. There was a gray wool pencil skirt that seemed to be part of the sexy librarian collection and a silver metallic blouse with a houndstooth print. Oh, and a hat, a gray flannel cloche bucket hat. A fucking bucket hat. Was this just stuff from his grandma's closet?

It was bizarre, and I didn't like the notion that Jonah felt that he could dress me up, as if I were now his doll. If he had gotten me a classic detective's trench coat, I would have been happier, but even then I would have had some reservations. Instead he got me the outfit of a Manic Pixie Dream Girl in her late seventies.

I put the clothes on anyway. It was that contrarian bit in me. I'd show Jonah Long. I was going to wear them and look ridiculous doing it. In front of him.

And for all their inappropriateness, they fit me like a glove. If I'd been more of a detective, I might have wondered why Jonah's clothes all fit me so perfectly.

———————◆———————

I had some misgivings about this morning's interview, but the deeper you get into unemployment, the less discerning you can afford to be. Even so, this was going to be the worst. It was a sketchy interview—there was no way around it. First off, it was taking place on a Sunday morning, which ought to make anyone suspicious. More damning was the fact that the interview was for Wash U's psych department, which, as far as I could ever tell, existed solely for the purpose of punking students in the name of science. Possibly some real learning went on there; I can't prove it didn't. But my impression of the place was that at six PM the entire faculty got into their single clown car and drove home, honking wildly and sputtering a trail of seltzer behind them. Probably I would get there and there would be no interview. There would just be money on the ground and a strobe light and grad students observing me through one-way mirrors. It would be like *Saw*, but with less bloodshed and more humiliation.

As it happened, there was an interview, sort of. Two grad students read questions to me in a monotone, and then stared at me with their dead eyes as I tried to answer them. I quickly came to the conclusion that: (1) I was not getting this particular job, because (2) there was clearly an internal candidate—what internal candidates beget are weird interview times and dead eyes.

I would have preferred the money on the floor and the strobe light.

The thing was a debacle—I'm pretty sure one of the interviewers actually had headphones on—and I wasn't even halfway through when I decided that I was going to stomp over to Plant and Microbial Sciences to give Jonah grief. For the clothes, not the interview, although my feelings at this point were spilling together a little.

Jonah had told me he was going to be working with his fellow TAs Sunday morning, and that I could "swing by" if I needed anything. And I did need something: I needed to yell at someone with money. Even if it meant not getting the second thousand dollars, Jonah was getting schooled, Dahlia-style.

I slammed the door as I came into the place. In part, I wanted everyone to know that I was angry, and in part I was trying to rev myself back up. I'm not a naturally angry person, and when I do get angry, it tends to wear off very quickly.

"I'm not your concubine, Jonah Long!" I yelled, hoping for the kind of line that would make an entrance. This worked, although it wasn't exactly the entrance I had imagined.

First of all, the place was tiny. I had imagined a cavernous hive of TA cubicles—that's what we had in business school—where my entrance would have turned a lot of heads. But the place was a cubbyhole, and I was yelling at people who were right in front of me.

They blankly turned to face me. Two people, neither of them

Jonah. There was a tall, bushy-headed kid with brown hair and a blond tank of a girl. I don't mean to say that she was fat—I mean that she had a scowling face that would have been well suited to extended land battles, and that she looked like she was prepared to trundle over my lifeless body in the name of the greater good.

The blond girl asked, not at all happily:

"Who are you?"

But the guy looked delighted and added, "Aside from *not* Jonah's concubine."

I was uncertain. I don't know what I had been expecting, but it hadn't been this.

"Is Jonah here?" I asked.

"He hasn't come in this morning," said the guy. "We've been waiting for him, actually. You don't know where he is, do you? I'm Nathan Willing, by the way."

I liked Nathan Willing. He was affable and cute, at least relative to the tank. I was about to introduce myself to him, but of course the blonde was not having it.

"Nate, why don't you finish typing up our project report?"

"Actually, I'd like to—"

And she repeated the question, with the kind of force that suggested that this was not a question at all, but more of a galactic imperial decree.

"Eh. I'll finish typing up that report," said Nathan agreeably. Easy come, easy go, Nathan. Or maybe that was the croupier's jacket talking. As Nathan took off, I could see two of the cubicles behind him. The girl's station was neat and orderly, lined with philosophy books and bedecked with a bonsai tree. The station next to hers must have been Jonah's, because it was messy and extravagant and had a poster-sized picture of Jonah shaking hands with the governor of Missouri. The blonde waited until Nathan was out of sight behind a wooden cubicle wall and we heard the rhythmic patter of a remarkably good typist.

"Do you have a message for Jonah?" she asked in a hushed tone of voice that suggested we were now under a cone of silence. The stubborn part of me wanted to answer in a yell, but it really wasn't worth the effort.

"Maybe," I said. "Do you know him?"

"Obviously. I'm Jennifer Ebel," she said. Then, seeing that this declaration brought no reaction, she continued. "I'm in his graduate program. Now, what's this about you not being Jonah's concubine?"

I noticed Jennifer's earrings now, and I don't know how they escaped my attention earlier. She was wearing a plain black shirt and pants and had a rather severe haircut, all of which contributed to her "serious student" vibe. But she had on what might have been the silliest pair of earrings I'd ever witnessed. They were Day-Glo pink, asymmetrical—with a large circle and square on one ear, and a jangling triangle on the other. I tried to put them out of my mind, but they kept pulling my attention, like some sort of terrible pink stereogram.

"These clothes," I said. "I don't want Jonah buying me clothes."

"Are you Jonah's girlfriend?" asked Jennifer condescendingly. "Is this a lovers' quarrel? Because I don't think it's appropriate to bring it to work."

She oozed brisk, judgmental efficiency, this Jennifer. I suppose she thought I was some sweet thing of Jonah's who would wilt under the force of her gaze.

"No," I said, leaving the cone of silence. "I'm not Jonah's girlfriend. I'm a private detective he hired. I agree with you that it's inappropriate for me to be here, but that's what happens when you buy your detective clothes. I'm not a dress-up doll, Jennifer. And besides which, these clothes are ridiculous. Look at me! I look like a goddamned Manic Pixie Dream Girl." I was going to add, "as imagined by someone who was color-blind," but as far as I knew, Jonah *was* color-blind, and I don't like picking at people's infirmities. I told you I wasn't good at anger.

Jennifer was not impressed.

"Jonah bought you those?" she asked, sounding not exactly jealous. Maybe curious. "They're not so bad. I think they're sort of interesting."

The enormous pink triangle on her left ear wobbled distractingly, reminding me that praise on an outfit from a woman wearing Day-Glo pink earrings should be taken with a grain of salt.

"Yeah, well, you can tell Jonah that I'm not going to meet Kurt wearing them."

Jennifer's face registered a sudden look of concern.

"You're not investigating Kurt? Kurt Campbell?"

"Investigating" would be a very loose term for my meeting with Kurt Campbell. Mostly I would be reading a prepared speech at him. But I didn't want to wade into the details.

"Can you tell me anything about Kurt? I haven't been told much, aside from he's quote unquote very charming."

Jennifer openly laughed at this—a quick, sharp snort of a laugh that was the kind of thing that could get wine up your nose at dinner parties.

"Who told you that?"

Jonah had told me that, but I didn't feel like telling this to Jennifer.

"It's the word on the street," I told her, improbably keeping a straight face as I got this whopper out.

"He's not charming. He's like a brain-damaged panda in human form."

It was my turn to scowl at her.

"Have fun," said Jennifer, shuffling me out of the office and closing the door. "I'll be sure to give Jonah your message: 'Not a whore, no clothes.' Thanks for coming by."

CHAPTER THREE

I had a lot of reservations about meeting Kurt at this point, but I had taken the money, and so there was no backing out now.

The "ambush" could not have gone worse. Everything about it was wrong. For starters, I was meeting him in a windmill. Technically, a restaurant shaped like a windmill, but a freaking windmill nonetheless, with giant arms that swung around in the breeze. I was feeling a bit silly about the whole thing and had hoped that the Bevo Mill would be a seedy bar, with a grizzled-looking barkeep who would say something like, "What can I get for you, angel?," which would help put me into the proper spirit of things. But no, it looked like the sort of place that would inspire a Koji Kondo score. The parking lot would have been well suited for a chicken-collecting mini-game. It did not steel the spirit is what I am saying.

I told the server that I was there for the Long party, and he guided me to a secluded table where a dapper, brown-haired twentysomething was nervously fidgeting with a menu. Maybe the whole thing was a farce, but it was a farce I had signed up for, and I jumped in with all the gusto I had.

I thundered onto the scene, yanked the wooden chair out from the table, and straddled it as I sat down.

"Okay, pal. I'm not the person you were expecting," I told him.

"No," said Kurt. He was a plain-looking guy, but he had these great Neil Gaiman eyes that looked enraptured by my arrival.

"I was sent here by Jonah Long. I'm a private detective."

Kurt's eyes widened. A-plus eyes on this guy. B-minus face, but ace eyes.

"I'm not going to pussyfoot around this, Kurt," I said, feeling that "pussyfoot" was the sort of word that a private detective would use. "I know that you stole the spear from Jonah shortly after he kicked you out of his apartment. That's a given. It's where we're starting from, you understand me? I'm not going to bother with your 'Oh, I'm innocent!' speech. I know you did it. The question before us is, what are we going to do about it?"

I looked at Kurt, who was, indeed, thoroughly disarmed. He just gaped at me, openmouthed. Maybe Jonah was right— maybe this was going to be just as easy as he had suggested. Then Kurt asked me:

"Are you sure you're at the right table?"

I had run through this conversation in my head many times on the way here. There were several responses that Kurt could have made that I had crackerjack answers to. But the question "Are you at the right table?" had never come up.

"Am I?" I asked this person, whom I now hoped was Kurt.

"I don't think you are. You called me Kurt."

"Isn't your name Kurt?"

"No," said not-Kurt. "My name is Silas."

"Did Kurt send you?" I asked hopefully.

"I don't know anyone named Kurt," said Silas. "So I would say no." Then Silas had a question of his own.

"Do I look like Kurt? Or is it that you do not know what he looks like?"

Well, no, Silas. I didn't know what he looked like, because his Facebook icon was a picture of him taken from a great distance away, so my notion of his face was somewhat pixelated. I had a very vague description, which, when you get down to it, could have been a lot of people.

I apologized profusely to Silas, who was delighted and tried to give me his phone number. This is what men want, apparently. Chair-straddling women who threaten them. I took the phone number to be polite, but I don't plan to see Silas's lovely eyes again unless I am in the seventh circle of hell.

I returned to the server and explained that I was from the *Long* party, and after much futzing we determined that there was no such party. I asked if anyone named Kurt Campbell was there and I was directed to another table, mercifully out of sight from Silas.

This Kurt did reasonably resemble the other one. Close-cropped brown hair but a rounder face, although his eyes did nothing for me.

Literally, they did nothing. They didn't even look up when I sat down.

I didn't have quite the swagger for this Kurt that I'd had for his predecessor. I plopped down across from him, feeling defeated, and said, "I'm Dahlia Moss."

Kurt was texting. He had a cell phone in his lap and was texting. Whatever this missive was, he also found it terribly funny, because he was giggling to himself as he made it. I did not immediately realize that it was a cell phone in his lap, since it was out of sight, and I spent the first few seconds of the conversation with the assumption that he was fiddling with his crotch somehow.

"I am Dahlia Moss," I repeated, trying to revive my dignity whilst simultaneously believing that I was being ignored by a boy who was readjusting his junk.

"Just one second," said Kurt. And it was at this point that I realized *cell phone*, because no junk could possibly require this level of repositioning. Also there were buzzing noises.

I looked at Kurt. He didn't look like a brain-damaged panda to me, but neither could it be said that he gave the impression of being an Adonis. Or even one of those young people my parents characterize as a "mover and shaker." He was not fresh-faced and up-and-coming. He was plain-faced, and if he had to be assigned a direction, it would be gently sloping downward.

Kurt laughed at whatever hilarious response had come back to him and placed his phone on the table, where he continued to look at it in happy anticipation, glancing only occasionally at me.

"Who are you again?" he asked.

"Dahlia Moss. I am a private detective."

This line had had such great effect on the other folks I'd interacted with—Charice, Jennifer, my old friend Silas—yet it did zilch here. So blank, so distant was Kurt's response that I repeated the line to make sure he heard it.

"How interesting," mumbled Kurt, and he looked at his phone, which had vibrated again. He glanced up at me with a look that seemed to say that he knew it was bad form to be paying more attention to his phone than me, but what are you going to do? The nonverbal apology dealt with, he picked up his phone, read the text, and dissolved into sibilant sniggering.

"Who are you texting with?"

"A girl," said Kurt with a pleased intonation on the word.

"Can you look at me, please? I have business with you."

Kurt put down the phone and looked at me, giving me the sort of expression an eighth-grader might make when you confiscate their DS. "Who are you again? Dahlia something?"

"Moss. I'm a detective."

"Yes," said Kurt, who already seemed to be thinking of something else. "You keep saying. Should we order now or wait for Jonah?"

"Jonah's not coming," I told him, and I could now see where Jennifer was coming from with her panda description. "He hired me to come here for him."

"Then let's order now."

Kurt opened his menu and was visibly smacking his lips as he thumbed through it. I had the impression that he already wasn't listening to me again, but I was going to keep this conversation on track. "I am here to recover the spear," I announced.

"What page is that on?" asked Kurt, turning through the menu.

"The Spear of Infinite Piercing. It's an item in the Kingdoms of Zoth."

He brightened up at this. "Oh, the Bejeweled Spear of Infinite Piercing, you mean?"

I felt that this was a breakthrough, and that it should logically lead to further conversation. If this were an adventure game, I should have unlocked colorful new options for conversations with Kurt. But it was not an adventure game; it was life—shitty, shitty life. Kurt went back to his menu.

"I'm here to recover it."

"At the Bevo Mill?"

31

"From the person who stole it."

"Did someone steal it?" asked Kurt. "When did that happen?"

Actually, I did not know when that happened. Jonah had been very loose with his chronology. And if I believed Tambras, it had potentially been stolen twice. But Jesus, could Kurt really have been that obtuse?

"You stole it from Jonah. I'm here to recover it from you."

Kurt stopped glancing at his menu and looked at me, really looked at me. I had finally broken through. And what was my reward? Sad puppy dog eyes.

"What? That's ridiculous. Who told you that?"

"It's what Jonah believes. The spear went missing from his account immediately after he kicked you out."

"Kicked me out? I moved out on my own. And why would he think that I took it?"

"Synchronicity?" I ventured.

"That's the stupidest thing I've ever heard," said Kurt. "And I can't even use the spear."

"What do you mean you can't use it?"

"I'm a ninja," said Kurt, shrugging.

Kurt did not bother to explain this any further, which I am offended by in retrospect. Why does everyone assume that I'm super geeky? I mean, yes, I *am* super geeky, but it wasn't as if I had advertised it at dinner. It wasn't as if I had come dressed as Trinity or Ms. Pac-Man. Is it like gaydar? Could Kurt just tell?

At any rate, Kurt's point was that ninjas can't wield spears. If his character in *Zoth* couldn't use it, why bother stealing it? It was a fair point, but I had a retort.

"You could still be denying it to Jonah."

"If I wanted to rob Jonah, why not take something useful? A

different item. Or money? I left my own sofa at his apartment. Why not take the sofa?"

My initial answer was that it would have been hard to transport, but I held on to the thought. We were both right. It was true that people would do things purely out of spite, but I was starting to feel like that wasn't the case here. As if to drive the point home, Kurt said:

"Tell Jonah that he should go to customer service. It's cool that he has minions and everything, but honestly, just email customer service. They'll recover it and punish whomever. It's really not that big a deal."

The weirdness of this all was getting to be too much. If it meant going off script, so be it.

"I spoke to a guild mate who told me that Jonah had stolen the spear."

"Jonah did steal the spear," answered Kurt.

"From whom?"

"The guild, I suppose. Usually there's a lottery for items among the people who need them. But Jonah just snatched it up before we could start the process."

A tacky thing to do, I thought, and yet was not very surprised.

"I see. So do you think that one of his wronged guild mates stole it back?"

Kurt paused so long that I was worried he had fallen asleep. Eventually, he burbled up an answer.

"I don't think so. The item is so rare that there was a server-wide announcement made when he acquired it. Everyone on our server knew that he had it. Probably he was just hacked by a Chinese gold farmer."

Again, I pretended not to know what this meant.

Kurt noticed my fake confusion and answered. "Just google it. Now let's get some dinner."

———————◆———————

The rest of the conversation was even more awkward. When we were done discussing the spear, Kurt returned to his texting, and course after interminable course passed in silence. I stumbled out of the Bevo Mill the way that you would leave a wake. It wasn't that one thing had gone wrong; it was that everything had gone wrong. Sure, I had made a thousand dollars, but the humiliation would stay with me for years to come. I now likened Jonah's cash to the sort of retainer a contestant would get for going on one of those reality shows where you kill a live pig or starve.

I trundled my way through the chill night air toward the bus stop. After a debacle such as this, there should be no luxurious cab rides. But I didn't make it out of the parking lot before a green Scion blocked my path.

"Hey there, *belle fleur!*"

I couldn't see the driver's face, but I knew it was Charice. She had purchased that Scion because she had read an article about how there are no flat paints in cars anymore, only shimmery ones. This prompted her to find the only flat-colored car in production and buy it new, on the spot. Because she is insane. Also she cycles through money like the evil stepmother in a live-action Disney film, because she makes upwards of $80,000 a year. Just to clarify—not to seem bitter—but Charice majored in dance. I didn't even know that was a major, aside from at the school in *Fame*, but regardless it strikes me as the sort of career that should lead to impoverishment. It's the sort of major that sets parents to shaking their heads and clucking.

But no, Charice is in marketing. She's good at marketing; she has an uncanny talent for talking people into doing unlikely things.

I got in her car. A ride with Charice was going to be at least as much penance as the bus. Maybe more.

"You followed me here," I told her.

Charice was ecstatic. "How could you tell? You're getting really good at this detective thing!"

This was patently not true, but I explained nonetheless.

"It's eight o'clock on a Sunday night, and we're both at a windmill. What are the odds?"

As deductive reasoning, it was a little weak, but it brooked no further discussion.

"So I've got some ideas about how to get back this spear."

Oh, the spear. I really did not want to talk about the spear anymore, but this was my penance, sure enough.

"How do you know I didn't get it back already?"

This was my stab at a dark joke, but a glimmer in Charice's eye, never a good thing, made me suddenly suspicious.

"How long have you been here?" I asked.

"Oh, you know, a little while."

I looked at Charice, who was trying not to beam. I also observed that there were four bags of trash in the backseat, which was out of character for her. Though she may have been an agent of chaos, she was remarkably tidy.

A dark, terrible vision ran through my head.

"Tell me you didn't."

"Didn't what?" asked Charice, with only the thinnest veneer of innocence. She wanted me to ask her what she had done. It was killing her not to shout it from the rooftops.

"You put some kind of wire on me, didn't you?"

"Maybe?" said Charice, with the tone of voice of a charming trickster goddess. Or Woody Woodpecker.

"Why would you do this?"

But we both knew the answer. Because she was herself, and this sort of thing was fun.

"How much did you hear?"

"Are you going to call Silas? He sounded very handsome. Very stentorian."

"Where did you find a freaking wire, Charice?"

"I picked it up at a novelty shop, and I put it in your purse this morning. As a private eye, you should really be looking out for that sort of thing."

Arguing with Charice was generally like trying to persuade a hurricane. Even so, I had to draw a line.

"This is a gross violation of my privacy. This is not cool."

"I know, I know. But I needed to know when you were going to be finished."

It was the trash in the backseat that she was referring to, somehow. I didn't immediately understand how it could be involved, but it was out of place and Charice wanted me to notice it, because she kept glancing at it and winking.

The certainty that she had planted a bug had hit me all at once, but the business with the trash was so bizarre, so frankly stupid, that I could only slowly hazard a guess.

"This trash is from Kurt's car? You stole bags of trash from Kurt's car?"

"Well, it wasn't bagged. It was all just loose."

"You broke into Kurt's car and cleaned it?"

Charice considered this. "Yes?"

"Why?"

"Because these are all clues! We are rich with clues, Dahlia!"

I tried to imagine what Kurt Campbell must have thought after leaving the Bevo Mill and finding that his previously trash-filled car was now spotless. Did he now think that he had been very, very thoroughly robbed? Or would he imagine this as some sort of bizarre pay-it-forward scheme? Perhaps he would think that his mother had sent minions to smite an abomination she could no longer abide. Four bags was a lot of trash.

"There were really four bags' worth?" I asked Charice, momentarily forgetting to be angry.

"The thing was filthy. I don't know what girl Kurt was texting with, but I'm willing to bet that she's never been in his ride."

CHAPTER FOUR

By the time we made it back to our apartment building, I noticed a rancid, egg-salady smell spreading through the Scion. Whatever else his shortcomings were, Kurt should have spent less time texting and more time monitoring decaying food-stuffs. I asked Charice to let me out at the door, both to escape from the smell and to register my disapproval with the whole trash-gate operation. I couldn't imagine anything useful coming from Charice's four bags of garbage, yet some part of me was curious. Mostly I was hoping for something that I could embarrass Kurt with, because I am occasionally petty, and this was one of those occasions.

I walked up the stairs to my apartment and was surprised to see two black men in the hallway walking toward me.

"Dahlia Moss?" The older of the two men looked at me quizzically, flashing a badge to show that he was a detective for the city of Saint Louis.

"Yes," I said, thinking, *Ah, this is how you do it.* Detectives don't run in, guns blazing. They make sure their mark is the person they're looking for before they start straddling chairs.

"I'm Detective Maddocks. This is my partner, Detective Shuler. Could we talk to you a moment?"

And at this point I was basically scared shitless.

Whenever I got pulled over, I always ran through a mental checklist of what I might have been doing wrong—speeding, illegal turn, brake lights out—and I almost always came up with nothing, which steeled my spirit, because if I couldn't think of anything, how illegal could it be? I ran through my checklist then: I hadn't driven my car in weeks. Should I have filled out an I-9 for Jonah? Surely there was still time. Then it hit me. The bags of trash. Charice had broken into a car and stolen four bags of trash. This made me an accessory.

"Um," I said. This is a very charitable rendering of my response. Honestly it was something like, "Aa-a-rrro-ooo-uuu-um," so it lasted about seven or eight seconds and involved several facial contortions.

Bags of trash. I was going to jail for bags of trash. I was going to go to prison and become one of those sad people featured in *News of the Weird*. I heard a *ding* from the elevator and thought, *Christ, it'll be Charice*. Once I finished fumbling with my keys, I all but yanked Detective Maddocks into my apartment.

"In," I told him.

He did not seem to mind the yanking. Detective Maddocks glided into my apartment. Honestly, glided—like he owned the place. I was reminded of inviting a vampire into your home. Okay, he wasn't a vampire, but the similarities were there. He was regal, demanded respect, dressed in black, and was extremely dangerous. He didn't look much like a vampire, and in fact, he had kind of a classic detective's face—great craggy features. He looked like he should be on the street, making grim deductions while it rained on him. But my nerves were rattled, so my impression of him was a bit vampiric.

It was easy to overlook his partner. Detective Shuler did not look like a vampire. He had entirely the wrong sort of face for drama. He smiled too easily, I think. Even when he wasn't smiling, it looked as though he might have been thinking about it. He had smooth light brown skin and a cute doughy face with overly expressive features. It was hard to imagine him nailing a perp, but easy to imagine him explaining the concept of sharing to children. Possibly while playing a ukulele.

"So you're Dahlia Moss." This was Maddocks again. "Do you know you seem to have been ahead of us all day?"

I am amazed I was able to correctly transcribe this, because I was scarcely listening to him. His lips were moving, and all I was thinking was *Trash, trash, trash. I'm going to jail for trash.*

He looked at me, and I was now going with vampire again because I felt like he was trying to read my mind.

"Would you like to sit down?" I asked. "Can I get you something to drink? Water? Gin and tonic? I'm kidding about the gin and tonic."

This was just verbal stuttering on my part. They sat down but were not interested in drinks. Because I am a terrible hostess, I made myself a drink—just tonic—while I tried to process what he had asked me.

"What do you mean, I've been ahead of you? Have you been following me?"

"We have not," said Detective Maddocks. "It's just that people I've spoken to seem to have all spoken to you first. Surprising."

And Maddocks said the word "surprising" as if it were a synonym for "disgusting." I tried to lighten the mood.

"Did you also interview for a secretarial position at WashU? Because I can tell you that you don't need to worry. I am not getting that job."

This got a short guffaw from Detective Shuler, and Maddocks

shot icicles at him for it. The room became silent again with his vampire magic.

I tried to be appropriately solemn, but I was becoming giddy with the thought that if they had been following me all day, then this couldn't be about the trash.

"How do you know Jonah Long?" Maddocks asked me.

"He hired me," I said, relieved that I wasn't going to jail on trash-theft charges. "He hired me to recover a stolen item for him."

"Why you?" asked Maddocks.

"You're the second person to ask me that today," I said, laughing nervously. Neither of them said anything. I don't know why I had thought this would have sufficed for an answer, but I was still surprised when the two men continued to look at me, patiently awaiting further elaboration.

"I don't know why he hired me," I said. "I guess he just felt I was the right person for the task."

It didn't feel like the time or place to go into the Hitchcock blond theory I had been formulating. Instead, I asked, "What's this all about?"

The two detectives shared a look as if they were privately deciding whether to let me in on a secret. As this happened, Charice entered the apartment carrying all four bags of trash. She glanced and saw the two detectives on my couch, technically her couch, and remained utterly unconcerned. Strange men in her apartment? No problem. She didn't so much as wave or say hello as she carried on with her trash-moving efforts.

"Do you need help with that?" asked Shuler, speaking for the first time since I had made his acquaintance.

"How gentlemanly," said Charice with typical nonchalance. "But I got it. Thanks, though."

Despite her saying that she had it, she was clearly carrying entirely too much trash for one trip. There was hardly any Charice visible, just a veritable Christmas tree of trash bags teetering dangerously down the hallway.

The hitherto laconic Shuler seemed intrigued by all this, and I wanted to yell out in a tone of voice that would sound helpful, and not at all alarmist, "Charice, these are policemen, potentially theft-investigating policemen," but it seemed hard to do this in a way that would not arouse suspicion.

"Why are you bringing trash into the building?" asked Shuler.

"Dumpster diving," said Charice.

"Isn't that usually done outside?" he asked. "That can't be your haul."

Charice stuck her head out from behind a bag and regarded Detective Shuler, who I imagine she did not realize was a detective but just another available guy. She gave him a look that seemed impossibly flirtatious coming from behind a bag of trash and said:

"I do my sorting inside."

I didn't want this exchange getting weirder than it already had, so I interrupted.

"You guys aren't here to discuss trash. What's this about?"

"Jonah Long is dead."

In retrospect, this was kind of a litmus test. They tell Dahlia that Jonah is dead and then study my face for some kind of reaction. I just looked at them, dumbfounded, and said the first thing that came to my mind.

"He owed me one thousand dollars."

I said it as if I were in a trance, which I suppose I was. It's a tacky way to respond to anyone's death, but give me a break. My annual income had been halved and I was in a period of mourning.

"We'd appreciate it if you could tell us about your interactions with Jonah."

The part of me that wasn't worried about money—admittedly, now a very small part—was thinking.

"Was he murdered?"

"Why would you ask that?" asked Detective Maddocks, somehow marrying the question to both his detective and vampire aesthetics.

"Well, when my aunt Pauline died, no one sent detectives around to ask me about my interactions with her. That's not usually how it goes."

Maddocks was skeptical but mollified by this response.

"There's an investigation. We'd appreciate it if you can tell us what you've been doing for Jonah."

"If you've interviewed everyone I've spoken to today, you must already know."

And Maddocks actually smiled at this. "Even so."

"Fine," I said. "I was hired to recover a spear that had been stolen from him. I've been going around today looking for him to ask him some follow-up questions, but he wasn't at work."

"And Kurt Campbell?"

"I was hired to intimidate him. Jonah thought his ex-roommate had stolen the spear, and I was supposed to shock and awe him into giving it up. Over dinner. Inside a windmill. Which is another thing I would have liked to speak to Jonah about."

Shuler, who had been keeping silent all this time, spoke again. "You seem like an unusual choice for a shock-and-awe mission."

"Are you saying that I'm not intimidating?" This was supposed to be a joke. It's obvious I'm not intimidating. It's like tapioca pudding asking if it's intimidating. But Shuler did not recognize the rhetorical nature of my query.

"I am gently suggesting it, yes."

"We know that you failed at your task," Maddocks explained.

This embarrassed me, but there wasn't anything to do but be honest and explain. "Listen, it didn't make any sense to me either, Detective. I don't even think Kurt stole the spear in the first place."

"Why would you say that?" asked Detective Maddocks, with a certain proprietary tone in his voice that suggested any theorizing was the domain of the police department.

"Aside from his outright denial, the tenor of our conversation, and his facial reactions, which were pretty conclusive from my point of view, there's the fact that he can't use the spear."

Maddocks scoffed. "He could use it as well as Jonah Long could have."

"No," I said. "He couldn't."

This prompted a staredown from Maddocks, who I suppose must have thought I was bluffing. When I didn't back down, he furrowed his brow and made the only guess that made sense to him.

"He doesn't . . . have arms?"

"No," I said. "Of course he has arms. What kind of suggestion is that? Have you not met with Kurt yet?"

"We spoke on the phone, and I'm meeting with him later. Tell me why he can't use a spear."

"He's a ninja. Ninjas can't wield spears." And for this I wheeled out the same tone that Sherlock Holmes would use to dazzle a room full of Victorians with his amazing deductive powers.

It did not have the same effect here. Maddocks regarded me with a combination of pity and mortification. This is what happens when people realize that you're not a casual geek but a full-blown professional.

"You understand that he's not a ninja in real life?" he asked with more uncertainty in his voice than I would have liked.

"Of course I understand he's not a ninja in real life. This is not feudal Japan. What does real life have to do with it?"

Maddocks spoke slowly, as if he were talking to a small child. "Because we live in real life. And in real life, anyone can pick up a spear."

We seemed to be in an unspoken war of condescending to each other. But I suddenly got where he was coming from. He didn't realize:

"The spear is digital," I told him. "You understand that, right? I've been asked to retrieve an item from a video game."

Maddocks was stunned for a moment and just said nothing. It was like he had had holy water thrown on him. He didn't apologize, but when he came back, he was less patronizing and more thoughtful. Which was even more terrifying somehow.

"Fine. Can you tell us more about this digital spear?"

And there was something about the way he said "digital" that set my mind to reeling. Before he had finished the sentence, I had a theory, and I wanted to test it right then and there.

I turned to Shuler, who looked blank but wary.

"Why would you have thought the spear was analog?"

Shuler gave me a poker face that could have broken banks in Vegas. But I had guessed the answer.

"Jonah had a replica made, didn't he? He used some service, some 3D-printing company, to have a replica made of the item. That's why you seemed so confident that I had failed to recover it from Kurt. You found a copy of the spear in Jonah's apartment and thought it was the real thing."

Then, a terrible thought hit me as soon as I was saying it.

"Jonah was stabbed with the spear."

It wasn't a question. I just said it to them. And neither of their faces seemed up to the challenge of contesting me.

I always thought that when detectives, and specifically I'm thinking of William Powell, made great intuitive leaps, there was supposed to be cheering and perhaps the clinking of champagne glasses. Instead everyone just looked at me as if I had committed a grave faux pas.

"Right," I said. "Sorry."

"We can't share information about that at this time," Maddocks said. And I felt bad. The next few minutes of the interview went on in that same flat way, with me filling in the police on what they didn't know about the Kingdoms of Zoth, which was everything. And about Jonah's hiring and Kurt and, well, the whole unlikely thing.

As we were finishing up, Charice reentered the room, having inexplicably changed into a black cocktail dress. She ran toward me, arms outstretched, which made me wince. Hugs from Charice were the kind of thing that haunted my dreams. I'm not huggy at all, and she embraced you like a Russian weight lifter on his third glass of Stoli. It's rib-crushing. And literally, you leave the ground. Charice majored in dance, and she's stronger than you would expect her to be.

"Dahlia!" she wailed. And there it was, the vise grip, and then I was airborne. I held my breath until it was over, but Charice took no notice and kept on talking. "I couldn't help but eavesdrop, and I heard the terrible news."

"Couldn't help but eavesdrop" was probably a euphemism for crouching at the door with her ear to a cup, but I wasn't going to argue with her in front of the police.

She looked especially somber, which should have set off

alarms, but I was mesmerized by her extravagant dabbing at completely imaginary tears.

"To think I saw him just yesterday," she said.

Then Charice shivered—how I could have possibly not realized something was up by this point is beyond me—and said, "Being gored to death, how horrible!"

Maddocks asked simply but evenly, "Did you know Mr. Long?"

"He was standing right here only twenty-four hours ago," Charice said. Detective Maddocks correctly recognized this as a dramatic rendering of "No, I didn't know him," and reacted accordingly.

"One last thing," said Maddocks, turning back toward me as Charice continued to mime mourning at us. "You're not a detective, Miss Moss."

"That's what I told Jonah," I said, noting that my voice sounded small and squeaky.

Maddocks gave me the evil eye. This was the kind of thing that brought Lucy Harker to her doom. "So you say. But you've told at least two other people that you were a private detective."

"A very, very private detective?"

This did not amuse Detective Maddocks, who was baring his proverbial fangs. "If you want to go around telling people that you're a detective without getting licensed, then you should move to Mississippi. In Missouri there are laws for that sort of thing. Is that what you want, to move to Mississippi?"

I told Maddocks that was not what I wanted. That was what no one wanted.

"Then I don't want to hear any more accounts of you telling people that you are a private detective. Or there will be hell to pay."

I looked at Maddocks, who glared at me, and at Shuler, who looked politely embarrassed.

"Of course," I said meekly.

I felt humiliated, but it must not have registered to Charice, who dived right in for another inappropriate hug—this time Detective Shuler took the hit—and the police were quickly out the door.

I was still trying to process what had happened, but as soon as they were gone, Charice had brightened right back up, as big as Christmas lights. She had put white headphones in her ears, and she was grinning as though she had a terrible secret.

"I've bugged the police," she said.

Yes, that was a terrible secret all right.

"Have you gone mad?"

"Shh!" Charice told me.

And against all sense or wisdom, I took one earbud out of Charice's ear and listened.

"I've had better interviews." It took me a second to recognize him—it was Maddocks, but he was laughing and sounded casual and different. "I don't know, Anson, what do you think?"

"There's more going on there than I would have guessed. She was clever. If you wanted to hire a geek detective, you could do worse." Charice was jumping up and down at this approbation, and I had to admit that my heart was fluttering a little bit. "Why'd you lay in on her like that?"

"If she wants to be a detective, she can go to school for it. What did you think about the case, Shuler?"

"Well, if the spear is digital, it opens things right up."

Maddocks must have been frowning pretty hard, because I could feel the force of it through the walls. "No," he said. "That's not it at all. Jonah Long was not murdered with a digital spear. He was murdered with a real one. It could have been a random break-in, for all we know. Since we know that Miss Moss was not involved with the real spear, we know that she's not important."

And it started to get staticky at this point.

Charice yanked the earbud from me. "The range on this is terrible," she said.

"Why would you have a bug that can only receive from twenty feet away?"

"I just got it from a novelty shop! Who knew an opportunity like this would present itself?"

And Charice was racing toward the door.

"I'm following them—hopefully I can get back in range. I'll let you know what I find out."

And out she went, but not before putting on a large black trench coat that was not particularly weather-appropriate. Presumably, this was for sneaking. That or it had Inspector Gadget–style paraphernalia attached to it; a remote possibility, but not impossible.

I would be lying if I told you that I wasn't intensely interested in what she learned. But chasing after Charice down a stairwell would have been ridiculous and just made matters worse. So I added the gin into my ginless gin and tonic and tried to process what the hell had happened.

After a few sips, I decided that not everything needed to be processed. Some things needed to be ignored and slept on.

CHAPTER FIVE

I woke up at 7:55 in the morning to repeated banging on our front door. Charice wasn't in her room, having apparently never returned from her tailing of Maddocks and Shuler. If I were a better person, this might have worried me. But I rather liked the idea of the detectives being called away to a pressing crime—pursuing a serial killer through the streets of the city, let's say—all the while being hounded by an invisible Charice, always at the edge of the shadows. That's Charice in a nutshell. Great fun as long as she's hounding someone else.

It was because of my certainty that the noise must have been Charice, however, that I elected to open the door in my nightgown and Ewok slippers.

Instead of Charice I found a redheaded thirtysomething with a death glare. She looked like a movie star—wavy red hair that was fit for a costume ball—but her outfit suggested business. She was wearing some orange-sherbet-colored cashmere jacket thing with a teal top, which I admit is not a color combination one usually associates with crisp efficiency, but it was about the details, the overall effect. And not simply that the cashmere thing appeared to be worth more than my car. This scowling redhead, whoever she was, was Put Together.

"What the fuck does it take to get you to open your door?" she asked.

But she wasn't all glares—there was an amused tone to her, that much was clear.

"Would you like to come in?" I said, more out of caffeine-less confusion than manners. But the question was silly; she was already in.

"So you're the detective?" she asked. "Not quite what I expected."

I nodded, forgetting in the confusion of the morning that Detective Maddocks had asked me to stop saying that.

"Well," she said, dubiously assessing me. "I suppose Jonah must have had his reasons. Anyway, I'm Emily Swenson," she said, holding out her hand, which had a lovely silver hoop on it, which, again, was probably valued at more than my car. I should stop saying that, though, because my car is an awfully low bar to clear. "I'm here to make your day," she said.

I was, at this point, very confused, because Emily had gone into the kitchen and was pouring a glass of orange juice. She was also assessing the contents of our refrigerator, mostly with a series of sighs and a "We eat out a lot, do we?"

I was incredibly confused, but my thought was that at least the apartment was looking good and not gussied up for some arcane theme party. And the place cleans up nice. People are always surprised by Charice's apartment in its nonparty state. Yes, Charice is as mercurial and eclectic a person as I've ever met, but our place is a parade of ecru and beige. Occasionally pops of color appear, but they never seem to stick around. The only permanent bit of frippery is this giant scowling Max Beckmann portrait in the kitchen, which is not a face you want looking at you while you nurse a hangover. The painting is so at odds with the apartment, Charice, and breakfast that I actually asked her about it, and she told me, gravely, "I don't discuss the Beckmann." She said it just like you're imagining, as though she were the heroine in a Daphne du Maurier novel. Probably she was putting me on.

But I digress. My point is that the place wasn't a post-collegiate hellhole of crusty shag carpet and spilled Dixie cups half filled with cheap beer. It looked good, and a judgment from a stranger about my living standards is the king of things that piss me off. Even though everything was Charice's, I wanted to reach for a clever retort, or at least a fuck-you, which is sort of like a clever retort, except for the part about being clever. But I was still so sleepy and confused—I was kind of running under a vague assumption that Emily was a reality-television host who was going to rate my refrigerator contents and then challenge a high-class chef to make a meal out of its contents. Is that a show? It could be.

After some bleary-eyed bleating at her, I eventually found the wherewithal to ask: "I'm sorry, why are you here?"

Emily was deep into the refrigerator. "I'm a lawyer for Jonah Long's parents. Like I said, I'm here to make your day. And possibly breakfast, since you appear to need it."

I don't usually let strangers enter my home and make me breakfast, but I was still emerging through the substrata of sleep. Having processed, at least dimly, what was happening, I was now in the vanity layer. It wasn't that I wouldn't have answered the door in my slippers and nightgown, but they would have been different slippers and a different nightgown. I closed up as much as I could. And my hair. I had to do something about my hair, which at this hour possessed topography-defying tendrils that suggested I was wearing some sort of fuzzy Cthulhu on my head.

Emily didn't appear to notice my distress at all but instead seemed dismayed that we had but a single egg, which she set on the counter and sighed at. My refrigerator is best described in terms of stark minimalism, and this too did not seem to please Emily Swenson. "Why don't you clean yourself up—you look like you've had a rough night—and when you come back we'll have breakfast and talk business."

It was a good plan. And on the one hand, Emily was actively offering me what I would have proposed myself, were I fully awake. And yet, I could feel myself beginning to bristle at her. This comely woman, with her cashmere charm and apparent cooking skills. I wanted to say, "I have not been drinking; this is simply what I look like in the morning," but I decided this would not improve my station with her. She'd probably lay me out on the counter and sigh at me in the same way as that lone egg.

I retreated to my room and did the best I could in two minutes. I grabbed jeans and a gray sweater off the floor—wrinkled, but better than my bare flesh—and stuffed my hair into the first hat I could find—a pink Jigglypuff toboggan cap my ex-boyfriend had bought off Etsy for me. I returned to the room to find that Emily had made a perfect little omelet for me.

Emily raised an eyebrow at my attire, but it otherwise escaped comment. "You had fresh dill," she said. "I wouldn't have expected that, but there it is."

I, of course, had nothing to do with the dill at all, but I took the praise anyway. I also ate the omelet, because hey, omelet, and now that I was awake I wasn't going to kill myself trying to impress a woman who had sort of broken into my home.

"You're probably wondering why I'm here," said Emily. "Probably you are starting to wonder if I'm here to sue you somehow. You were hired by Jonah as a detective, and then he's murdered later. I suppose in some lights, this might be considered a poor performance at detecting."

I hadn't wondered that, actually, although now that Emily was spelling it out, it seemed like a thing that I should perhaps have been worried about. I would have done a spit-take, but the omelet was too good and—especially with just the one egg—I didn't want to waste it.

Instead I said, with food in my mouth, "You're not here to sue me."

"Oh?" said Emily, cocking her head. "What makes you say that?"

I swallowed the last of my food. "A hunch," I said. Which is really the last resort of the cornered detective. Still, it made Emily smile at me, more than the fresh dill even.

"I'm not here to sue you, at least not today. Today," said Emily, sitting down at our kitchenette bar with me, "I'm here to hire you."

"Hire me for what?" I said, and I would have done the spit-take now if I had any food left.

"Finish the job. Jonah wanted you to recover something called—I believe it was—the Bejeweled Spear of Infinite Piercing, from the Kingdoms of Zoth. Jonah's family would like for you to continue in that task. As you may know, Jonah was murdered by a copy of the weapon, and so the family has taken a particular interest in *Zoth*."

"The police don't think that *Zoth* is related to the crime," I told her. It perhaps wasn't the most politic thing I could have said, but it made her smirk at me.

"Now where would you have heard that?" she asked.

"Just from a source," I said, neglecting to explain that the source was a five-dollar-and-ninety-nine-cent sound recorder from the Tamayochi Corporation. But it was a good answer, because I went up three more spices in Emily Swenson's estimation. I was up to marjoram now.

"I've heard that as well," said Emily. "And I'm inclined to believe—for the moment—that the police are correct in their estimations. But the family would obviously like to play all of the angles. Recovering Jonah's spear would, at worst, do no harm to the case and fulfill one of Jonah's last wishes. Which would be a comfort to my clients. And at best, well…it may prove useful. The police are not"—and here I felt there was an unspoken *unlike myself*—"completely infallible."

I felt that Emily was gauging my face for some sort of reaction. I wasn't sure what reaction I was supposed to give, so I just drank orange juice instead. This is probably what Sam Spade did when lawyers broke into his kitchen. Only with bourbon.

Emily continued. "Obviously, the task now is more difficult than simply taking a boy out to dinner. What's expected of you now is more complicated, and you will be compensated accordingly."

Emily slid a check facedown across to me on the counter. Either she was a prestidigitator or she had been holding it the whole time. Probably the latter, although the more I knew her, the more skill sets she seemed to have. I turned the check over and promptly fell off the swivel stool I was sitting on. I don't mean that metaphorically—I fell off my chair. I didn't land on the floor because, legs—but to perfectly clear: Ass left chair. And why wouldn't it? The check was for ten thousand dollars.

At first I thought it was a typo. Well, no, at second thought I thought it was a typo—my first thought was *AAARRRGGGH!*— but

I checked both fields and there it was, typed out: ten-thousand-dollars-and-no-cents. At that point I began to babble.

"Listen, Ms. Swenson," I began.

"It's breakfast; I'm fine with Emily."

"Emily, I'm not the person you want for this. You can find someone more qualified, you can find someone more experienced, you can find someone more—"

And she cut me off, Emily Swenson, with the same cucumber-scented efficiency with which she had entered my apartment and cooked me an omelet. "Let me give you a friendly piece of advice, Dahlia. Don't talk yourself out of a good thing. And besides which, this decision was not made idly. There are three strong reasons you are a good choice for our little job. One, you're the person Jonah wanted, which is not to be understated. Two, it is eight in the morning and you are wearing what appears to be *Star Wars* slippers and what I believe is a Pokémon hat. You know your way around the world of geeks, which, as clever as I am, I do not. And three? You're a complete no one, and if things go badly, the family can throw you to the wolves."

She shot a smile at me, which suggested that she was joking. And also that she was, on some deeper level, probably not. "Take the ten thousand dollars."

"Detective Maddocks has made it very clear that I'm not to represent myself as a detective."

"I don't recall mentioning detective work," Emily said with a smile. "I believe I have carefully avoided the phrase."

"I thought you wanted me to—"

"The family would like to hire you as a funeral planner."

This was a wild line, even for someone as smooth as Emily Swenson, who had to keep talking lest she break character.

"A funeral planner in *Zoth*," she added. "Not the real world.

Put something tasteful together in the next few days. And of course, you'd want to meet with all of Jonah's guild mates, to make sure they were apprised of the situation. And ideally, we'd like to see Jonah's character respectfully retired with all his possessions."

"You want to bury the spear with him," I said, seeing where this was going.

"The family would like that. But no detective work, you see. Just talk to people, plan a service, possibly find the spear if you could."

I was still processing it all when Emily hit me with the kicker.

"And of course, let us know if you find anything interesting."

———————◆———————

I saw Emily out, and it took another hour and a half to get properly dressed. I may have been in something of a state. All of it was disturbing, but perhaps the most alarming part of it was that people were coming to my door. The apartment was my sanctum sanctorum. Aside from whatever craziness Charice was involved with, I was always safe from the horrors of Saint Louis. No one came looking for me at Charice's—not my ex-boyfriend, not my old friends, nobody. It was like being hermetically sealed from everyone I wanted to avoid, albeit with a crazy woman. It was a trade I had been happy to make.

Once I had finally put myself together, I gathered up the check the Longs had written me and started to head out the door for the bank. I wasn't sure what to make of their request, but I wanted to get the check deposited quickly, before they came to their senses.

I opened the door to go out, and there it was: someone violating the sanctum sanctorum a third time.

Nathan Willing, the cute botanist Jennifer had banished from talking to me, was crouched on the floor, blocking my exit.

"I knew that would happen," said Nathan, standing suddenly. "I was wondering on the way up here what would be the least-opportune moment for you to open your door. Because I knew that's how it would happen."

Nathan was wearing a maroon sweater and black skinny jeans. He also had a bright-mustard messenger bag, which certainly suggested that he was not dressed for sneaking or surveillance.

"A strange biologist is huddled in my doorway," I said to him. "Explain."

Nathan smiled at me. "Not that strange," he said cheerfully. "I was leaving you a note."

Nathan passed me the note, which I glanced at but didn't bother with other than to observe that Nathan's handwriting was very tiny and very square.

"Thanks," I said, "but I'm going out. You want to give me the CliffsNotes version?"

"I wanted to apologize for putting the police on your trail."

I raised an eyebrow at him and sighed. "Why don't you come inside?"

Nathan happily entered my apartment. So happily, in fact, that I idly wondered if he'd been crouching out there for a while. He collapsed grandly into the sofa, even though I hadn't invited him to sit down. There was something familiar about Nathan—not familiar as if I had met him before in disguise— just familiar.

And he was pleasing to look at, Nathan. He had dark brown hair that looked like something you would find on a Lego mini-fig. It was improbably thick—mini-fig thick—with a buoyancy that was either achieved with molten plastic or a lot of hair gel. He had the classic hipster black-rimmed glasses but had eschewed the bearded-youth look in favor of scruffiness. I'm not a fan of scruff, but it suited him, especially when he smiled, which was always. He looked like an adorable cactus is what I am saying.

"Did you get roughed up by the police?" he asked me.

I sat down on an armchair opposite him. Talking to Nathan made me feel prim, although I couldn't have told you why.

"The police did not rough me up. What do you mean you tipped them off to me?"

"Well," said Nathan, "the police came by after you left and asked a lot of questions. Jennifer didn't mention you to them, so it was left to me to rat you out. I felt very guilty."

Nathan opened his messenger bag and procured a bento box from it. He then opened the bento box and began to eat matchstick carrots and radishes that had been cut into star shapes. When he noticed that I was watching him do all this, he asked: "Carrot?"

"No, thank you," I said, less offended and more confused. This was the sort of living theater that Charice usually gathered, but now it was mine. "The police did come by," I said, "but it wasn't the end of the world, and I'm sure they would have found me eventually. So I appreciate the apology, but really, it's fine."

"I couldn't believe that Jennifer didn't mention you. It was the most exciting thing that's happened all week, a private eye coming by to clarify that she's not a sex worker."

"A concubine. I used the word 'concubine.'"

"So you are a sex worker?"

Nathan seemed to be flirting with me, but I wasn't sure. Flirting was, for me, an ancient language, like Phoenician or Ammonite, the particularities of which have been lost due to lack of usage and also antiquity.

"I never told you I was a private detective," I said. "Were you eavesdropping on my conversation with Jennifer?"

"Oh, completely," said Nathan. "I practically have a transcript. As do the police, now, which is why I came by to apologize."

There were a lot of thoughts going on in my head. One was that Nathan was kind of adorable. Adorable goes a long way with me. And he smelled like cucumbers. I was still smarting from my last guy, though, and I was looking for a way to shuttle him out. Sanctum. Sanctorum.

My other thought, however, was that he probably didn't know that Jonah was dead. I didn't want to tell him, but at the same time it felt wrong not to mention it.

"You heard the news about Jonah?" I asked, sounding him out.

"Murdered," said Nathan, now gnawing on a radish. "By some ornate spear, is what I hear. That's what you were looking for, weren't you? Jonah had told me about it."

This was very anticlimactic.

"You don't seem very broken up about his death," I said.

Nathan flashed a look of embarrassment. "I'm the strong, silent type who buries his feelings?"

"You have a messenger bag," I said.

"I have hidden depths," said Nathan happily. "And I didn't know him very well, honestly."

"Except that you knew about the spear," I pointed out.

"You are very detective-like," said Nathan. "But Jonah was always going on about *Zoth*. He tried to get everyone to play with him. I took a cab with him once after a party, and he tried to get the cabbie to play with him."

I would have pushed at this more, but the truth of it was that I wasn't very broken up about Jonah's death either.

"Oh," said Nathan, snapping his fingers. "I almost forgot. I'm also supposed to apologize for Jennifer. She's usually a lot nicer. Quote unquote. I'm supposed to tell you that."

"Is she usually a lot nicer?" My experience with her had strongly suggested that stern was her default mode.

Nathan considered this. "Well, perhaps 'a lot' is overstating it. She's usually a degree nicer. But that whole sex-worker thing set her off. She was dating Jonah only last week, so a pretty lady dressed in the outfits of Atelier Long is the sort of thing that freaks her out. After you left, she was sharpening dozens upon dozens of pencils. It was good that you got out when you did."

There were two things in this explanation that had not escaped my attention. One was that he used the word "atelier," which, between that and his bento box, was rapidly propelling him into the upper echelons of hipster geekery. The second was that he called me a "pretty lady." I wasn't going to pursue those things, but I noticed them. The sex-worker line I could let slide.

"Well," I said, "apologies have been made. Thanks for coming by."

I got up and Nathan stood quickly, stashing his bento box back into his bag. I was all but physically shuffling him out the room, but he was stalling me. If he were a Pokémon, this would have been where he revealed his super-effective stat reduction on me. He made pouty eyes and scratched at his neck.

This worked surprisingly well.

"Don't laugh, but I kind of wanted to hang out with a private detective," he explained. His embarrassment lasted nanoseconds, and he was bright again. "Makes you feel like you're in on something. You know, put the squeeze on the old up and down. Derrick the gin mill. Hoosegow the bean shooters."

"You're just stringing together nonsense words."

"Maybe," said Nathan. "But you have to grant that I've got the cadence down."

"Out of my apartment, please."

Nathan took this well, like a game-show contestant happy with his parting prizes. "You can't blame a guy for trying. That's the Willing family motto."

"Yeah? The Moss family motto is 'I Never Thought My Life Would Be This Way.'"

This is actually true—it wasn't a line to get a laugh out of Nathan, although it did. Obviously it's not ancestral; it's not written in Latin on our family crest. But it's gotten a lot of usage.

"I'll bet there's a story behind that," said Nathan.

"Yes, and I'm not going to tell it. Out of my apartment, pretty boy."

And he jetted out. I hadn't intended to call Nathan "pretty boy" to his face. This was probably not a good sign.

CHAPTER SIX

When I finished recovering from the curious visit of Nathan Willing, I triple-checked that I had everything I needed and made my way to the bank. I have a somewhat complicated relationship with my bank tellers. Since I have been subsisting on garage sales and craft fairs, I deal largely in cash, and every time I make a deposit or withdrawal, I feel the judgment of the teller as he or she quietly observes the paltry amounts in my checking and savings accounts. This disgust is particularly noticeable when I try to deposit large amounts of coins, or in the circumstances when I have needed to withdraw less than twenty dollars.

So it was with great pride that I walked into my bank and deposited a ten-thousand-dollar check. I waited in line, letting people go ahead of me to see James, the least judgmental of tellers (although he too has flashed me looks of pity), and waited for Clara.

Clara is evil. I imagine that when everyone leaves and the bank closes, she leaps into the vault and swims in giant vats of money, like Scrooge McDuck, only creepier. I don't like Clara.

She was there today, wearing a sad black blouse and a pin that told me to ask her about a savings plan. It was a tempting notion, but I had other ideas. She looked at me with undisguised resignation as I came toward her.

"How can I help you today?" she said. Only Clara could make this sound angry and petulant. Well, and also Renee. And Walter, but mostly he did drive-through, and I had a very unreliable car.

"Hello, Clara," I said as though I were addressing my archenemy. "I'd like to deposit this check."

I slid her the check.

"For *ten THOUSAND dollars.*"

I didn't really mean to say it like that, in a Dr. Evil voice, but damn it, I was happy. I had expected more of a reaction from her, honestly. She looked at the check, and me, and just sort of clucked in a sad, resigned way.

"ID, please."

More like, ID? Please. You remember me, Clara. I'm the woman who made you recount a ceramic Death Star filled with pennies. Don't pretend we don't have a past.

But I didn't say any of that. I gracefully removed my ID from my purse and slid it over to Clara, who studied it deeply, looking for some sort of forgery, I presume. Because This Could Not Be Happening.

Clara sighed and did some typing. After a moment she handed me a receipt of deposit. It was strange—holding the check didn't affect me, but having the receipt of deposit made me feel like my hands were on fire.

"Have a nice day," she said tonelessly.

I was still living large, and I wasn't yet ready to walk away.

"Do you have mints?"

"Mints?" said Clara with a sigh, now regarding me as though I were wasting the bank's very valuable time.

"You know, complimentary breath mints? Like in a candy dish?"

"Those are for children, ma'am."

"Do children like mint?"

"Would you like me to get a children's mint for you, ma'am?"

I believe that I was now being sassed.

"Two," I told her, "if you don't mind. I'm feeling very parched. After earning all of this money I just deposited."

The effort Clara had to expend to get my two mints was minimal, given that they sat in a candy dish on her side of the desk. But she managed to move her hands in a slow, exaggerated way, suggesting that she were moving mountains, or accomplishing some great Herculean, godlike burden that had been placed on her.

She dropped each mint into my hand, separately, with a dramatic pause between each one.

"Thank you," I said, lording over the moment.

"By the way," she said darkly, "I'm sure you're aware that with large checks like these, it sometimes takes longer for them to clear."

"How much longer?" I asked.

"Five to seven days," said Clara. "Sometimes even longer than that, if the bank deems it suspicious. You can call our customer service line if you have any questions."

I tried to be sunny, but I couldn't help but frown at her. This, of course, made her brighten.

"Enjoy your mints," she chirped. "And have a nice day."

It was about the time that I would have started genuinely worrying about Charice that I got a text from her.

"Chinese food," it said.

Which was a typical missive from Charice Baumgarten.

Nothing about where she has been, nothing about what she has learned from the police. And it made no immediate sense. So it was good to know that she was her usual self.

My guess was that she was asking if I wanted Chinese food, perhaps tonight? So I texted: "yes?"

I went to the library for the afternoon and tried to find some books about becoming a detective. There's less on the topic than you might imagine. When I got home I found no Chinese food, and immediately, no Charice. All the lights were turned off, and the place seemed to be lit by candlelight coming from the dining room. Two possibilities immediately sprung to mind—one was a candlelit dinner, which would have been lovely. I can't say who might have prepared a candlelight dinner for me—Charice, possibly?—but setting aside reason, I occasionally like to be optimistic about things.

It wasn't a candlelit dinner. When I got into the dining room, I observed that someone had covered our table with a fancy red cloth and that Charice was gathered around a folding table with four people who I did not recognize. Four of them were dressed solemnly, practically in funeral garb, although Charice was wearing a hat that looked like it had been assembled from the remains of a violently murdered peacock. The fifth person wasn't dressed solemnly at all. Her blond hair was pulled into a ponytail and she was wearing an inexplicable poodle skirt.

"I came from a sock hop," she explained, apparently feeling my eyes on her.

"Ah," I said. I didn't want to get involved.

"I didn't have time to change," she said, sounding more irritated.

"Sure," I said. But I must have still looked skeptical, because she looked put out.

"It was for a charity," she said. "Why is everyone giving me a hard time about this?"

I didn't want to get into the weeds about a sock-hop fundraiser with this unknown woman, so I asked the more relevant question.

"Charice," I said, faking calmness, "tell me that you aren't planning a séance."

"We are not planning a séance," said Charice. "The planning has passed. We are séancing."

I got out my best ice-dagger glare, mostly out of habit, because it never did anything on Charice. It was more the principle of the thing.

"I'm sure I don't need to point out that it would be in amazingly bad taste to try to contact Jonah Long."

"Who would be so tacky?" asked Charice, in a rhetorical question that begged to be answered. But I held my tongue. "We're just going to have a séance and see who shows up."

I should make very clear, although I'm sure it's unnecessary, that Charice has no special abilities at communing with the dead. She does about as well with a Ouija board as she does with Catan, which is a game she wins only by stealing wool when people aren't looking. My eye was drawn to Ms. Poodle Skirt, who did look familiar somehow.

"I'm not participating in this séance," I told her.

"Oh good," said Charice. "You have a bad psychic energy. Just sit on the sofa."

By "bad psychic energy" Charice meant that I was troublesome about not pushing the pointer where she wanted it to go. But I sat on the sofa and watched, because I knew it would make Charice happy, and there was often value in that. A man turned out the last light, and Charice started talking.

"Great spirits of the beyond, we contact you now."

There was the associated pause and a Y-E-S-? skated its way across the board.

"Can I ask with whom I am speaking?"

Poodle Skirt helpfully read the words aloud as the spirit "spoke."

IT IS I, WILFRID LAURIER.

"Who's that?" asked one of the somber-looking men at the table. He looked genuinely confused, so either he was a good actor or he wasn't in on the joke.

YOU HAVEN'T HEARD OF ME?

"No," said Charice.

AMERICANS.

"Where are you from?"

CANADA. I AM CANADA'S MOST FAMOUS PRIME MINISTER.

"Really?" asked Charice.

WELL, TOP TEN.

"So, Wilifrid...," started Charice, but she was interrupted by a jerking of the Ouija board.

WILFRID. IT'S WILFRID.

"Right, Wilfrid. So there's been a..." And Charice looked at me as she spoke now, testing to see how far she could reasonably push me. "...a disturbance around here lately. Is there anyone there with anything pressing they want said?"

HOW FARES ONTARIO?

I noticed a smile starting to crack ever so slightly on Carnation Lapel Guy.

"It's fine. I could google it for you, if you want," said Charice.

AND HALIFAX? HOW IS THE GEM OF THE EASTERN SEABOARD?

"You know, I've never been," said Charice.

OH, YOU SHOULD GO. IT'S VERY NICE. PEOPLE ALWAYS JUST THINK OF PRINCE EDWARD ISLAND FOR VACATION BUT HALIFAX IS A DELIGHT.

"So do you have any clues, or..."

IT'S LIKE BOSTON BUT WITHOUT THE CRIME.

"Anyone recently murdered around there?" asked Charice.

LOTS OF GOOD BARS TOO.

"Any souls crying out to be heard? Even a cryptic message might be helpful."

GOOD LOCAL BEERS.

I could tell that everyone at the table was in on this farce, simply because of how completely ashen-faced they all were. If one of Canada's top-ten prime ministers were legitimately giving you drinking advice, you would probably at least crack a smile. I was about to get up and retreat to my room when there was an honest-to-gosh thunderclap. It must have been close to us, because it sounded incredibly loud, and the power in the apartment dimmed. Maybe I'm misremembering it, but I think there was some serious candlelight flick-age as well.

Whether it was a spirit or simply Charice not being one to waste an opportunity, the Ouija board wheeled out one final message.

D-O-U-B-L-E-_-L-I-F-E

———————◆———————

Charice was not willing to let go of that DOUBLE LIFE line. I might have somehow believed that it had been somewhat real, given the overall spookiness and suddenness of it all, except for her hounding me about forever after.

"Double life, Dahlia!" she kept repeating. "I wasn't even moving the pointer. It was a message."

I let a lot of things slide here, as I usually did with Charice. First of all, her insistence that she wasn't moving the pointer for DOUBLE LIFE was more or less an indirect confession that she was moving it the rest of the time. Not that I had genuinely expected that PM Wilfred Laurier was seriously using me as a window into Canadian affairs. Furthermore, even if Charice were telling the truth, there were a lot of other people at the table. Finally, DOUBLE LIFE is an impossibly vague sort of statement. When your clue from beyond the grave is too vague for a fortune cookie, it's probably not worth spending a lot of time on. I mean, if you believe that Jonah Long sent me a final message—which I don't—let's consider it. Ten letters in DOU-BLE LIFE. You could do a lot with ten letters. If I were a spirit with ten letters, I'd just spell out the name of the murderer. IT WAS TOM. Heck, with two characters you could do the guy's initials. Even if I didn't know what the guy looked like I could give a description. LLWBRIMLEY. (That would mean that the attacker looked like Wilford Brimley.) Not sure if they'd get that, but I'd try.

"I'll keep that under advisement, Charice. I'm writing it down now and putting in my big book of clues." I had told her that as a sort of sarcasm, but it seemed to mollify her anyway. She apparently thought I did have a big book of clues. Maybe I should have a big book of clues. Isn't that what Encyclopedia Brown did? (Please turn your page upside down for the answer.)

To be fair, Charice was also sated by the story of my getting $10,000, which admittedly packed a wallop. Also, she got rent money, which continued to cheer her. I even told her about Clara and the mints. She had never heard me mention Clara before, but I was riding high. She cleared out the séancers and celebrated. I drank a gin and tonic, retreated to my room, and tried playing a round of *Dota*, a computer game that marries my triplet loves of deep strategy, quick reflexes, and collecting clothes for the walrus. After I was throughly buzzed and I had made a reasonable dent in my MMR, it was time to get to work.

I had business in *Zoth* to arrange.

I needed to create a new character, but my fingers were now pleasantly numb. Not frostbite-victim numb, just cheerfully floopy. Like a giant squid attempting to play an Elton John song.

I was done with my archer, though. I did not want Tambras connecting me to that particular interview. I needed something new, and because I was a little floopy myself, I wanted someone who would express me.

This general light-headedness is probably why when I attempted to name my character "RedRadish" it came out as "RedRasish." I did not realize this until much later, when a sugarplum fairy instructed me that gathering ten dumblemoor flowers from the Fetid Swamp would bring glory to the Red-Rasish family name. I read that initially and thought, *Is this fairy drunk?* It was then that I realized that I was the drunken fairy.

Of course, if I had spelled it correctly, I would muse later with the benefit of sobriety, the game wouldn't have let me in, as the game already had a RedRadish in it. Which was me, a year earlier, under my ex-boyfriend's account. RedRadish was a happy, carefree ogress, with dreams of financial gains and a certainty that her boyfriend was not cheating on her with a dental hygienist. She also had tremendous facial scarring and an enormous tree trunk that she used as a sort of club. This was because the old me wanted to be badass. The dreams of youth.

Despite the fact that I had no intention of really playing the game—my business here was to meet up with other guild members and do a little reconnaissance—I found myself taking an inordinately long time picking out my character. First impressions were important.

RedRadish had been an ogress with a facial scar. RedRasish was a delicate-looking fairy, with rosy-pink skin and on whom I spent ninety-nine cents for especially elaborate hair. Yes, this was the gin, but ninety-nine cents for candy-colored hair with thick curls that coiled on the top of my head like a luxurious apostrophe seemed appealing at the time. I was looking for the girliest starting class I could find, which I assumed to be dancer, but then I discovered a new god named Usune, (new gods crop up in *Zoth* relatively frequently), and by becoming her priestess, I would get to carry a harp.

So it was in this way that a drunken harp-wielding fairy with fabulous hair entered the Kingdoms of Zoth. Clovemince, a surprisingly stern-looking sugarplum fairy, gave me a brief but efficient description of the current state of the fairy kingdom and strongly suggested that I would be doing both myself and Usune a favor by wandering into a deadly swamp to gather flowers for our people.

I ignored her request, as well as that of a handsome green fairy man who wanted to know if I was a girl in RL, and looked for the guilds tab. I needed to find Jonah's guild so I could interrogate its members. I could have just sat there and queried names, but I wanted more of a personal connection this time around.

And I did not feel like putting off the provocations of a green fairy man, who seemed to want to sit on me.

"Ur hot," he was saying.

I certainly didn't want to gather flowers while battling the mud people who would shamble out of the swamp. I just didn't. I realize that this was a privilege that other people paid for (and that technically I had paid for), but as far as I was concerned, RedRasish was just an elaborate, badly spelled disguise. Squashing mud people was just not part of my wheelhouse. Besides, what was a harp going to do to them, anyway?

I dialed Kurt Campbell, whose phone number Jonah had given me, "in case of an emergency." I had fully expected it to go to voice mail, and then I would end up in the swamp after all, but lo, there he was.

"Hello?" he said.

He must have seen my Saint Louis cell number and assumed that I was someone who knew him.

"Hi, Kurt. This is Dahlia."

Silence.

"Dahlia Moss? The—" I was going to say "detective," but I remembered Detective Maddocks and rethought it. "...The woman you ignored at dinner on Sunday?"

"Why are you on my phone?"

The way he phrased it made me sound like I was some sort of insidious lolcat. "I in ur iphone, calling ur contacts." But I was not having this. Why shouldn't I be on his phone? I was a somewhat legitimate businesswoman.

"Well, I've logged in to the Kingdoms of Zoth and I was hoping you could show me around."

"You're what?" That got him.

"I'm on the edge of a swamp. Some fat purple fairy is trying to get me to gather flowers."

"Do you know about Jonah?"

"I do. In fact, his parents have hired me to manage his online affairs."

"Jonah's dead and you're still after that damned spear?"

Something about Kurt suddenly made me think of Clara. Not that I thought Clara was involved—although it was a fun idea—but in the same sense that he did not want me to succeed. I found myself briefly wondering if he didn't want me finding the spear, or if he was just generally bad tempered. Our text-filled dinner together certainly didn't give the impression of him being a people person.

"Primarily, I'm here to arrange a funeral for him online. Some sort of open service, I was thinking. Of course, if you know anything about the spear, I'm sure that Jonah's parents would be happy to learn of it."

"*Sylvia* hired you?"

It was nice, for once, to hear the question with the emphasis somewhere other than the word "you."

"Indirectly," I told him. "I was hired by their lawyer."

This seemed to relax Kurt, although I couldn't tell you why. Did he not want me speaking directly to Jonah's mother? Why?

"I'm glad that's settled," I told Kurt. "So, how about this swamp?"

"I'm not going to game with you, Dahlia."

"I'm not looking to play, Kurt. I just want to talk to other people in the guild."

Kurt sighed—not a real sigh, actually. The sort of audible stage sigh you would make so the people on the back row would know that you were sighing.

"Go talk to them, then. We have a webpage. I'm sure you can look everyone up."

"I could do that, or you could introduce me to everyone and explain that I'm a friend of the family who's putting Kurt's affairs in order."

"Why would I do that?"

"It will sound better coming from you."

"That's why *you* would want me to do it; why would *I* want to do it?"

It was like dealing with Clara. I don't know why I hadn't realized it before. Weirdly, even as I made this realization, I decided to try an approach that I would never dare to take with a battle-hardened bank teller.

"To make amends? You were a real jerk to me over dinner."

"You accused me of a crime."

"You were rude well before that. And besides, this is a good thing to do. Don't you want Jonah's affairs settled? Wouldn't you like to see some sort of remembrance for him online?"

Kurt paused for a second, and I took it to mean that the conversation was going even worse. But his response sounded rational and even.

"Fine," said Kurt. "Meet me in two hours. Let's say…at the Broken Sickle Bar in Hochstein. That should be easy enough for you to find."

And he hung up on me. I'm not sure if smirking makes an audible sound, but if it did, that was definitely the sound I heard before the click.

CHAPTER SEVEN

Something about the tenor of that conversation—perhaps coupled with the memory of my ex huddled over his laptop while vampirically draining bottles of Mountain Dew—made me realize that I had better alcohol down and caffeine up. I was going to meet a bevy of gamers, one of whom was possibly a thief and a murderer. This was a time I not only wanted my wits about me; I wanted them styled with cute blond streaks and smelling like echinacea and hibiscus.

A quick trip into Charice's cabinet of wonder had me drinking coffee with butterscotch, which pairs *great* with ramen. Once I was fortified, I did some wiki searching and I figured out why I had the vivid image of Kurt smirking into the phone.

Visiting the Broken Sickle Bar as a level-one character was a little like a four-year-old visiting the top of Mount Everest. Good luck with that.

Hypothetically, I could get there. All I had to do was hike south for a few minutes, hop aboard a flying Chinese dragon that would carry me to another continent, follow the shoreline for another several minutes, then cross the water at some shoals, hack through some jungle, visit a fortune-teller and breathe in her "magic herbs," go back through the shoals, and walk through a newly visible cave until I came upon the Field of Ghosts, from which Hochstein, a sad little mountain in the midst of a barren field, was clearly visible.

It would take me two hours to do this, but I figured it was a kind of test and I wasn't about to be shown up. I got killed a few times on the way to the Chinese dragon, but I eventually realized that if I stuck to the roads, I'd be mostly okay. The worst were the shoals, which were filled with horrible crab-men and -women that would pull me beneath the water and strangle me. This happened, like, six times. I only got by when some other schlub came along and got through while they were strangling him. The fortune-teller was also dead when I got there, which struck me as another murder to solve, but after a few minutes her body vanished and then later respawned.

By the time I got to the Field of Ghosts, I had been skewered, drowned, burned, buffeted with arrows, poisoned, and killed by an evil doppelgänger of myself who hit me in the head with my own damned harp. I had also been mocked by lots of gamers, mostly on horseback, who would dash by me with shiny suits of armor and particle effects, laughing.

One woman was driving a giant winged snake and told me, "lol. get out of this zone, noob."

The aggravating thing about the Field of Ghosts was that you could clearly see the Broken Sickle Bar. But you could also see that it was separated from you by an insurmountable number of the walking dead. Presumably, characters who belonged here could fight their way through, but these were ghosts that killed me not by breathing on me but just by contemplating the idea.

I know it's unbecoming for a gamer girl to do this, but I /sat down on the ground and decided to /cry. Frankly, RedRasish's cry was not very moving. It sounded a little like the noise you get when you poke the Pillsbury Doughboy. But for my own private disappointment, it was a good a soundtrack as any.

A harpy came swooping down by me, I assumed to eat me, which isn't actually a death I had experienced yet. Instead she sat on the ground next to me and started a campfire.

"Why the long face, little lost fairy?" she typed.

Her name was Vothvoth, which I knew not from detective work but because the letters were floating over her pointy, misshapen head.

"I'm not lost. I'm trying to get to that inn over there, and I'll never get across this field of undead. I've been walking for, like, two hours."

"Oh," said the harpy, who was now cooking a live bird. "Did you run out of invisibility oil?"

The whatnow oil?

"Here," she said, giving me five stacks of invisibility oil. Then she bit the head off her cooked bird and flew off.

Fuck this shit. I mean, that had been one nice harpy, but there's fucking invisibility oil? I had to fight a fire-breathing camel at one point, and there's invisibility oil? This is the kind of thing I hated about these sorts of games. Everything's obvious once you already know it, but woe unto the private dick who has to cross a shoal of angry crab-people and doesn't know about invisibility oil.

By the time I made it to the Broken Sickle Bar I was already tired and wanted to stop. But of course, this was the reason I had come here. In this case, the getting there was not part of the journey at all. In this case, it had just been a horrible trial along the way.

Given the ramshackle appearance of the bar—a run-down

shack in an abandoned ghost town—and the fact that it took freaking forever to get here—I found myself shocked at how many people were squeezed into this bar. It was packed. I had been to nightclubs with less action—good ones.

I had assumed that meeting up with Kurt would have mostly been a matter of saying hello to the only person around, but now there was all of this. Plus, I didn't know what his username was, or what he looked like in-game. I did know that he was a ninja. But what did that look like?

Also, I was invisible, which is not useful when you intend to rendezvous.

I yelled, which meant that everyone in the room could hear me. "DOES ANYONE KNOW HOW TO TURN OFF INVISIBIL-ITY OIL?"

I realized that it was an irritating thing to do; but I had spent much of my evening being devoured by crab-people and irritating was feeling more promising than irritated, which is where I had been. Still, there was karmic payback, because I was helped by the worst possible person.

His name was Atheun, and he was a tall, handsome elf with revoltingly nice cheekbones.

I knew Atheun. Atheun was the name of my ex-boyfriend's character. I knew the name well because Erik had written a song for him. In retrospect, it should have been easy to see that our relationship was in trouble given all the presents Atheun got that I didn't. Atheun was on T-shirts, imprinted on custom action figures. No one's ever written a song about me.

What was agonizing was that he actually looked like Erik. He had the same ridiculous '90s haircut, the same tiny body with loose-fitting clothing, the same smirk on his face, even. Only Athuen looked charming and mysterious, whereas Erik had looked...Ah hell, who am I kidding? Erik had always looked charming and mysterious too.

But his cheekbones hadn't been that good.

Atheun came up to me and typed, "you should be able to right-click on the invisibility buff to take it off."

Which was straightforward enough. Although now I was less certain that I wanted to be seen. I hadn't actually spoken to Erik in months, and then under somewhat arranged circumstances, and meeting him here in a fairy costume was not the image I wanted to convey.

"It's not working," I typed at him. "Thanks for helping anyway!"

And then I thought I would hide. Which was ridiculous, given that I was already invisible.

But Atheun would not leave well enough alone. He had to be helpful. In three years, he had never washed a dish, but when it came to invisibility oil, he was Johnny-on-the-spot. Three years I dated this goon.

"Don't worry, I've got some vapor of appearance," he said, and a puff of pink dust appeared around me.

"Oh, hello little fairy," he said. "You've wandered pretty far, haven't you?"

I /curtsied. This was worse than Facebook stalking, but I had come by it honestly.

"RedRasish? Is that an Indian name?"

"I wanted to be RedRadish, but someone had taken it."

"Oh. Ha ha."

I honestly don't know what I wanted to happen here, or what I was afraid of happening. There probably exists some alternate universe, sitting very close to this one, in which Erik confesses to me that his wonderful ex-girlfriend whom he was missing terribly used that name, and how his dental hygienist is a pale shadow of what a wonderful girl she was. And from that alternate universe, there are branches in which I tell him off and RedRasish flies off on her gossamer wings while he cries into his drink. And there are branches, probably multiple branches, in which I take him back and have his babies. And there's that universe that I'd rather not consider, in which he confesses that RedRadish was this awful hag of an ex who could never play games like this and had chosen a scarred ogress for her avatar, which was truthfully not that far off the mark.

All of those could have happened. And probably more. And, forgive me, they're all more interesting than what occurred in the actual universe, in which Atheun then said:

"Oh well, off to go raiding! Good luck, little fairy!"

And he was gone.

It had certainly been a more friendly communication than the evening in which we had broken up. I could have used a "good luck, little fairy" then. I seemed to be getting them in spades now. Something about being a fairy, I suppose. I had never gotten a "good luck, little ogress." Perhaps this was how pretty people went through life. On little gossamer wings.

My pontifications on beauty and race were quickly interrupted by an old bald man with facial scars of his own. If I had to guess his class, knowing nothing about *Zoth*, I would have led off with Beggar. He was shabby-looking. People in this bar were decked out in all manner of shining zoot suits and glowing plated mail. Not this guy.

"Dahlia. This is Kurt."

He bowed at me. For some reason, even though I knew full well that it was Kurt, and I knew what Kurt sounded like, I imagined the voice of a wizened sensei. If you had a long white

Fu Manchu, the long flat vowels of a Midwesterner should not be coming out of you.

"I'm impressed you made it this far."

"How did you know it was me?"

The old man, whose name was "Disfigurement"—which I again knew because it was floating over his head—waved his hands at me in order to suggest that it had been obvious. He did not look like a ninja, nor was he especially disfigured.

"You mentioned the Fetid Swamp, which is part of the fairy homeland. No other fairies here. Plus you're level two. Also, you're carrying a harp."

"What does that have to do with anything?"

"I don't know. You seem like someone who would carry a harp."

Although it may detract from the narrative, may I briefly espouse the virtue of everyone's names floating over their heads all the time? People who have not played MMORPGs may find it disquieting, but I feel that this should be happening all the time. Every party I attend should have this technology. Google Glass, get right on that.

Meanwhile, Kurt was throwing silly guesswork at me. Was this the same kind of thing as fairydom? When you're a fairy, everyone wishes you well. When you're a detective, everyone shares random theories with you.

He was right, though. I *was* the kind of woman who carried a harp. Ideally, I'd bring them to the parties with the floating names, and if there was alcohol involved, you'd have your whole evening worked out right there. But I digress.

"It was hell to get here. You were completely putting me on, right? You thought I would get lost along the way."

"I thought you would make it, but just find it very

challenging. And I was putting you on a little bit. Welcome to Zoth."

It was strange how much faster Kurt could type responses to me than he could speak them. In real life, he was off-puttingly slow. In *Zoth*, he was Chatty Cathy.

I wanted to tell him that it wasn't my first time here, but truthfully RedRadish's excursions were nothing special. Mostly they consisted of me jamming at buttons ineffectually while Erik yelled things like "Turn off your goddamned bloodlust" at me from another room. Instead I said:

"So you're going to introduce me to the rest of the guild?"

Kurt ignored the question. "Why do Jonah's parents want the spear?"

"I'm just a gun for hire, Kurt," I said, issuing from my mouth the least plausible combination of words I had ever delivered. And yet it just rolled right out. "I don't grill my clients about their motivations."

I couldn't help but notice the gorgon sitting at the bar drinking wine. Probably she was afk, but something about the black gaze of her dead eyes made me feel that she was eavesdropping on me.

"Shouldn't we be whispering?"

Disfigurement /whispered in response:

"You know a little about *Zoth* after all. But are you really that paranoid?"

I responded in kind:

"I'm more than that paranoid. I've got a lot of money on the line here, and I want to make sure my clients are satisfied. They want the spear, and I don't want things getting derailed."

I'm sure it was the caffeine, but for a moment I could have sworn that Disfigurement winced, for just a second.

83

"I've met Jonah's parents. They don't need a digital weapon. You're telling me that they're going to create *Zoth* accounts, and, what? Run around the hillside battling imps?"

"I don't know and I don't care. I'll probably just send it to Jonah's account through the in-game mail. Whatever they ask for."

"He can't log in! You'd be sending it to oblivion!"

Even with his ninja face hiding Kurt's own, it was clear he was pretty testy about the spear. I had pegged early on that he hadn't taken it, and though it might still have been folly, I was pretty sure I was right. But he cared about it a lot more deeply than he had let on before. Was this just an academic's interest, the way a geologist gets upset when someone tosses an unusual pebble down the garbage disposal? (I've had some odd boyfriends, and this observation comes firsthand.) Or was it something else? I'd come back to it later.

"It's really not my problem," I said. "So can I join your guild? I obviously need to talk to a lot of people."

"No. I don't actually have permission to add new members. Only Oatcake and Clemency do, and they're not online right now."

"Well, I assume you're all on a vent server or something, I'm sure you won't mind if I join that."

He wasn't expecting that I would know about that, clearly. A vent server, in case you're not in the know about these things, is a server where people in a game can get together and speak to one another as they play. I imagine this involves yelling, "Turn off your goddamned bloodlust" a lot, but I have a somewhat limited perspective. The trick about them, however, is that they are never a part of the game you are playing on. This is by design, because if the game crashes, it is still useful to be able to speak to one another. Thus, there is absolutely no reason I shouldn't be allowed on their vent server.

Save for Kurt not wanting me to talk to anyone.

"I don't want you to talk to anyone."

Well, so much for subtext.

"And why not?"

"No one actually knows that Jonah's been killed yet."

It was my turn to type /surprise.

"You didn't tell them?"

"Oddly, I haven't been playing much lately, after having lost my job and home."

"You're here now," I told him.

"It's difficult to bring up."

"Haven't they been asking about him?"

"A few people asked where he was, and I said I wasn't sure. Philosophically speaking, that's technically true."

"Let me speak to them," I typed.

"No," said the old ninja, who was fading from Kurt's voice in my mind, back to my stock sensei. "You'll just make everyone feel weird. I'll spread the news and let them know that you plan to ask them questions."

"You brought me all the way out here for nothing."

"Not for nothing." The old man smiled. "Have a drink."

CHAPTER EIGHT

I went to bed sleepy and dissatisfied. Things were going my way financially, but everything else felt wrong. I don't know what I had expected from Kurt, but his sending me home with digital liquor wasn't it. I kept thinking about Detective Maddocks's impatience with me. It's one thing to be a failure; it's another to be a fraud.

At two thirty in the morning I was awakened from my troubled sleeping by Charice, who either hadn't bothered knocking on my door or had taken my nonresponse as implicit instructions to enter and kneel by the side of my bed. In other circumstances, a thin, wispy woman whispering, "Dahlia, Dahlia," in half darkness at your bedside would be horror-movie material. Maybe it still was.

The best I could manage was light chagrin. This was not the first time that Charice had awakened me in the middle of the night. And of course, sudden influx of money or no, she was still paying the rent. So I could put up with her eccentricities.

"Dahlia," she whispered again. And "whisper" isn't really quite the right word. "Death gasp" is really more descriptive. It was an inflection designed to produce troubled dreams.

"We don't want any," I told her in a pretend sleepy voice. Better to put her through the paces a little.

"I need your advice," said Charice.

This is a fantastically un-Charice comment to make, as Charice usually rejects advice as though it were pitched outside of the normal of range of human hearing.

"What kind of advice?" I asked.

"It's curtains for you, Dahlia Moss."

I got out of bed and followed her into the common room. I don't know what I expected, but it wasn't that there would be absolutely no curtains anywhere in the apartment. At least I had a decent pair of pj's, because I was visible to the greater half of Saint Louis.

"What's happened in here?"

It was obvious what was happening, however. There were enormous Rubbermaid containers all over the floor and the apartment smelled like Rit dye.

"I'm doing a little redecorating," said Charice. "I'm just a tad worried I've left these in for too long."

"That's what you got up from sleep for?"

Charice was very skilled at not responding to this sort of question and just lifted what had previously been a white curtain out of the Rubbermaid container.

Dear God.

"Are these too yellow?" asked Charice.

Chernobyl had never been this yellow. If I closed my eyes, I could still see yellow curtains. If Charice hung these in the apartment, we would never need coffee again.

"They are a little vivid," I told her, which was putting a good face on it.

"Maybe I should throw some pink dye in there," said Charice. "We could soften it with an ombre effect."

Two thoughts. One was that the last thing these curtains needed was more dye. Any more color and they might supernova and destroy us all. The other thought was that I needed another task, quick, because when Charice starts using the word "we," watch out.

"Yes," I said. "Soften it. By all means. Charice," I said, trying to make a casual transition, "as much I'd love to help with this important curtain dye situation, I was thinking of going through the trash you had gotten so expertly from Kurt's car."

This was a good transition, because it also had the benefit of being true. Not only had I been thinking about it, I had been dreaming about it, which was like thinking, but with Jungian symbolism and a little sex.

"I threw that out," Charice told me. "It was making my room smell like egg salad."

Despite living with Charice for a number of months now, she continually found new ways to irritate me. Whenever I recalibrated to her insane whims, she would compensate to keep me equally exasperated. It was a cycle. Ours was not a Betty/Veronica relationship but Bert/Ernie. Still, this was an impressive bit of maneuvering on her part. To recap: She had broken into a car, gathered clues, professed at great length as to the power and importance of those clues, and then, when I wasn't looking, threw them out.

"Why would you do that, Charice?" I asked.

"You said it was a dumb idea."

Technically, this is true. But I say that ideas are dumb with a lot of frequency. I began making this point to Charice, but it proved to be one of those statements that sounds unhelpful the moment it begins to form in your mouth.

"Did you throw it out recently?" I asked.

"Very," said Charice. "I'm sure that its on the very top of the Dumpster out back, if you wanted to look."

"And are you going to tell me what you discovered from your late-night tailing of the police?"

Charice feigned confusion.

"I know you've been dying for me to ask you about it. Remember? You were chasing after police detectives with a novelty-shop microphone?"

"Nothing came of that. It's very hard to run down stairs faster than our elevator. And I got a late start on them."

I could tell that Charice wanted me to ask her where she had been all that time instead, and so I specifically avoided the question. When she saw that I wasn't going to take this particular bait, she told me:

"Top of the Dumpster, black bags, purple tie."

It wasn't on top. It wasn't even close to being on top, but in fact rather firmly in the middle. And the ties were blue, but let us not dwell on petty details.

Oh hell, let's dwell a little, because it was a nightmare. This was not one of those sitations where Nancy Drew twitched her nose and bumped into a wall of clues. It was a Dumpster, in the dark. And to make matters worse, I ran into our neighbor Mr. Tei.

Mr. Tei is an elderly Chinese gentleman who seems perfectly nice but whom I dislike because I only seem to run into him when I am drunk or otherwise in a terrible way. This is partially bad luck and partially because he keeps very strange hours. I ran into Mr. Tei the night Erik broke up with me. I was drunk and crying, and he did what he always did, which was give me A Look.

I'm completely projecting, but every time I see Mr. Tei I feel like he's thinking, *What is wrong with the youth of America?* Like I'm not just a tragedy in and of myself but emblematic of a greater systemic problem. I'm dragging down the reputation of millennials, is what I'm saying. I realize this isn't rational, but it's what I think when I see him, every time.

"Did you lose something important?" asked Mr. Tei.

It was the first time he'd ever actually said anything to me. I'd imagined that he'd speak with an accent, because he spoke Chinese to his dog, but no. Another wrong deduction from Dahlia Moss.

And I had lost a lot of important things, actually. I could have delivered them to him a cascade, but this might have left me sobbing, and I was really trying to make a better impression on Mr. Tei than my usual interaction, which was tough enough given that I was talking to him from inside a Dumpster. I was sober this time—that had to count for something.

"I think maybe there are some clues in here."

"Clues for what?"

I had no idea what kind of clues. Maybe something that implicated Kurt in the spear theft, or murder. This seemed positively insane to say aloud.

When I didn't answer, Mr. Tei asked, "You're not going through my trash, are you?"

"No," I said. "Just some things I threw out earlier."

This pleased Mr. Tei, who said, "Good. Your roommate wonders if I am a spy for the Chinese government."

"Why would you say that?"

"She asked me if I was a spy for the Chinese government."

"That's ridiculous," I told Mr. Tei.

"Yes," said Mr. Tei, who put a bag of trash carefully next to me and then went inside. I'd say it was a net wash for American millennials.

Sorting through bags of trash is slow and disgusting, but I found myself deeply pleased by the work of it. Part of it was that Kurt had been kind of a dick to me, and I figured that even if there weren't any clues, there was surely something in the mix that he would be embarrassed by. An unflattering photograph or a receipt for some sort of weird pornography. I wasn't planning on throwing any of it in his face, but it could at least give me a tiny moment of superiority. Or hell, maybe there really would be a clue in there. I was starting to believe my own hype about being a geek detective.

And maybe finding a clue wasn't the point anyway. Maybe the point was that I was trying.

I put everything into four quadrants: "Toss," "Save," "Interesting, Save for Emily," and "Oh My God, Kill It with Fire."

To be perfectly honest, most of the stuff belonged in the "Kill It with Fire" category. Foodstuffs! So many rotting foodstuffs. Old crumbling peanuts, gummy bears encased in multiple layers of dirt, partially empty Greek yogurt containers soured to a point close to madness, a half-eaten burger, grocery store sushi that had hardened into something sinister and diamond-like, and all these disturbingly indefinable bits, some of which were sloshy, some of which were sharp. Kurt's car must have looked and smelled like Cormac McCarthy's *The Road*. Probably it had a similar relationship with women.

The "Toss" category was mostly foodstuffs too, just ones that weren't completely disgusting. Lots of cherry cola bottles and detritus of food consumption that hadn't become totally gross yet: empty bags that had contained potato chips, old sandwich bags, and some Zebra Cakes that looked as fresh as the day he had bought them. Probably in the aughts. I'd kind of expected the sandwich Baggies to smell like weed, but honestly they smelled like sandwich. It was equally disgusting and disappointing.

Lots of clothes in the "Toss" pile too—some abandoned winter wear: a black glove, a scarf, a St. Louis Blues toboggan cap. There was a pair of jeans that had been stained with what I hoped was Greek yogurt, and the first embarrassing bit: a pair of pink Jockey shorts. Or rather, a pair of white Jockey shorts that inattentive washing had turned pink and that had been left in Kurt's car to die.

I describe all this to you not just so you get a sense of what a slob Kurt was but also to reiterate that I didn't just suddenly stumble my way into a big clue. I sifted through trash. I earned these clues.

In the "Interesting" pile: a cardboard box with the word TOP-ICO printed on the side in a fake-stenciled font. The box was empty except for a very interesting note printed in a computer serif. It read:

"Embroidery in childhood was a luxury, but sometimes you need luxury. Love, Tambras"

Well now, this was interesting. Tambras had gotten Kurt a present. A *love* present. Maybe it was the pink underwear, but my first thought was that Kurt must have been having a secret gay relationship with the troubadour, the stupidity of which was apparent as I turned over the box and saw the return address. Someone named Ophelia Odom of Boston, MA. So, not a gay relationship, because Tambras was a lady. I felt knuck-leheaded for even assuming otherwise. I really should have known better—assuming she was a dude just because her avatar was one. So what? My avatar had been a dude. He was also an elf. And he had great hair. I had nothing in common with him at all. People's *Zoth* avatars are not themselves. Sometimes they might give you insights into their characters—healers tend to be supportive, wizards like to be the center of attention, rogues are assholes—but sometimes not even that.

So, Kurt and Ophelia.

What was the present? The box certainly held something aside from the note. I googled "Topico," which apparently made clothing. Something embroidered, I guessed from the message. But there was no packing slip, so I couldn't know for sure.

Still, I found myself wondering about Ophelia. Kurt had cooed at dinner that he had been texting with a girl, and here was a woman who had gotten him a present. Was this the per-son who had been sending hilarious texts throughout dinner?

If her name had been Elizabeth Jones, I would have stopped there, but with a name as particular as Ophelia Odom, web searching is too fruitful to resist. A few keystrokes revealed that there have been only two Ophelia Odoms in the recorded his-tory of mankind—and thus she was either born in 1865 or a music teacher who occasionally played viola in the Boston Pops. I was tending toward the latter.

I even got a picture of her—from an article in the *Boston Globe* that featured a shot of the violists. Assuming that the attribu-tion of names was in the right order, and that she really was the third from the left, well, she was a stately-looking gal, Afri-can American, with a short Afro and very dark skin. Not what I would have immediately guessed for Kurt's girlfriend, and certainly not from what Tambras looked like. She was frowning in the photo, and it seemed hard to reconcile the frowning, stately violist with the sheer nerdiness of *Zoth*. But we all have secret depths.

It seemed even harder to imagine someone as classy-looking as Ophelia Odom—even her name seemed classy—stealing a spear, but it was worth knowing. Tambras could use the spear, unlike Kurt. And maybe she could have gotten the password. She lived in Boston, but maybe she had come to visit.

I was going to call it quits there, but there was something about that card. "Embroidery in childhood was a luxury, but sometimes you need luxury." It felt like an inside joke, but I couldn't make any sense of it.

Anyway, I was feeling pretty clever about all this, until I got to the bottom of the bin. Because here was a clue that dwarfed everything else. It was a small teardrop-shaped ruby. Exactly like you would find on the bejeweled spear.

Charice had been downstairs, washing the dye out of our curtains. I had a terrible feeling that this meant that everyone in our building would suddenly have yellow-tinted clothing, but I did not address this point. Instead I showed her the gem. She was delighted, if a little uncomprehending. She had pointed out to me, savvy jewel person that she was, that it wasn't a real gemstone, just cheap glass. But the spear wouldn't have been made with real jewels, anyway, or so I assumed. So this was the real thing. The fake, real thing. I went back to sleep excited, but I tried very hard not to overreact. I hadn't seen the "real" jeweled spear yet, so I didn't know for certain that my gem went on it or not. And if even if it did, that didn't necessarily mean anything. But I couldn't figure out any other reason Kurt would have a paste gem in his car.

I felt like I was onto something.

As a way to ward off my thinking about the murder, I decided to focus on thinking about the theft. The theft I could handle. Or so I thought. This put me, more or less, instantly asleep.

When I got up, I made a list of the folks in Jonah's guild. I then went through each class, one by one, and figured out who could wield spears. There was no way to find an alibi for any of these folks but I could at least determine motive. I knew already that Kurt couldn't use the spear, since ninjas aren't allowed to use spears in the game.

When I was done, I had three names. Clemency, Thread-work, and Tambras. Tambras was tingling my danger sense like Dr. Jekyll frolicking on a three-legged trampoline, but I'd look at everyone. Just two more people to interview, and I'd have my primary suspects. Of the non-Chinese-gold-farmer variety.

In addition to fretting about the case, I also checked my phone to see if Nathan Willing had messaged me. He hadn't. This was something I was going to have to take into my own hands.

Did I message Nathan because he had cute spindly limbs and reminded me of a slightly sexy walking stick? Or did I have some professional purpose? I suppose the truth was mostly column A. I told him I wanted a little more insight into Jonah's life. But I could have gotten that from lots of places. It was just that Nathan seemed a lot more promising than a lot of my other options.

He responded to my FB message instantly, which should maybe be off-putting but wasn't.

"How about you crouch in front of the doorway of a fine Saint Louis eatery?" I messaged him.

"When and where?" he had responded.

Yes, this was going to be bad indeed. I put on my sexiest clothes, then, worrying that I had overshot the mark, opted for my Jigglypuff cap. It was cold, and Jiggly helped send the message I wanted to send, which was apparently that I would like Nathan to fall asleep so that I could write on his face. (This is a hard-core Pokémon reference and if you do not get it, I apologize. If you do get it, I apologize even more deeply.)

We met at a Thai place on the Loop that I liked. There are better places for Thai, fancier places, tastier places, but there was something nostalgic about the joint for me, although I couldn't have told you why. Just Friday nights with friends, I suppose, but sometimes that lends enough memory that you're willing to overlook lousy service.

Nathan had arrived before me and was sitting there in a striped green polo, smiling at me as I came in. He was also munching on a piece of celery, which they did not serve here. Did he just travel around with healthy food?

"What inconsistencies in my story have you come to grill me about?" asked Nathan as I sat down, a little too hopefully, I thought.

"Is that what you were looking for? A grilling?"

"Is that something you offer?"

"I'm more of a gal who singes lightly, but arrangements can be made."

The tone of this was probably flirtier than I can easily describe here. Professionalism had gone out the window. Somewhere, the scowling disembodied head of Jonah hovered disapprovingly over us. His parents' money was buying this meal. Perhaps I should bring it down a notch.

"Okay," I said, "so we've established that you're adorable."

"Adorable, really? That's not a word that's usually used to describe me."

"How about narcissistic?"

"Closer."

"That's not the point, Nathan. The point is that you're adorable, and that I'm single, and what was I saying?"

"You have a job to do?"

"Right."

"So the grilling?"

The waitress came over and took our orders, which for some reason or another seemed to put sort of a chill on our conversation. She always seemed not very far away, just looking for an opportunity to refill my glass of water. It was unnerving. It's not as if I thought she was eavesdropping, and judging from her accent, I'm not sure she would have followed much if she had been, but it made the dinner feel more illicit to know that there was another set of ears not too far away.

My voice dropped a little closer to whispering when I resumed our conversation in earnest.

"So, Nathan, I think I should begin with a confession."

"I like confessions."

"Then here goes: I'm not really a detective. I mean, I was hired as a detective by Jonah, and later, his family, but I don't know what the hell I'm doing."

Nathan seemed to take this very lightly, clinking the ice around in his drink jovially.

"That's your confession?"

"Yes. Were you expecting more?"

"Well, the police did tell me that already."

"What? Those bastards."

Detective Maddocks just seemed like the sort of person who wanted fun to be stopped. I imagined him showing up at my high school reunion, explaining to everyone that I wasn't a real detective, and telling people other true but embarrassing things like "Although Dahlia claims to speak German, she only knows like fifty words," and "Those cool shoes she's wearing are borrowed."

Nathan did not notice my furrowing brow and went on.

"Anyway, I told them that I thought they were wrong. I think that you are a detective."

"They're not wrong," I said, sighing.

"No," said Nathan. "They're wrong. What you're telling me is that you don't have a lot of experience as a detective. To that I say: No matter! There is something decidedly detective-like about you."

"Is it my hat?" I asked, tugging at my Jigglypuff cap.

"You have an interrogative manner."

It had gotten a lot less flirty, but I was liking Nathan more and more by the minute. Then our courses were here. Nathan had gotten something complicated and unpronounceable, whereas I was sticking with my tried-and-true green curry with vegetables, which is the Thai restaurant version of ordering vanilla ice cream. I guess this place really was all about nostalgia for me.

"Still," said Nathan, looking thoughtful—and I liked boys who looked thoughtful—"it begs a question. If you're so sure that you're not a detective, why take Mrs. Long's money?"

I had planned to answer Nathan by telling him that I was

basically a terrible person, but my lips went renegade and spit out something altogether different.

"I want to know why Jonah hired me. It doesn't make any sense."

"Aha," said Nathan. "I was right! You *are* a detective."

What the hell was I saying? My brain took executive control of my lips again and tried to steer the conversation to the safety of the shore.

"I'm *not* a detective. I'm an unemployed millennial with an overly expensive business degree."

"Nope. Painters paint; sculptors sculpt; and detectives detect. You are a detective, because you are detecting."

"I'm not doing it very well."

"I didn't say you were a good detective. Probably you aren't. But you've got a spark, a little glimmer. Why do you think Jonah hired you?"

I probably should have found this patronizing, but I didn't. And Nathan had distracted me with a question regardless.

"Not because of a spark," I said. "He had never even met me."

Nathan looked puzzled. "I hadn't known that bit. That is a little weird."

It comforted me to hear this, because I'd floated the same theory to Charice, who lives a world of insane coincidences and would not accept anything unusual about it. Now that I had a receptive audience, I was willing to try out my actual theory.

"Ever read one of those old private-eye mysteries where the detective gets double-crossed?"

"I suppose," said Nathan. "I'm really more of a sci-fi guy."

"But you knew all of those noir words!"

"Google," said Nathan.

"Well, it's a thing. Sam Spade is in his office, or wherever, and some dame with great legs comes in and asks him to find her sister."

"Did Jonah have nice legs?" interrupted Nathan.

"He had nice pants, but let me finish. The dick takes the case, and when he finds the sister, he discovers she's dead, gets framed, and besides which it wasn't the dame's sister anyway."

"And the great legs were prosthetic," added Nathan.

"Exactly," I told him.

"There never was a dame; she was a hologram."

"Yes, you're moving into sci-fi."

"The sister was a Cylon."

"Now you're just being derivative."

There was something catlike about the way Nathan flirted. Probably that he practically purred when you complimented him. I felt like if I rubbed his face, he would jump into my lap.

"All right," he said, stretching. "So that's a thing. Are you saying that Jonah hired you just to frame you for murder?"

"It sounds paranoid when you say it."

"I could try it again in a different intonation."

It did sound a bit half-baked. But there was something so smug about Jonah when he hired me—he was up to something. I was clearly supposed to find something, do something. Maybe it wasn't Jonah who made the wrong step. Maybe it was me?

"So I'm paranoid," I told Nathan. It was feeling less like a date and more like a confession.

"Well," he said, not remotely put off by the suggestion. "It's only paranoia if they're not really out to get you."

Nathan and I talked for a few minutes about things other than the case, and out of privacy and self-preservation, I shall not mention them here. I did learn that he had a model train hobby, which is a positively ridiculous hobby for someone under fifty. I learned a few other things as well, including the existence of his half-Japanese ex-girlfriend who he had broken up with eight months earlier but who he was still sharing an apartment with. I couldn't decide, and still can't, if such an amiable breakup overrode the creepiness of living with his ex this many months later. But I digress.

———————◆———————

After I ditched the boy, I found myself lingering in the Loop before I headed back to my apartment. It was hours from when I could log back in to *Zoth*, and I felt that my investigation was pretty much stalled out until I got online and actually, you know, met some suspects. Perhaps it was my newfound optimism, or that my confession to Nathan went shockingly well, but I found myself wanting to hang around a bit.

The Loop, incidentally, is a straight line. It's a little neighborhood of shops in University City that is named for the fact that once, billions of years ago, streetcars used it as a point to loop around. Now it was just odd little shops with great antiquarian books and hipster stores. I had always liked the place, but I hadn't actually been down here in ages, and I suddenly wanted to see it again.

Yes, it was probably optimism. If they say pride comes before a fall, cheeriness surely comes before massive depression. But God help me, I was cheery.

I was in one of those stores, looking at a naked magnetic refrigerator *David*, who I had dressed in magnetic pink boxer shorts. I thought the look suited him, and I was contemplating his eyewear when I heard a voice.

"Investigation coming along nicely, then?"

Occasionally, even idiots like me have good moments. And this was one of my rare good moments. I knew who was behind me; I recognized the voice. That, or I just imagined who would be the worst person to be behind me and just ran with it. It was an intuitive leap that would have made me look stupid if I had been wrong. But I went with it without even a moment's thought. When you're juggling flaming torches, why not throw a knife into the mix?

"Just you today, Detective Shuler?"

I did not turn around—in part out of fear that I had screwed up—but instead deliberately focused on sliding oversized white sunglasses onto *David*'s perfect little face.

"Did you see me come in?"

And I turned around now. He was alone and looked surprised and impressed. In my heart of hearts I wanted to do a little dance, maybe shout "Boo-yah!" or words along those lines, but I felt pretty certain that it would blow the moment. Instead, I was honest.

"I just had a feeling you would show up."

"Good God, are you wearing a Jigglypuff cap?"

Right. I made a mental note not to wear Pokémon-related headgear while conducting future investigation. But given that the game was up, I sung a quick bar of the Jigglypuff song. "Oh-ho-o!" When Shuler grinned, I asked:

"Why do you know who Jigglypuff is, anyway, Detective?"

"Everyone knows who Jigglypuff is," said Shuler with fake nonchalance. "He's famous."

"No," I told him. "Only geeks and children know this."

Shuler cleared his throat. "Well, I picked it up somewhere."

Yeah, I thought. *Somewhere like an unabridged Pokédex.* I knew a closet geek when I saw one, and Shuler was a classic example.

Usually I ride folks like this to the point of tears, but today, I decided, I was going to show compassion.

"What exactly are you doing, Dahlia Moss?"

It was not a question I had expected. I was originally planning to answer it in a glib way, like, "I'm putting sunglasses on Michelangelo's *David*, you?" but there was something so unexpectedly genuine about his tone that I just looked at him.

"Where is Detective Maddocks?" I asked. Not able to come out in daylight?

"It's funny you should ask that. Because if he finds out that Jonah's parents hired you for ten thousand dollars, he's going to murder you. With his eyes."

I considered this. It seemed plausible.

"How did you find out?" I asked him.

"Jonah's mother told me. The family has hired all sorts of people. There's a private detective looking at their business; there's someone looking at—" Here Detective Shuler paused, thinking. After a second he continued. "Another angle I shouldn't mention to you. And some other detectives, investigating things that"—he paused again—"I also probably shouldn't mention."

So I wasn't the only flower in Emily's garden. It made sense, but I felt a little betrayed nonetheless. One more professional who thought I didn't have what it took.

"Oh, good," I said. "Well, hopefully I'll just get lost in the mix. Hey, you can't, by any chance, let me see the murder weapon that Jonah was killed with?"

Detective Shuler's eyes boggled at me.

"I grant you that was probably a reach," I said. "Could you maybe just show me a picture?"

"No," said Shuler with a finality that I frankly hadn't expected from him. "That would not be a good idea."

There was a pause, as if he were considering his answer to my question after rather than before making it, and Shuler looked very worried. I liked Detective Shuler. Maybe they were just playing good cop/bad cop on me, but Shuler's furrowed brow of worry was more compelling to me than Detective Maddocks's angry hypno eyes. (Although I probably was just saying that because he wasn't around.)

"Do you think that it's that bad an idea to investigate the *Zoth* angle?" I asked.

"I think it's a terrible idea for *you* to investigate the *Zoth* angle, even under the cover of being a funeral planner. Especially under that, actually," Shuler answered, still looking worried.

"If not me, then who? You guys aren't taking it seriously."

This snapped Shuler out of his concern for me and back into his proper role of being suspicious.

"Where did you hear that?" he asked.

"Jonah's mother told me," I lied. It was a lie that came to me easily, which is the best kind. Shuler obviously went for it, because he visibly relaxed.

"I don't think Detective Maddocks realizes how fanatical people can be about games like *Zoth*. To him, they're just, well, games. As far as he's concerned, it's just a complicated version of *Candy Crush*, and no one ever got killed playing *Candy Crush*."

Shuler had obviously never met my aunt Lorraine, who played *Candy Crush* while driving seventy and passing slower traffic. But I knew what he meant.

"If that's as close to your approval as I can get, I'll take it. Honestly, I just don't want to cheat the Longs. If I find the first remotely interesting thing, I'll be sure to pass it along to you."

As I spoke, I toyed with the jewel in my pocket. The jewel I had found among rotting foodstuffs and the items from Kurt

Campbell's car, and the jewel I suspected belonged on the spear that Jonah had been stabbed with. I was telling Detective Shuler that I would share everything with him, and yet the jewel stayed firmly in my pocket. It wasn't that I was playing the police. I just didn't want to look like an idiot. I didn't want to explain where it came from, and I didn't want to deal with the pitying look I'd get from Shuler if I was wrong. I decided, then and there, the jewel was staying with me until I could somehow get a look at the analog spear.

But my prevarications went unnoticed by the detective.

"Just be sure to share them with me," said Shuler. "And not Maddocks." He eyed my work with the magnets in front of me. "And for God's sake, show some respect for Michelangelo's *David.*"

CHAPTER NINE

Sure enough, Kurt had heralded my coming, because a great many of the Horizons had arrived to meet me at World's End Tavern when I logged back in. This was not strictly necessary; I could have spoken to them perfectly well just on the vent server, but even with fake avatars, it's nice to see who you're talking to.

Also, they all had scads of glimmering weapons and whatnot, and I suspect they wanted to show off.

There were altogether too many Horizons—more than a dozen of them in the guild—but even though I was pretending just to be an online funeral planner, I really didn't want to waste my time with folks who couldn't use the spear. I was looking for a thief, and Kurt had a point. Why steal something that's useless to you? I had cross-referenced a list of guildies with classes that could use the spear, and that left me with just three names. That's manageable, right? Tambras—who I'd spoken to already—a human healer named Clemency, and a catfolk Fatespinner named Threadwork. Yeah, I didn't know what "Fatespinner" meant either.

But as soon as I was in the bar, I was set upon by a Horizon I didn't want to speak with. Most particularly, there was a giant tree—or I suppose treant—who was easily twice the size of everyone else in the room and had to bend down to get into the bar in the first place. She was all face, this tree—a huge nose made of bark and yellow-green leaves that twitched about as she spoke. And there was no escaping her. She wanted to talk to me, and when a giant tree wants to have a conversation with you, you listen.

"Oh, it's been so dreadful. We're all in shock. You're the funeral planner, yes? I loved Jonah so much, and it's been such a terrible situation. Please let me know if there's anything I can do to help."

To make the affair slightly more strange—that is, stranger than a greeting from a tree squeezed into a dilapidated bar—the treant—Orchardary, as the letters above her head told me—spoke in a musical Indian American accent. It was a pleasing voice, the sort of voice that made you glad to be speaking on a vent server and not just typing, but I don't know if I could have picked anything more incongruous.

At first I just sort of stared at her. "Sure," I said, double-checking that she wasn't on my list of spear-users. "I'll get back with you on that." I could just spot the blue-gray fur of a cat-man sitting at the bar behind her, and musical voice or not, I'd just as soon use my time productively.

"Interesting line of work," said Orchardary, who now blocked the path between myself and the bar. "How did you stumble into being a online funeral planner? Do you have a website?"

I hadn't given my cover story a lot of thought. "No," I said, "I'm more of a friend of the family."

"Oh," said Orchardary. "What's your name?"

Pushy, this Orchardary.

"Dahlia Moss," I told her, trying still to walk around her,

which took some doing because she was wide like a sequoia. "Did you know Jonah personally?"

And Orchardary sort of bobbed at me, as if she thought this question were ridiculous. "He lived in Saint Louis. Who knows anyone in Saint Louis? But I knew him well for never having met him, if that makes any sense. A wonderful man."

You couldn't have known him that well, I thought, although maybe I was being bitter about that Saint Louis crack.

"Do let me know if I can help," she repeated, although now in a more slightly bored tone. I had just finished circumventing her when she took off altogether, not even saying good-bye. She just made like a tree and leafed.

At the bar, not only was a cat-man named Threadwork looking at me expectantly, but suspect number two was there as well, with a drink in her hand. They made quite a pair—she looked like a Pre-Raphaelite beauty dressed for a wedding—lace everywhere and actual flowers in her hair—and he looked like some sort of dapper pirate cat. Puss in Boots, but sexy.

"Oh, thank God you're here," said Threadwork, in a voice that I first mistook for sarcasm. "Now we can finally talk about something other than babies."

"I've barely mentioned the topic to you," said Clemency. She had a voice that was a little huskier than her avatar would suggest. "You're so touchy on this subject."

Threadwork picked up a oversized pipe and blew a smoke ring at her.

It was a weird place to enter the conversation, but here I was. I felt like I had interrupted some kind of quarrel—and particularly a quarrel that was none of my business—and so I cut straight to the chase.

"So," I said brightly. "I'm here to put something together for

Jonah's funeral in *Zoth*. I was going to ask you for advice—I don't suppose he had any favorite zones?"

"I love that you don't open with an expression of grief, or asking about our well-being, whether we're in shock, that sort of thing. I find your mercenary attitude completely refreshing." Threadwork's cat eyes looked at me. I honestly couldn't tell if he was being genuine or sarcastic.

"Don't mind him," said Clemency. "He's in a disagreeable mood."

He was right; it probably was bad form. In my defense, they hadn't seem particularly broken up when I entered the conversation. But my bedside manner could use some rethinking.

That said, Threadwork went on in a tone that was more magisterial than grief-ridden. "Besides which, I don't know if favorite zones are the way to approach it, my child, because Jonah's favorite zone was probably the Pit of Yagwath. It would be an extremely distasteful place for a funeral, in that it looks very much like hell."

Clemency giggled at this. Threadwork, who clearly loved the sound of his own voice, kept right on talking.

"The floor is mostly lava, there are walls of flame, and frequently little red devils scamper about with pitchforks. That's not even mentioning the sacrificial altar of Alt'thum."

"The devils are really very cute," said Clemency. "It's not like they're scary."

"While that's true," said Threadwork, "I think it would certainly send the wrong message. Besides, my favorite place is Arby's—I don't want to be buried there."

As Threadwork spoke, his accent drew increasing attention to itself. It was, quite plainly, a put-on. It looked great coming out of his avatar—this great puffy Ian McKellen/Alec Guinness affectation—but its consistency left a lot to be desired. There was something particularly off about "the floor is mostly lava," which came out a bit less old England and much more South Boston. Still, it was fun.

"Well," said Clemency. "What about the Zinnia Jungle?"

"Too much foot traffic," said Threadwork. "And Jonah would have hated it. All those bees!"

"I feel like we should ask him," said Clemency. At first I thought she was referring to more Ouija board nonsense, but then she explained, "It doesn't seem real that he could be dead."

Threadwork was genuine, I think, for a very brief moment. "No," he said, dropping his accent. "It doesn't."

Clemency was about to volunteer another location when I cut her off. The truth of it was that I wasn't particularly vested in a final resting place of digital Jonah Long. What I wanted was a spear. Or more to the point, I wanted the thief.

"Also," I said, stealing an idea from Emily, "Jonah's parents would like for the Bejeweled Spear of Infinite Piercing to be buried with him. You don't know anything about it, do you?"

"Are you asking if we stole it from Jonah?" said Threadwork disdainfully.

I hadn't expected such a frontal assault, so I stumbled a bit. "Me? What? No! Was it stolen? Where did you hear that?"

"Tambras was saying so," said Threadwork. "Apparently Jonah had been telling new people that it had been taken from him. He never mentioned it to me."

"Really? I hadn't heard that at all," said Clemency. "I suppose it would make sense."

I couldn't reconcile why no one in the guild seemed to know that the spear had gone missing. Why would Jonah care enough about it to give a stranger $1,000 to hunt it down but not enough to mention it to anyone else? Jonah had seemed sure that the thief was Kurt—had he been trying to save his ex-roommate from embarrassment?

"Why would it make sense?" I asked.

"Well," said Clemency. "He took the spear, but we never actually saw him use it. I just assumed that it was because of bad blood."

"What bad blood?" I asked.

"He ninja'd the spear," said Clemency. "It was really terrible. We were supposed to roll for it—high number wins—Jonah, Tambras, me, and Threadwork—and before we even roll, he just takes it."

"Before you rolled," said Threadwork. "I rolled an eighty-seven." He could manage a good Ian McKellen impression when he put his mind to it.

"Were you angry about it?"

"Of course I was angry about it," said Clemency. "And not just the spear—it's a huge violation of trust. We are a guild; there are rules for these things."

"I couldn't care less about the violation of trust," said Threadwork. "I was just angry about the spear."

This was interesting and corroborated what Kurt had told me over dinner. But it didn't put me closer to finding a thief.

"So what do you think happened to it?" I asked.

"Well," scoffed Threadwork. "Clemency certainly didn't take it. She'll be leaving *Zoth* in a few months anyway—why bother with a memento?"

"I'm not leaving *Zoth*," said Clemency.

"Everyone leaves *Zoth* when they become parents. Look at what happened with Viper. Look at what happened with FuzzyStigmata."

"Those guys were pretenders," said Clemency. "I'll be back," she said.

I had two reactions to this: One, Threadwork was probably right, and two, Clemency was remarkably unconcerned with defending her innocence. I figured that meant she didn't do it or at least didn't care whether she got caught.

"Anyway," said Clemency. "Threadwork didn't take the spear, because he couldn't stand to keep the secret. We would all know that he had taken it in a few hours because he would tell everyone."

"I can keep secrets fine," said Threadwork puffily.

"Why does everyone know I'm pregnant, Threadwork?"

"Who have I told? No one."

"You told this fairy just now!" said Clemency, sounding exasperated.

"I did no such thing," said Threadwork. "I made the vaguest implication."

"Guild mates are sending me booties in the mail, Threadwork."

And as if on cue, an enormous green-and-black beetle scurried up to the table. Perhaps it's redundant to say that a giant beetle at a barstool is captivating, but it was. The beetle's carapace was beautiful, boldly patterned with an iridescent sheen, in a schemata that was vaguely hypnotic. But under the carapace it was terrifying, sharp and furry and ominous.

"Congratulations, Clemency," said the bug in a friendly plain female voice. "I hear you're with child."

"Ugh," said Clemency.

"I had nothing to do with this," said Threadwork. "I am a blameless vessel."

Blameless vessel or not, Threadwork was looking to change the subject, and so he asked:

"Perhaps you could discuss Jonah's funeral with this fairy—she's putting something together in his memory."

And I heard a terrible sort of *zzzzzzzrrrpp* sound, like feedback from a mic.

"oh crap," typed the insect after a moment.

"What happened?" asked Clemency.

"i dipped my microphone into this champagne glass. by accident. you know how those long fluted glasses are."

"Why are you drinking champagne?" asked Clemency. Clemency was generally sunny, but you could hear irritation creeping into the edges of her voice.

"to celebrate your fecundity," typed the bug.

"I didn't tell her," said Threadwork, just as Chtusk typed "threadwork told me."

"Perhaps I may have hinted," added Threadwork.

"Booties in the mail," said Clemency again. "I'm getting booties in the mail."

This conversation was quickly devolving into a sort of friendly bickering that I wanted to escape from. It made me think of an old married couple, or more specifically, Erik, my ex. I had gotten pretty good about not thinking about Erik in the past few months, although my techniques for doing so had involved excising massive parts of my life. But I was punished for thinking of him now, because the game beeped at me. It was a beep that would signal trouble.

CHAPTER TEN

The beep meant an email in-game, which I knew because a little black bird flittered at the corner of a screen with an envelope in its beak. Despite elves, dragons, and a preponderance of mystic portals, there is nothing in *Zoth* so magical as a smartphone, and when one receives mail, you have to walk it to a mailbox to pick it up.

It wasn't that I expected the mail I got to be that interesting—very few people at this point knew my username. I suppose my expectation was that it was going to be an advertisement—"Enjoying your first two days in Zoth? Sign up for your next month now and get an extra week free!" Or something of its ilk.

And I had been enjoying my first two days in Zoth. I was feeling downright chipper, actually—it was a strange thing to say about visiting a fantasy world, but the otherworldly climes of Zoth somehow made me feel more like myself. This probably says less about Zoth and more about the sad state of my personal life, but even so. With so much focus on one thing, I had allowed myself to become a Person Who Did Nothing but Fail at Job Interviews, which was no good. Now I was person who was failing at all sorts of things, which was much easier to take. I had diversified my portfolio of failure. Missed clues, a murdered client, and I had been killed in-game by a camel. If nothing else, it'll give you perspective.

The email was not an advertisement. It was from Atheun—aka Erik, my damned ex-boyfriend. I would have preferred an email filled with wasps. Or that girl from *The Ring*—I wonder what she's doing these days? I had entire subsystems dedicated to not dealing with Erik, and this was going to disrupt all of them. I just stared at the letter, refusing to open it but unable to back away. Another new thing to fail at.

The subject heading was "hey," just like that, with nary a capital letter. He probably put that there just to placate me—with Erik you were likely to get no subject heading at all.

I opened the email, wincing through one eye as I read it. It didn't take long.

```
just wanted you to know i wasnt involved. erik
```

No caps, no apostrophe, and it was missing a "that." And yet, the damned thing was making me tear up, stupidly. Can you be rational and irrational about something at the same time? It was all so stupid—I knew it was stupid, and yet there was still this part of me, most of me, actually—that felt like it was being crushed. What the hell, right? It wasn't just Erik that I needed to get over, apparently. I needed to get over myself.

I logged out of *Zoth* and consoled myself by playing a different video game, one that I actually liked. When enough rude Internet boys had been Walrus Punched—this took about an hour of punching, mind you—I came back to the email.

Fortified by *Dota*, I now had a few questions. Like: How did Erik know RedRasish was me? A lucky guess, possibly, but Erik was not a great intuitionist. And not involved with what?

Certainly not that dental hygienist, because he was decidedly involved with her. I was eagerly awaiting their engagement announcement so that I could set it on fire and laugh at the flames.

Still, what was he talking about? Not involved with the spear theft? Well, duh. He wasn't part of the guild, and as a necromancer, he couldn't use the spear anyway. Yes, I dated a necromancer for three years. He was good in bed. Sometimes.

Or was Erik saying that he wasn't involved in Jonah's death? Did he know Jonah? The message begged for clarification, but I wasn't willing to reinvolve myself. Besides—and I know that this sounds naive given that he cheated on me for three months while I was living with him—but Erik was nothing if not honest. He *never* lied to me about the cheating—he just assiduously didn't mention it. If I had ever asked: "Say, you're not cheating me, are you?," he would have folded like a paper umbrella. But I never asked, and he didn't volunteer. If it hadn't been for an email from the hygienist, God knows how long that might have gone on.

Redrasish was outside the bar, now sitting cross-legged in front of the mailbox, as I had gone idle. She looked appropriately overwhelmed, which I drew some consolation from. I was still deciding what to do about Operation Erik when Tambras showed up, juggling those knives and looking as snarky as ever.

"Who are you, really?" she asked. "You're not a funeral planner."

———————◆———————

I've glossed over some of the technical details about vent server channels, but I should mention that I quickly moved Ophelia to a private channel. She had caught me deeply unawares, but

I was not so lost that I was willing to let other guild mates hear me stammer around.

"What gives you that idea?" I asked once I'd put a password on the channel just to make extra sure no one walked in on us. Told you I was paranoid.

"Hmph," said Ophelia. I had thought it goofy when she had typed it, but to hear her say it seemed utterly right. Honestly, everything about Ophelia's character seemed right. With Clemency, there had been a kind of disconnect between her smoky voice and Pre-Raphaelite digs, and one might expect that here. But something about Ophelia's stately little voice—I could just see her at home, dressed in pearls and a classy black dress—that felt perfectly placed coming out of this lanky goth troubadour.

"That's your answer, *hmph*? I'm glad to know you're comfortable accusing total strangers of wrongdoing."

"Someone spoke to me a couple of days ago, said Jonah had mentioned joining our guild. A level-one character?" Ophelia made this question sound uncomfortably accusatory.

"I'm level two," I said, like an idiot.

"Why would Jonah invite a level-one character into the guild? And an archer? We don't need archers. Whoever that person was—she was lying. *And* she knew about Jonah's spear being stolen."

I did not like her choice of personal pronoun, given that I had been masquerading as a guy. I felt like protesting, meekly, that this had nothing to do with the funeral I was planning, but it didn't seem worth the effort. The last thing I wanted was to invite funereal etiquette questions. I kept mum and let Ophelia have her say.

"And now you show up, supposedly planning a funeral, but then you go around harassing people about the spear. And only the people who could use it. What kind of funeral planner does that?"

"All right, fine," I said. "You got me."

"You're just after the spear for yourself."

The conversation had been slightly humiliating up to this point—not Silas at the Windmill humiliating, but humiliating—but when Ophelia hit this wrong note, I instantly cheered up. She was just as bad a detective as I was. Maybe worse. I turned her own emoticons against her and /guffawed at her.

"Wait, what? I don't want the spear. That's ridiculous," I said.

So attuned was Ophelia to her avatar's emotions that she /scowled at me again. Probably she typed these things without even realizing it.

"Why should I believe you? Who are you really?"

"I'm a detective," I said evenly. "I was hired by Jonah's parents to get the spear back. And yes, I'm planning his funeral as a sort of cover operation to investigate."

Ophelia's avatar /crossed his arms at me. "I don't believe you," Ophelia said. "What are Jonah's parents' names?"

I admired Ophelia's stubbornness, fending me off as if I were some sort of online infidel. I told her Jonah's parents' names, which she /scoffed at. Then, amazed at the serendipity of being able to do it, I gave her a parlor trick of my own.

"Believe me, or don't. But I'm looking at all the angles. I know about you, for example."

Ophelia said nothing, but she/narrowed her eyes at me.

"Your name is Ophelia Odom; you live outside of Boston and occasionally play viola for the Boston Symphony Orchestra and Pops. You're involved in a long-distance romantic relationship with Kurt Campbell, and..." I felt like there should be a fourth thing, because these kinds of things go in threes, but I was out of ammo. But it didn't matter, because Ophelia gasped. Not /gasped, but a straight-up real-world gasp, the kind you would get in a Victorian novel.

"Who told you that?" she asked, sounding less impressed than I would have hoped but definitely irritated. "That's a secret."

"Secrets are my trade," I said. This was such a whopper that I half expected God to come down from the sky and smite me and RedRasish both, but nothing happened.

Ophelia sighed. "I guess you're legit," she said grudgingly. "Don't tell anyone about me and Kurt. We're kind of in a wait-and-see-what-happens phase."

Less embarrassing if things fall apart? I could hear that. "Fine," I said smartly. "Don't tell anyone about me being a detective."

"And the viola," added Ophelia with an edge of conspiracy in her voice. "Don't mention the viola to anyone."

This was not the turn I was expecting the conversation to take.

"Why can't I mention the viola?"

"Viola jokes," said Ophelia. "When people find out you play the viola they like to make viola jokes at you."

"What are viola jokes?" I asked, but I was already alt-tabbed to google them.

"I can hear you typing," said Ophelia. "Tell me you are not googling viola jokes in front of me."

She did have a preternatural ability to guess what I was doing, that Ophelia. That didn't stop me from reading a joke to her anyway.

"You mean like: How do you keep someone from stealing your violin?"

Ophelia /clucked at me and said, "Listen, RedRashish, whoever you are. I know like thirty violists. I don't care how far away you live, or clever you think you are, but if you start with the viola jokes, I will gather all thirty violists up and we will come to your house and FUCK YOU UP."

Technically, the correct answer was "you put it in a viola case," but Ophelia's answer was compelling too.

CHAPTER ELEVEN

I finished the night by sending out a mass email to the Horizons asking about material for a eulogy for Jonah. I stayed up entirely too late waiting for responses, because I got not a single email in return. Was Jonah just not that liked, or was it just too depressing to come up with material for a eulogy? At any rate, when morning rolled around, I slept in. It wasn't something I usually did, but so far doing things unusually had been working out for me. So when my alarm rang at eight, I acquainted myself with the snooze option. I honestly don't think I had ever used it before. However, fifteen minutes later, I was hating myself because my iPhone had shot out a stern reminder that I had to be across town in a half hour for yet another sad job interview.

I saw the reminder and thought, quite vividly: "Fuck it." But I didn't say it aloud, and I didn't do anything differently. Such are the silent, sad rebellions of Dahlia Moss. Instead I got dressed with less time than it would usually have taken, and began my day in a grand tradition of half-assing it.

I had learned nothing from my last bombed job interview, because when I arrived at the agency, dressed far too casually in a tatty gray blouse that would have been pushing my luck on casual Friday, my mind was still swirling with questions. I couldn't get over that initial hunch that Jonah had hired me to shake down someone who he himself didn't think had stolen the spear. I was probably being cocky to trust my instincts so much—I had zero detective experience, as Maddocks had reminded me. But I couldn't let go of it. Something told me that this was an important piece of the puzzle.

The waiting room was filled with applicants who in other circumstances I would be scowling at and studying. It was disheartening because you would often see many of the same faces. But this time I was in another world altogether, thinking through what had been said last night. I wasn't exactly amassing a treasure trove of clues. There wasn't any reason to suspect anyone, except perhaps Ophelia, and even then, my evidence was mostly that she was kind of crabby.

I couldn't even tell you how long I was waiting out in the lobby. Someone eventually called my name, and I was shuttled down a long corridor to a colorless, coffin-shaped room where I was interviewed by someone named Beth. Interview rooms were always colorless. Never had I been interviewed in a room painted vividly in chartreuse. Maybe it would have riled candidates up too much. Or maybe I was applying for the wrong jobs.

Beth was in her thirties, and looking at her, I was reminded of Jennifer Ebel from just a few days earlier. She looked like a downmarket version of Jennifer—same black dress, same efficient manner, but not as put together. Although, she lacked ridiculous earrings, which had to be a point in Beth's favor. She was droning on about the virtues of her company, but I couldn't honestly say that I was listening to her. Instead, I was thinking about Jennifer herself. Maybe it was a mistake to limit my investigation to the world of Zoth. Jennifer probably didn't steal the spear, sure. But she could give me more insight into Jonah's life, and the news of Jonah's murder just might have melted part of that icy exterior of hers. Detective Maddocks probably wouldn't love it if I talked with her, but that was part of being a private eye, right?

I'm sure she'd have great ideas about an online funeral.

"I *said*, Miss Moss, it looks as though you've been unemployed for quite some time."

Oh dear, Beth was speaking to me. And she was complaining about me being unemployed, which was a riddle I never had patience for, even in the best of times. It works like this: Once you've been unemployed for too long, you're somehow deemed unhireable, because you've been unemployed for too long. It was a cruel circular logic. Generally, I would give my standard answer about being especially keen to make my mark on my career as a whatever I was trying to get hired for. But I suddenly couldn't remember what I was interviewing for that day. This was clearly destined to go down the tubes, although this time I was very resilient to the anguish of it.

"Have I? I've been so busy lately," I mumbled.

Beth regarded this statement with a polite skepticism.

"You ought to update your résumé, as your new activities are not reflected in what you've given us."

This is where I would ordinarily be backpedalling to try to recapture the interviewer's favor. But this time I was still distant, even thinking about the case a little.

"Well, let's see how it works out first," I said. "Before I put it on the résumé."

Beth was undeterred. I suppose she thought I was lying. "What are your new activities?"

"I'm wary to say, because it's slightly insane."

And she perked up at this. I suddenly realized that Beth's job must be terribly boring, interviewing the same identical schlubs for a job none of them wanted. I got tired of seeing them all in the waiting room every interview; at least I didn't have to maintain a dialogue.

"Go on." She was perking up, all right.

"I've been working as a private detective."

"Oh. Why is that insane?" Beth asked, a little more disappointed than I expected. I guess she was hoping for actually insane, not merely slightly so.

"You've got my résumé. I don't have the background for it."

"Meh," she said. "People transition into jobs all the time. Is it working out for you?" She was being unexpectedly kind, but skepticism had begun creeping back into her voice. I'm sure people lie to her outright all the time, so I didn't take it personally.

"I've made eleven thousand dollars in five days. So it's been going well in a financial sense, I suppose. I don't know if my investigation is going well. I've definitely learned things, but I don't have a supervisor or any sort of rubric to tell me how I'm doing."

I knew people like Beth appreciated words like "rubric," so I made a point of throwing it in, and it did indeed seem to please her. "So, why are you applying for this job?"

It was a good question. Even if Beth was a little snotty, it was fair to ask. I thought for a moment before I gave my answer. I think this unnerved Beth more than anything—someone calmly considering a completely bullshitless answer.

"I don't even remember what this job is," I told her. "I

applied for it before this all happened. I probably shouldn't even have come. It's embarrassing, really. Even when I succeed, I'm slightly embarrassed; it's like discovering that you're really good with a garrote. Detecting is not a respectable skill."

"Respectable skills are overrated. The job market is saturated with them. But yes, you probably shouldn't be here if you don't know what you're applying for. Why did you come?"

"Habit? I was also thinking I would make more progress on the case somehow, if I wasn't thinking about it all the time."

Beth seemed to regard this as interesting.

"Did that work?"

"I haven't ever stopped thinking about it," I said, sighing. "It's like when you've looked at the sun and then close your eyes, how you can still see its outline."

"Maybe try the Botanical Garden," said Beth. "I've always thought it's a good place to clear your head. It's where I send applicants when they start crying mid-interview."

"Does that happen a lot?"

"Often enough. And you never know the questions that will set people off. I asked one woman if she could use Microsoft Excel, and she starting bawling and threw a chair."

This was clearly the strangest interview I had ever had, and I had applied to be one of the people who scares you with a bladeless chainsaw at a corporate haunted house.

"Well, thanks for coming in," said Beth. "We'll keep your résumé on file. For what that's worth."

"Hey," I said, "how about I ask you a quick question about my case? I told you I needed a supervisor."

"Is that appropriate?" asked Beth. She was trying to bristle, but her eyes told me that she was enjoying this.

"I didn't realize we were bothering with appropriate," I said.

Beth shrugged, but she couldn't completely repress her smile. I took that for a yes.

"Here it is: If you were sure that your friend hadn't committed a crime, why would you tell a detective that you thought he did? And then send that detective to investigate him?"

"I'm one hundred percent sure my friend is innocent?"

"You have no doubts," I told her, despite the fact that I had plenty.

Beth thought about it and gave an answer that was the kind of wormy little response that I would expect from Human Resources.

"Maybe I'm sending a message."

"What kind of message?"

"Maybe I want the thief to think I'm on the wrong track. Or maybe I want to visibly threaten someone who's innocent to make the thief feel bad."

Ophelia had a connection with Kurt, and she could use the spear. Was Jonah's hiring all a show to get Ophelia to give the spear back? There were worse theories.

Beth was looking at me expectantly.

"Is that the right answer?" she asked.

"Could be. Ask me again in a week," I told her.

"Sure," said Beth, amused. "When I call to tell you you're hired, you can give me an update."

———————◆———————

I didn't know what to make of Beth, but I did find myself taking her advice and making an unexpected trip to Saint Louis's Botanical Garden. It was not on my way. Going there meant killing hours of my day, and yet now that the idea had been planted there, it seemed like the only possible course of action. I'd always liked the place. But it was somehow another of these locations that the combination of my failed career and disastrous breakup had made toxic. Most of the best parts of Saint Louis had this aura, come to think of it. Lately, I had been living in fear of running into people I knew. They would ask questions, and the answers invariably prompted these looks of involuntary pity.

I do not love involuntary pity. In fact, it's my least favorite kind of pity. If I want to be pitied, I absolutely require it to be the sort of pity that I am actively clamoring for. As in, I'm pretending to be out of gas in a strange town, and I'm scamming you out of ten dollars. That sort of pity is okay, and even then only in limited circumstances. When I ran into people I knew, it was instead the kind of pity you gave to a dog that was hopping around on one leg. Dahlia, who has no job. Dahlia, whose friends all sided with her ex-boyfriend. Blech.

And yet something felt different. It was a typical morning—an interview for a job that I certainly wasn't going to get—but I was electric. I didn't want to jinx it, but I think I felt like my old self. And my old self was awesome.

When I got there, I beelined to the Victorian District, always my favorite part of the gardens. Something about its cobblestones and statues was always inviting to me. I'm sure the botanists in Jonah's program would have considered it the housewife's choice. Screw those ivy-loving elitists. I sat down on a bench, studied a lovely hedge that had been cut into a spiral, and tried to put the case out of my head. For some time I had the creepy sensation that someone had been following me, but I had put it out of my head as baseless paranoia. It wasn't.

My head was covered with a plastic shopping bag.

"Guess who?" a voice asked me.

There was no need to ask who might have sneaked up behind me outside a hedge maze and dumped a plastic bag over my head, even if I didn't recognize the voice, which I certainly did.

And she didn't wait for an answer anyway.

"It's Charice!"

"Yes, Charice. What are you doing here?"

"I've been tracking you."

The next obvious question would be for me to ask how she was tracking me, and I really, really, really wanted to skip over this part, but I couldn't help but wonder—how was she tracking me?

"Fine," I said. "If you take this plastic bag off my head, I'll ask how you're tracking me."

She removed the bag, and I bit.

"I've got your iPad. I'm using the 'Find My iPhone' app. Pretty great solution, eh?"

"A solution for what?"

"For not being able to track someone."

I was not sure that it was that great a solution, no. For one, it involved slipping my $400 iPhone surreptitiously on someone. Which was a large, bulky, easily findable thing. Which would lead back to me. And cost $400. But these were not details I was going to waste on Charice right now.

"Why have you tracked me, exactly?"

"To give you an update!"

"You are aware that I have my iPhone, clearly. You could have called me."

"Well, I also wanted to test my tracking system."

"What's your update, Charice?"

"While you have been uselessly playing *Kingdoms of Zoth*, I have been out cashing favors."

For Charice to say that was ominous. Almost everyone seemed to owe her, somehow, and who knows what strange circumstances would occur from a cached favor?

"What sort of favors?" I asked her.

"Photography."

Well, it could be worse. I crumpled the plastic bag with my hand, a gesture that I felt more than adequately expressed my desire for Charice to get on with it.

"As of this moment, I have a rotating squadron of members from the WashU photography club monitoring entrance and egress from Jonah's apartment."

Not exactly what I was expecting, but I continued to let the crumpling do my talking.

"For Jonah's funeral on Thursday, I will also have photographers on hand taking photos of all attendees. Am I not Very Helpful?"

I had to admit, this didn't seem like a hindrance, which, when dealing with Charice, was often as close to helpful as one would expect to get. But I had to confess that I didn't fully understand her plan.

"Do we expect that the person who stole the spear will go to the funeral or Jonah's apartment?"

"The killer always returns to the scene of the crime," Charice told me with more vehemence than I would have expected from her.

"Who's talking about a killer? I just want a spear thief."

"You'll find both. Besides which, this information can only help you. You should be thanking me."

And she was right. I should have been. That's the thing with Charice—she's all hot and cold. One minute you're sick to death of her, and the next she's cashing in personal favors in a slightly misbegotten effort to help you out. I hadn't learned much about the case today, but the interview with Beth had taught me one thing: I wasn't so bad. And if I had value, there was no reason to be snippy with Charice. It was sort of paradoxical, but now that I wasn't an unemployed mooch, I could afford to be generous to Charice. Well, not financially generous. But I didn't have to be so damned bitter all the time.

"You're right," I told her. "It's cool, and while it's maybe a long shot, who knows? Maybe it will give us the clue we need to break this case wide open." The "break this case wide open" was pure schlock, I know, but I'd lived with Charice long enough to know the kinds of things she liked to hear.

She grinned cheerfully and said, "Fantastic. One last little tidbit—you can't go to the apartment tonight."

"I need to go to the apartment tonight; I need to get on *Zoth* to look for suspects." And to pick a funeral site—it was dull relative to the rest of this, but the funeral wasn't going to plan itself.

"Nope, sorry. There's going to be a production of *Godspell* in our common room."

"I'll just sneak in my room before it starts."

"We'll be using your room for storage."

I sighed.

"I suppose this was one of the favors you had to grant in order to get the photographers?"

Charice looked visibly surprised by this question, then contorted her face into an obvious visage of guile. "Yes, Dahlia. That's how it happened."

CHAPTER TWELVE

I followed Charice back to the apartment, taking advantage of her working vehicle. I wanted to get some things if I was going to be out for a while. I also made an impetuous and undoubtedly unwise phone call to Nathan.

"Hi there, Detective," he said.

"So Charice is kicking me out for the evening."

"Did you have a fight?"

"No, there's a musical theater occurrence that's taking place here—don't ask a follow-up question, please."

"Done."

"I was wondering if perhaps I could come over to your place tonight. I know it's a little forward, but I actually just need a computer so that I can play *Zoth*."

"I see," said Nathan, who sounded a little disappointed. Or perhaps it was distracted.

"I mean, I'd like to see you as well, obviously. But I need to finish interviewing suspects."

"No, that's no problem. I can set you up."

"Well, it's not going to be quite as easy as that. The game takes hours to download, so you're going to need to start work on that ASAP."

And Nathan was back to his usual amiable self. Whatever had troubled him there had been just a momentary blip.

"I can't wait," he said. "I'll pick you up in a couple of hours."

I was entirely too excited by this, and not just because I might be dating someone who had a car. A car! Excited because I was getting a little googly-eyed, which I am known to do. I am moderately ashamed to admit that I spent the next few minutes searching for information about Nathan on the Internet, which is the modern equivalent of repeatedly writing your new name after you marry the boy you like.

I was not cyberstalking Nathan. The line between checking out someone on the Internet and straight up cyberstalking them sits at the twenty-minute mark. Five, ten minutes of checking them out? Awesome. You're being a conscientious person and a good date, as you will have excellent conversation starters in hand. Thirty-five, forty-five minutes? You are a psychopath. I realize that's not a wide berth between the two, but them's the rules.

I can state these rules, because I've not only drifted into psychopath territory, I planted a small garden there, with perennials and a nice bed of marigolds to keep away bugs. Point in case: Todd Hudsell. Todd was a guy I had met through some board-gaming thing, and we were but a brief possibility—he gave me coffee beans, and I gave him wax. But he was weird, and dressed well, and he really seemed to like me. Things probably would never have worked out—he was way too old for me and actually even had an ex-wife, which I don't even know how to address. But let's not kid ourselves, our chances bombed not because Todd was a few years past dream-date age but because I had googled the *hell* out of him. I practically doxxed the man.

I was so armed with details about Todd that I could have had our date without him. Probably that would have gone better. We went to this Ethiopian place and he kept telling me things about himself that I had already learned. Todd—cute, well-buttocksed Todd—was boring me to tears. The date was like watching an episode of *Game of Thrones* right after you read the novel. Fine for somebody, I suppose, but not for me.

It was my own fault—part of the joy of dating is the slow reveal of information. Like stripping. Just to clarify (hi, Mom!), I've never stripped, but *were* I to strip, I would try to do it in a slow, revealing, and hopefully seductive way. It wouldn't be *Bam!* Nakedness! before the waitress had even seated us. And this doesn't fit in with the stripper metaphor, but in case you do cyberstalk: Never tell the other person information about themselves that they don't already know. It doesn't end well. Such as, just for example, that their ex-wife remarried last weekend and apparently neglected to mention it. Ethiopian food just isn't going to smooth that one over.

I dredge up Todd for no reason other than to say that I did not want to Todd Nathan. I liked Nathan. I was even willing to admit to Google that I liked Nathan, even though that meant that when I checked in at the Mary Sue later there might be cute pictures of Nathan in the sidebar. Cookies.

So: I gave Nathan exactly nineteen minutes of Internet searching. I used an egg timer, because as we've established, I can get carried away. Not Charice carried away, which I would assume involves some combination of kidnapping and elopement, just Dahlia levels of crazy. This mostly involves going *just* a bit too far while repeating in an even and convincing tone of voice that it's not big deal and that Charice would do much worse. This is an important and often neglected aspect of the Bert and Ernie relationship. Bert can, upon occasion, go absolutely apeshit crazy and do whatever he wants because really, what's Ernie going to say?

I started with Twitter, where Nathan's profile was a surprisingly unflattering photograph. This made me like him more, but he already had an unreasonable head start on that point. And then I burrowed in.

Twitter is quite a repository of information for the patient. It's all there if you think about it; nothing ever goes away. Your whole life, right in plain sight.

I was reading old tweets from Nathan Willing, nineteen whole minutes of them. I wasn't trying to bore in on Nathan's personal details so much as checking out for warning signs. Gay, womanizer, crazy, alcoholic. The basic food groups of bad relationships.

And I did find a warning sign, although it wasn't one the basics. Sixteen minutes in, I found a picture, posted directly to Twitter, of a JPEG invitation for a party at Nathan's. What alarmed me wasn't the theme (Vice Presidents) or the font choice (Curlz MT) but the address: 97 Euclid. It's a memorable address because ninety-seven was how old my grandpa was when he died and Euclid was the name of his mistress. He claimed nurse, but I think mistress. Euclid didn't seem to know the first thing about medicine. I mean, yes, she was also in her nineties and perhaps a little senile, but you should still know that a syringe doesn't go in your mouth. But I digress. The point is: This address, for whatever reasons, had caught in the craw of my memory. And it caught there earlier, when I was looking at the box of clothes that Jonah Long had sent me. This was his address.

Forget gay, forget womanizer. Forget the ironic hipster–y party choices. I had a brand-new problem with Nathan Willing.

He lived in the same building as Jonah Long. He was a fucking suspect.

I went out for a walk. I spent a good quarter mile brooding over what to do with Operation Nathan—like, seriously, was he trying to lure me to his lair now?—when I got a call from Emily Swenson.

I didn't immediately answer but just looked at the phone in the sort of slow, creeping horror that Lovecraft likes to write about. I felt certain that this call represented Emily taking back all this misspent money.

It did not.

Instead, Emily spoke to me in a cool, almost collegial tone. This shouldn't have brightened me, but it did—Emily Swenson was like your cool older sister who you wanted to impress.

"Dahlia," she said, "if you have a moment, you might want to swing by Jonah's old apartment. I have something I'd like to share with you."

"Oh," I said, still a little stunned. "What is it?"

"I believe you might call it a clue."

"As it happens," I said, thinking of Nathan's pretty little head, "I was heading over there anyway."

———————◆———————

I can't say that I visited Jonah's apartment with completely maximal speed—I could have headed back home and broken out my jalopy. But I decided that the risk of my car breaking down was not worth the advantage of the fifteen minutes' walking that it would gain me. Plus, if I ran into a shuttle, I could pretend to be a med student and take it down toward the West Campus. These are the kinds of tricks that poverty teaches you.

Jonah's place was over on Euclid, in a neighborhood that was half chichi, and half student slums. The place looked modest from the outside, an old brownstone with keyhole windows and a roof that looked like it could use a little attention, but after I buzzed myself in I could see the appeal. It was cool-looking—not swank, exactly, but cool. The lobby had a black-and-white-checked floor, and the furniture seemed like it had been cobbled together from flea markets across the ages.

The security around here was minimal—when I say I buzzed myself in, I mean just that. I pressed a button at the door, and it buzzed and opened. Chalk one up for the police's break-in theory.

Then again, cool and hipster-y though the place might have been, was this really a place I would go trolling around looking for an apartment to rob? Only if I wanted a wicker sculpture of a moose wearing a fedora, and that hardly seemed worth killing for.

When I arrived at the door, I didn't even have to knock. Emily Swenson simply opened it as I got near, probably with one of her preternatural skills. It was unfair how some people seem to have preternatural skills, and I couldn't even scrounge up regular ones. If I had taken too long to get here, though, Emily didn't register it.

It took me a second to adjust to the apartment's smell, which, it had to be noted, was oppressively guy-like. And not guy in a sexy way, but more in the way of spilled beer and mismanaged laundry. The place looked like you would expect it to, bachelor-pad furniture and serious first-apartment vibe. The only thing that might tip you off that this was a rich kid slumming was the artwork, which wasn't your typical M. C. Escher posters, but actual artwork. I wasn't so gauche as to check, but I think there may have been a genuine Jacob Lawrence.

"Dahlia," Emily said. "I was just expecting you to show up. What do you make of this?"

"This" was a brown cardboard box that looked like it held IKEA furniture. It was not especially interesting. More interesting was Emily, who had changed clothes since I had seen her last—knitted pink top, lime green coat, white pants—and despite unusual clothing choices, she seemed as intimidating as ever. Let's face it: She dressed like an ice-cream parlor. A nice ice-cream parlor, one that sold Italian ice, but it was nonetheless unnerving to be in the presence of someone who considered Dolores Umbridge as fashion inspiration.

"It's a box?" I said.

"Open it," she said.

As I looked down at the box, it was clear that it had already been opened—it had plastic binding that had been cut—and that someone, presumably Emily, had closed it back up. Why would she do this? She wanted to see my reaction to what was inside? It was just a guess, but the idea made me open the box that much more slowly. When Charice wanted to see your facial reaction when you opened a package, it would be dramatic indeed. Could a corpse fit in there? The box was as tall as a refrigerator but only about a fourth as deep and wide, so probably not, at least not without some folding.

I pulled open its hinge, and there, only partially obscured by Styrofoam peanuts, was the gaudiest thing I had ever seen. There should be a word for something that is so sublimely gaudy that it somehow manages to end up just sublime. Even seeing only part of it left you in a kind of kitschy awe.

It was a spear, sure. But the handle was long and gold, and it had ornate carvings that spiraled along its side. There were also wisps of ruby? garnet? red glass? that spiraled along the handle in the opposing direction, although nothing that obviously matched the gem I had found in Kurt's car. Still, there were about a thousand places a gem could fit on it, and I'd want to spend a little time with it before I'd know for sure. The blade itself was sharp and shining, surrounded by a halo of pink opalescent glass at its midpoint, connected to the handle of the spear by a silver framework. Sharp enough to do the job.

"How did this get here?" I asked, genuinely dumbfounded.

"A courier delivered it, to this address. I'd been having an intern check Jonah's mail, but he thought I should look at this directly."

At the risk of coming off as completely callous, I should admit that I hadn't really deeply considered Jonah's murder. Not in an emotional sense. But holding the weapon in my hands made me realize: This was real for someone. I'd always thought of the notion of a *Zoth* player committing the crime as an outside chance, but with a garnet-handled spear in my hand, it seemed like a dim possibility and more like a sort of karma. But sensation faded, thankfully, as soon as I put the weapon down.

"Is it the spear that killed Jonah? But—"

"No," said Emily. "It is a copy of the spear that killed Jonah. Or, more probably, yet another copy of the spear you're looking for."

I don't know what it was about Emily that made me want to impress her. While it was true that I had spent the past thirteen months in a blurry nightmare of job interviews, I had managed them without being overly concerned with any one person's impression of me. Perhaps that was why I still hadn't gotten a job. But here I was—I wanted to awe Emily. She reminded me, inexplicably, of my older brother, Alden, shlubby, geeky, effervescent Alden—who, on the face of it, had nothing in common with her. I would try setting the two of them up, if it weren't for the whole thing about Alden already being attached. And gay.

But I didn't want to ask another dumb question. I started to look for the address on the outside of the box, hoping that would give me some kind of clue, but Emily was there with an envelope.

"This mean anything to you?"

I opened the envelope, which had a note in it, printed in thirty-six-point Helvetica. "THIS LEVEL LIFE TOO HAS ITS SUMMIT."

"Did you already eat the fortune cookie this came in?"

Emily sighed but didn't look disappointed. "It didn't mean anything to me either. For a very brief moment I had wondered if it was some kind of threat."

I told her it sounded less like a threat and more like a rejected Fiona Apple album.

"It was the way it was addressed that made me consider it," said Emily, showing me the shipping label.

It was addressed to DISFIGUREMENT.

"Oh," I said. "This is not Jonah's," I told her. "It's for Kurt. 'Disfigurement' is his name in-game."

"The ex-roommate?" And now Emily looked pleased, which was a good feeling.

"Yes," I said. "It must have been ordered before he was kicked out. But why would he…" And I dissolved into silence. If mental gears turning made a sound, Jonah's place would have sounded like a sweatshop. Emily was the first to break it.

"That's the boy you met for dinner."

One of them, I thought, setting Silas and his lovely eyes aside. I still had that paste gem in my pocket—I had been walking around with it for days, partly for luck, partly because I thought that Charice might steal it. I fished it out of my pocket and held it to the spear.

"And what do you have with you?"

139

"A gemstone," I said. "I found it in Kurt's car. Don't ask." I would have been feeling much more clever about the whole thing except for the fact that the more I looked at it, the clearer it was that my gem had nothing to do with the spear. Kurt's gem was penny ante, cheap-looking even from a distance. The spear was probably just made with colored glass, but it had panache, and not a part of it looked cheap.

"I don't plan to," said Emily. "Doesn't match though, does it?"

"No," I said.

Emily was practically purring, however. An idea. "Why don't you deliver the spear to him? You can see what he thinks, and maybe he'll know what the note means."

I didn't particularly want to mention to Emily that I didn't have a car that worked precisely, and I certainly didn't want to lug a conspicuously bejeweled spear three miles on foot back to my house. It's one thing to be a pedestrian in Saint Louis—a state that merely inspires light pity. But to be a pedestrian carrying something enormous and awkward? I may as well tattoo the word "unemployable" on my forehead.

Perhaps it was the guy smell that permeated the apartment, because I suddenly thought of Nathan. Not an obvious person to call for the lifting of heavy objects, as he was rail thin and essentially muscleless, but it was the thought I had.

"Sure," I told Emily. "Let me make a phone call to get someone to help me with this."

I dialed Nathan, who picked up on the second ring.

"Here's a weird request," I told him. "I've got something kind of awkward to carry. You think maybe you could do some lugging for me?"

Nathan sounded less amenable to this idea than I would have immediately guessed, but again, musclelessness.

"I suppose," he said. "Where are you?"

"Downstairs," I said. "In Jonah's apartment."

"Oh," he said, brightening at what should have been a somewhat macabre admission. "I'll be right down."

I suppose I meant this to be something of a test. *I know you live above Jonah Long, murderee, Nathan. I'm onto your games. What do you make of that?*

And what sort of a response did I get? A chipper *I'll be right down.* Nathan was positively scampering downstairs to see me. Who even reacts that way to being in the apartment of a murdered man? And yet, damn it, I still sort of liked him.

"I have the worst fucking taste in men," I told Emily.

CHAPTER THIRTEEN

The rest of it was awkward. I think I would have felt less strange if Emily had asked questions about who Nathan was and why this moving boy was able to appear so suddenly, but she was utterly mum. This didn't stop Nathan from trying to make small talk, joking about how heavy the package was and comparing Emily's outfit to an Easter parade float. "Why can't she help you carry this thing?" he asked. "We're only going upstairs." Lovable, chokable Nathan.

Nathan and I bid adieu to Emily and ascended the staircase with the hastily reboxed spear. I was fuming, incidentally—maybe it was unfair, but I was feeling mightily irritated that Nathan had neglected to mention that he lived above Jonah Long, Murdered Client. Nathan, for his part, seemed not to notice my anger in the slightest but kept laughing and joking around. He pretended to drop his half of the spear three times going up the stairwell. Lovable, and chokable.

When we opened the door to his apartment and were thoroughly and safely out of the ears of Emily Swenson, I let loose.

"Why did you not tell me that you lived above Jonah Long?"

Many things became apparent to me at once. I will enumerate them in the order of least important to most important.

1. Nathan's apartment was improbably small. It was like entering the TARDIS, but in reverse. It seemed as though it should have been bigger from the outside. Part of this, probably, was an ambitiously large sofa sectional, which had a lilac floral print and was so enormous and distasteful that it threatened to leave the room and cascade down the stairs.

2. Nathan's rumored half-Japanese ex-girlfriend Masako was in the apartment, phalanxed by lilac-printed cushions. She was eating alfalfa sprouts, not even with bread, just shoveling them raw down her face, where they spilled onto the sofa and became camouflaged among the foliage. She looked embarrassed that I had caught her in a particularly unseemly act of eating, but I was not, in the moment, in a pitying mood.

3. Kurt Campbell was there, sitting cross-legged on the floor, between Masako and Nathan, which was insane given the abundance of sofa. He looked not at all surprised to me again and was wearing a red hoodie that was, I distinctly noticed, embroidered with a monogram: KVC.

I had a lot of questions. Among them: "What the hell?" and "Lilac floral print, really?" and "Why is Kurt Campbell here?"

Instead, I asked a perfectly ordinary question, but as wrath personified.

"And how is everyone?"

Which is really a query that you can put a lot of force behind when you put your mind to it.

"Welcome to chez Willing!" answered Nathan, who looked utterly untroubled and who picked spilled sprout off the sofa and instantly ate it. "This is my roommate, Masako."

"Nathan is very taken with you," she told me. Which I assumed was her sneaky way of trying to not make me angry, and that was upsetting mostly because of how potentially effective it was. I was still angry at Nathan, but I now instantly regarded Masako as an ally, probably because I needed someone as an ally at the moment.

"And this is Kurt Campbell," said Nathan, rubbing the back of his neck, in that sheepish/cute thing that he does. "I believe that you've already met."

Nathan, of course, was as delighted as ever. I realized in that moment that he would have been perfectly happy to have a *Thin Man*–style party in his apartment, where we all drank a lot of booze over five courses and dessert and have the murderer revealed in the most dramatic way possible.

"Anyway," said Nathan, still sounding more affected than genuine, "I'm sorry that I didn't tell you that I lived above Jonah. I assumed that you already knew that, actually."

Which was maybe a dig at my detecting skills.

"Nathan, dear flower," I said to him. It sounded sweet, but four concerned eyebrows went up elsewhere in the room. "Would it be possible to adjourn to your room so we could discuss things privately for a moment?"

"I would be happy to do so."

Masako and Kurt watched with concern as Nathan led me into his room and closed the door behind me.

I will describe his room to you later, when I am less angry. Scratch that—I won't describe it at all, except to say that Nathan clearly had a thing for concert posters.

"Nathan."

"Dahlia."

"I am very, very cross that you did not mention to me that

you live one floor above Jonah, who was brutally murdered a few days ago. Around the time that I met you."

"Honestly, I thought you knew that. And I don't see how it's relevant."

"For one, it makes you a suspect. I don't know if I want to keep hanging around with you."

"What? Get out of town."

"Have you seen the first episode of *Murder, She Wrote*?"

"I've seen *an* episode of *Murder, She Wrote*. Aren't they all the same?"

"Not the first one, no. Jessica Fletcher is this widow, right? She stumbles into a murder and because she is awesome, gradually she figures it all out. At the same time, she meets an old guy who seems sweet, and she starts thinking, *Hey, maybe I'll date this guy.*"

"I have not seen that one, no."

"Yes, well, it goes on. She figures out that the old guy she's interested in *is* the murderer. She confronts him, thinking that he must have had some sweet, entirely reasonable explanation for why he committed the crime, and then he tries to kill her."

"And then the sheriff pops out."

"Not in the pilot. In the pilot, she thinks with her heart and nearly gets murdered."

Nathan seemed to think this story was hilarious. "Are you telling me that you're concerned that I'm going to murder you?"

"I'm saying that I haven't ruled it out as a possibility."

Nathan was laughing to the point that it was not fashionable. I don't just mean that it was irritating and insulting; I mean he was actually making a ridiculous snorting noise. The kind of private, awful laugh you use only when you're alone, or you've really lost it. He also dialed someone on his phone.

"Hold on a second. I want you to speak to someone."

I stared at him. I was still angry, but what can you do? He was gradually beginning to make me feel silly, but perhaps this was a lure so that he could murder me more thoroughly. Regardless, it could not be ignored that he lived alarmingly close to the victim.

"Hang on a sec—I want you to hear something." Nathan giggled into the phone, which he held out to me. "Explain your theory to the man on the phone."

"Who is on the phone?" I asked.

"It's my dad," said Nathan as happily as ever.

I was beginning to feel like I was the straight man for a couple of pie-wielding clowns, but I dutifully spoke my lines into the phone.

"I have some concerns about spending time alone with your son, because I think that he might have murdered Jonah Long and, in turn, may murder me if I learn too much."

I couldn't even finish that sentence before the elder Mr. Willing lost it. I believe the sound he made was something along the lines of *"Aaaaaaaaah!"* Seriously, I was lightly worried about him having a heart attack. This went on for about thirty seconds before it devolved into a crazy attack of tittering and he said, "Can you repeat that for my wife? She needs to hear this."

I repeated my statement for Nathan's mother, which prompted Nathan to lie down and start stamping his foot repeatedly. I can only imagine what Masako and Kurt were thinking in the other room.

My fears were gradually—make that rapidly—morphing from a concern that Nathan lulls me into trusting him before he murders me to a concern that I was going to end up marrying Nathan, and I would have to hear this story at every holiday dinner from now until I die. Literally, flashes of little

Nathan-and-Dahlia-spawn danced in my consciousness, and they chortled, saying things like, "Mommy, tell the funny story about thinking Daddy was going to strangle you." On the one hand, it felt like a little victory, being able to effortlessly imagine a future with someone other than my ex, but on the other hand: every holiday dinner until I die.

I walked out of the room, leaving Nathan to collect himself.

Masako and Kurt didn't even pretend to be interested in anything else. I appreciated their candor.

"Nothing on TV?" I asked.

"Nothing as exciting as that," said Masako. Did I say "ally" earlier? Make that "neutral party."

"All right, Kurt. Since Nathan is apparently too giggly to answer my questions, I'll ask you. Why are you here?"

"Jonah kicked me out, and I didn't want to stay with my parents."

"But that only explains why you're not there. Why are you here?"

"If I want to look for a job in Saint Louis, it helps to live here."

"Okay, that puts you in the city. Why are you *here*?"

"I asked Nathan if I could crash here for a while, and he said sure."

"There's a spare room?"

"No, I'm in Nathan's room."

Well, there you have it. Nathan Willing was literally sleeping with suspects. This would have to be something we worked out later. At my place. When the production of *Godspell* was over. I don't know why I was surprised—Kurt, Jonah, and Nathan were all grad-student buddies together. So was Jennifer Ebel. I wondered, suddenly, if she'd ever crashed here. But I put the thought out of my head because there was actual work to be done.

"So, I got a package for you. You'll never guess what it is."

Kurt appraised me with uncertainty. I think for a moment he thought perhaps my package was my fist. His face transformed, sad panda–style, as he figured out my meaning. "Oh, you mean that giant box."

I thought this couldn't have been plainer, but I suppose no one expects to get a giant spear in the mail.

"Yes," I said. "The giant box. Guess what's in it."

Kurt looked thoughtful. He wasn't checking his phone now, but he still didn't seem entirely present. After a beat, he ventured an answer.

"Maybe a parasol? Like, an oversized one, for a picnic table?"

On the one hand, this was the dumbest thing that I had ever heard. Who busts in on you and wants to gauge your reaction while you unveil an industrial parasol? Who buys industrial parasols, aside from the Saint Louis Bread Company? On the other hand, he did at least pick out something that, dimension-wise, would fit into the box. Which is more than could be said for my first guess of corpse.

Kurt, faraway though his emotional manner may be, detected that I didn't exactly admire this answer, and so he clarified, unnecessarily, "Like, an industrial picnic table. For a restaurant with a deck. On the ocean."

Poetic, but still wrong.

"Open it," I said. I figured I'd at least get his facial reaction; although, given my experience with Kurt thus far, it would probably be muted. But even that was ruined.

"It's not a spear like the one that killed Jonah, is it?"

Masako still had a lap filled with sprout, and I wanted to tackle her.

"Why would you guess that?"

"I don't know," said Masako. "You're making such a big deal about it, I feel like it should be something dramatic. That, or a corpse."

Masako was joking, but Kurt still was earnest. "The corpse would have to be folded," he said. "Or cut up."

"It could be a baby," offered Masako.

"But why would the box be so long?"

"Maybe it's three babies, head to toe."

"Just open the box," I told them.

And despite all this tomfoolery, the Bejeweled Spear of Infinite Piercing was just gaudy and awesome enough to still make an impressive reveal. Light shot in through the window and onto the box, so when Kurt finally opened the damned thing, part of the room actually glimmered with refracted light.

"Golly," said Masako.

"It's not the spear that stabbed Jonah to death?" asked Kurt, unwilling to handle it, either because of fingerprints or superstition.

"No," I said. "The police have that one. This is just a copy."

"Well," said Kurt, now touching it, "it's very shiny."

It was very shiny. It continued to be shiny. Its shininess is a point that possibly cannot be overstated. And yet I wasn't as drawn to it on this second viewing—maybe my detective was kicking in and I was watching Kurt's face, which seemed to be lost in a sort of private reverie. In retrospect, though, I think it was because it didn't stand out as much in Nathan's apartment. Nathan and Masako and Kurt too were strange and frivolous people (and I say that with esteem and admiration) and the Bejeweled Spear of Infinite Piercing—or even its replica—belonged in a place like their apartment. It should exist in a world of spontaneous alfalfa sprouts and terrifying sofa sectionals. It did not belong downstairs, in the empty apartment of a dead man.

"There's a note," I said, handing him the envelope Emily had given me.

" 'This level life too has its summit,' " I told him. "You don't know what that means, do you?"

Kurt didn't respond to me until he had opened the envelope and read it himself, three times. I know it was three times because his mouth moved as he read. Whether he thought I was going to lie to him about the contents or he just couldn't handle the multitasking, I'm still not sure.

At any rate, when he was done reading it, he gave me a puzzled look that was so extreme, so goofily confused, that you could have snapped his picture, written something snarky in Impact, and started a meme right then and there. I resisted this impulse and instead asked:

"So you don't know what it means?"

"No...," said Kurt with exceeding slowness. But his face was slowly transforming from utter confusion to creeping suspicion. It was like watching a glacier move.

"Hang on," he said, suddenly standing. "I need to check my email."

Then he left, going into Nathan's room. That left just me and Masako, whom I had never wanted to meet, much less be left alone with.

She must have sensed this, because after a long and uncomfortable silence, she tried comforting me. "Please don't feel threatened by me," she said. "I abdicated any claims on Nathan months ago."

I was trying to seem smooth, and so I laughed. I was shooting for cool hip girl in a vodka commercial. But the laughing lasted a beat or two too long, and I ended up landing closer to not-hip girl who was on her fourth shot.

I had reason to be nervous. Masako Ueda was not the half-Japanese girlfriend that I had imagined. If you will forgive my slight racism and massive paranoia, I had taken Nathan's ex to be a giggling pixie girl, slight, wispy, perhaps with imaginatively colored hair and one of those thin, delicate frames that sets boys to searching the Internet one-handed. I had prepared for that. But Masako was none of these things. For one, she was built like a truck. It wasn't unattractive, but she wasn't wispy, and any protracted conversation with her compelled one to look into doing sit-ups. She also, despite wearing a pastel yellow sundress, managed to seem kind of Goth-y. I guess what bothered me was that Masako seemed less like an idea and more like an actual person. Troublesome and contradictory and, goddamn it, sort of likable.

"You know, maybe the message is an anagram," said Masako, looking for solid ground for conversation. "I think I've got an app for that."

Masako started fiddling with her phone—and I just dropped the subtext and let her have it.

"Why did you break up with Nathan?"

I sort of winced as I asked this. It was a tacky question, but I wanted to know. I couldn't tell you why I was worried about her answer, given that Nathan was supine in the other room, still chortling about my apparent concern that he might murder me.

"It's somewhat complicated," said Masako, in a completely uncomplicated voice, "but the gist of it is that I left him for my sister-in-law's midwife."

"And that would be a woman?" As relationship-threatening answers go, switching to the other team was as good as I could hope for.

"It would."

"So you're a lesbian."

And Masako half smiled, which is as close as she gets to smiling most of the time, I would later learn. "It would seem not, no. But at the time, it seemed very reasonable to double-check."

This answer was less reassuring. Masako could read my face—I might be good at making guesses and deductions, but I did not have a private eye's inscrutable face. When I tried to look inscrutable, mostly I gave the impression of mild constipation. And even this required an embarrassing amount of concentration to maintain.

Masako had the opposite problem—her face would have been great for police interviews. Squeezing an emotional response out of her face was like trying to get the last bit of toothpaste out of a tube. It was as if she had been born Botoxed, and frowning, to boot. She was trying, mostly unsuccessfully, I should note, to look friendly now.

"I am not interested in Nathan, so you should not worry about it. I am emphatically so not interested in Nathan that it was completely unnecessary to move out."

"I can still hear you," shouted Nathan from the other room.

Masako said loudly, "He is very handsome, however." Then silently mimed the words to me, *Not. To. Me.*

And there you have it. I decided to trust her. At least about that. I wasn't ruling out that she hadn't gone downstairs and speared Jonah to death, just on principle, but when two people emphatically insist that they're not interested in each other, sometimes it's best to just let go.

I sat down on the sofa and asked, "What do you do for fun around here?"

"Anything that does not involve model trains," Masako said.

At which point, Nathan entered the room and collapsed into the armchair across from us, in a clear rebuke to the yardage of sofa. He did not sit in the chair like a normal person but instead draped his legs over the side of it, affecting a pose of amused decadence.

"Do you have an anagram?" he asked.

"Hmm," said Masako, poring over her phone. "Foist themselves a lithium Stoli?"

There was a silence as we all considered the ramifications of this.

"You've cracked this case wide open," I told Masako.

"I don't know. I think it's very practical," said Nathan. "I believe that foisting a little Stoli on ourselves is exactly what we need."

"If it has lithium in it, I'll pass."

"There's always wine, if you want a softer approach," offered Nathan.

And suddenly we were all sitting on the floor, drinking a rosé. For detecting, it was probably not helpful. But it was sweet and good, and I realized that I had not sat on a floor and had wine with friends in entirely too long.

Kurt stumbled back into the room. He hadn't had any wine yet; he just stumbled.

And he sat down, on the floor too. We were all on the floor now. Fields of sofa, and we just sat on the floor. But it felt right somehow.

"Your email?" I asked. "You thought you would find something in your email?"

"You were very dramatic about it," noted Masako, pleased.

"I didn't," said Kurt. "But I think I know what it's about. It's the Left Field Games Summit. He wants me to go to the Left Field Games Summit."

Left Field Games was the company that made *Kingdoms of Zoth*. I knew this because every time you logged in to the game, you had to watch their silly little three-second logo of a baseball landing in grass. Sort of a gaming equivalent of the Columbia Pictures woman holding the torch. But markedly less grand.

"So this was an apology," I asked. Nathan poured another mug of rosé. No fancy wineglasses here. Mugs. I think Nathan's had the molecular structure of caffeine on it.

"That's how Jonah did apologies," said Kurt. "He could never manage them head-on."

"This level life too has its summit. The Games Summit. Why are you frowning? I think it's cute."

I had taken that Kurt wasn't fond of wordplay. He frowned even more deeply now and said, "I'm not going. It'll be terrible."

"Have you ever been before?"

"No, it's in Phoenix. Who goes to Phoenix?"

"How do you know it's terrible if you've never been?" I asked him.

Nathan was still lounging on the chair. "This is why I said you have an interrogative manner."

"I've been to things like it. One con is like any other. Probably."

"Do what you want. It's your theory, after all. But it sounds like Jonah intended for you to have a good time on his behalf."

Kurt's frown grew deeper still. I wasn't sure why the idea troubled him, but it apparently did. "Yes, you're probably right. That's just the kind of big gesture that Jonah was fond of."

"So...yay?" I hadn't intended it as a question. I wasn't sure what was so horrible about the notion of going to the Games Summit. I wasn't even particularly into *Zoth*, but conventions were fun. People in costumes, visiting a new city, and late-night drinking with cute nerds. Or, at least, alcohol could make them seem so.

"It's just such a burden. It's exactly like Jonah. It's a big gesture, but with very little thinking behind it. The Games Summit is this weekend. Do you have any idea how much money it will cost to buy a ticket to Phoenix on such short notice?"

Masako said, "You're not working, you're not in school. You could take a road trip."

"Not in my car," said Kurt, which was a notion I could identify with.

"It's the last request of a dead man," said Nathan with the carelessness and the caprice of someone who would not have to fly to Arizona. The comment deflated Kurt, however.

"Right, then. Well, time to go to Zoth."

CHAPTER FOURTEEN

Kurt, by the ancient rule known as firsties, was stationed at a very nice computer indeed, and I was splayed out on the carpet using a laptop of yesteryear, which meant that I had a frame rate that made *Steamboat Willie* look like Pixar. However, given that I wasn't actually playing, and that I just flittered about the dangerous fields of Zoth with a harp, it didn't matter terribly much.

It did not take long to find out that the Horizons were in chaos.

Everyone had gotten Bejeweled Spears of Infinite Piercing. That was wave one of the shock.

"It's fabulous," said Clemency with a reverence I hadn't yet heard from her. "I don't know what to say."

"It's beyond fabulous, Clem. It's mythic. We are now living myth." Threadwork was not made speechless by the spear exactly, but even he was choosing his words with a solemn care. And he sounded a little less catlike and a little more plain than was his custom.

All the Horizons were there, all logged on. I haven't mentioned most of them, as they aren't strictly relevant, but taken altogether they made quite a group. They seemed very international, sort of like the X-Men. There was their leader, who was some Canadian kid given to saying things like, "Pretty flash, eh?" There was Terrible Southern Accent Guy. And speaking of dreadful accents, Orchardary and Threadwork seemed to be in a war of seeing who could dominate the conversation most.

"It is, without a doubt," she was saying in a thick Indian American accent, "the most outlandish thing I have ever seen. How much would such a thing cost? It is unthinkable."

Canada Guy was stammering. Kurt sounded like he was going to cry. Threadwork kept spitting out superlatives—this group, who was usually very restrained about everyone talking over one another on Teamspeak—was utterly disarmed. It dissolved into a cacophony of conversations.

Only Ophelia was unamused. "This is the least practical present anyone has ever been given."

"It's just an ornament," said Orchardary. "Granted, it is too heavy to put on my mantel, at least when nieces and nephews come to visit."

"I can't believe it," said Scarred for Life with His Southern Accent Guy. "I mean, I was slightly pissed at him for stealing the spear, but I never imagined this."

"He was full of surprises, wasn't he?" said Clemency.

And that was just wave one. At eight PM, on the dot, everyone in the guild got mail. From Jonah.

It happened like this—the wave of burbling about the spears, it mostly died out into a stunned silence, which was solemn and felt meaningful. Until Orchardary broke it with a speech, going on about the spear's market value, which suggested she had planned to hock the thing later in the evening. I interrupted this speech and reintroduced myself—because, frankly, I think everyone had forgotten about me.

"Guys, I'm here to plan a funeral for Jonah. I'll email you all the details about that, but I'm also here to talk to you about the theft of the spear."

"So you're a funeral planner and a detective both?" asked the Southerner, through that Mississippi drawl of his. "What else can you do?"

And then it turned eight o'clock. I had thought that everyone must had registered this clown's line as some great burn on me, because it was dead silent after that.

"Well, yes," I said. "I am doing both of those things. I grant you it's a little unusual, but this is what I was hired to do."

But I needn't have bothered. No one was listening to me.

"Did anyone else just get mail in-game?"

"Yes," said Threadwork. "I got one from Jonah."

"As did I," said Captain Canada.

"Oh, dear lord," said Orcharary, who was sounding more than a little frayed.

"we all got them," typed Chtusk.

"You've got to get that mic fixed," said the Canadian guy.

"it's a new mic. i don't know why it isn't working."

"This is not the time to berate each other over technical problems, Oat. We all just got mail from a dead guild mate."

I, of course, hadn't gotten an email from my dead guild mate, but I knew better than to interrupt this.

Threadwork spoke again, his cat-voice turned down to such subtlety that I thought I knew what he must have sounded like in real life now. "Does everyone else's email just contain some TinyURL links?"

"Yup," said Oatcake. "In other circumstances I wouldn't recommend clicking on these because there's no telling what kind of virus they might link to."

"Yes," said Clemency. "In other circumstances."

There was still a round of stunned silence. We had gone from everyone talking at once to no one talking at all. I was still working out how a dead guy had sent email. The way I saw it, there were three possibilities. Either Jonah had arranged for the email to go out in advance, before he died, or his parents had recovered the account and they had sent it. Or, and this was the alarming possibility, this email was sent by the same person who had hacked his account and stolen the spear in the first place. It could be a virus, a keylogger—or, if the person who stole the account was also the person who had murdered Jonah, something far more sinister.

When you put it that way, I wouldn't have wanted to click on the link either.

"Fortune favors the brave," said Threadwork, sounding much more resigned than brave.

What I heard next was an agonizingly long period of typing and mouse-clicking, followed by a parade of gasps and a "Well, shit" from Southern Guy. And then silence again.

I wanted to just yell out, "For chrissakes, just tell me what they linked to," but it seemed wrong to interrupt the stunned silence.

"Well," said Clemency, "it looks like we're all going to the Games Summit."

And then they were all talking again. Apparently they were links to vouchers for plane tickets and boarding accommodations—a hotel suite, rental cars, all of it. They were going to the Games Summit, and they were going in style. I don't know if it was because Jonah was dead, or the double dosage of generosity or what, but I might have been participating in the weepiest chat-room channel in the history of the Internet.

Oatcake was clearly, openly crying. "That bastard," he was saying, "he was such an asshole sometimes. But he was our asshole."

Typed out, it might not look like the sweetest epitaph ever written, but somehow, those were the magic words that just sent everyone weeping. And cursing. There was a lot of cursing as well. But this was the Internet.

"God bless Jonah," typed—not said—Chtusk, who was apparently still having mic problems.

"He stole the spear from us," said Tambras. "But he wanted our respect. Oh, fuck him. I'll miss the bastard." And she was crying too.

I tried to listen for someone who sounded especially bristly or guilty somehow, but it felt ethically incorrect—and beyond that, impractical. Everyone felt guilty, it seemed to me. When someone dies and posthumously gives you extravagant gifts, it's impossible to feel any other way, isn't it?

"He was much cleverer than I had given him credit for," Orchardary was saying. At least it wasn't the Southerner going on and on—her accent was at least musical and fun to listen to. "It's a literary joke. This level life too has its Games Summit. Ho, ho."

Kurt, whom I could hear in surround when he spoke loud enough: "I don't get it."

"It's from 'A Walk to Wachusett' by Henry David Thoreau. Hang on, I'll google it." A moment later, she was reading.

Remember within what walls we lie, and understand that this level life too has its summit, and why from the mountain-top the deepest valleys have a tinge of blue; that there is elevation in every hour.

And she paused, clearly having a sense of drama to her.

And we have only to stand on the summit of our hour
to command an uninterrupted Horizon.

"Jesus fucking Christ," said Tambras.

And the rest of the Horizons were expressing similar shock.

"It really is an apology," said Clemency. "It's kind of a beautiful apology. I didn't know that he had it in him. It's so...un-Jonah."

Tambras made a grunting noise that suggested that she was somehow amorphously skeptical of the whole apology concept but could not exactly explain how.

The Horizons were all in a state about Jonah Long, and it dawned on me that I would have no better moment to state my case.

I reminded them, now with much more agency, that Jonah's online funeral would be held tomorrow night. And then I went in for the kill.

I hate being overly earnest. I'm good at it; it just hurts. Like Delirium from the Endless can make plenty of sense when she needs to; it just damages her. This was my Delirium moment.

"Guys, I just want to remind all of you that I'm looking for the Bejeweled Spear of Infinite Piercing on behalf of Jonah's mom." I was originally going to say "parents," but I veered toward "mom" at the last second, sensing that it painted a better picture. I told you I was good at earnest.

"I'll be honest with you: I'm not a *Zoth* person. But I've played other games like this, and I know how inside of you they can get. If someone disrespects in *Zoth*, it feels like they're disrespecting you in the real world too." Pause, assess. "And in a way, they are."

161

And they were silent, every last one of them. And they say a Priestess of Usune can't spellcast.

"I also know that Jonah's making off with the spear was contentious at best, and probably kind of a dick move. All I can tell you is that his parents wanted it back, and their wishes are for it to be deleted with his character."

"Deleted" was the wrong word choice—I needed something more evocative: "erased," "entombed," "buried." I probably should have used "mom" again too, but I hadn't lost them.

"If you know anything about it, *anything*, please let me know. I'm not looking to place blame. I'm not trying to sell anyone down the river. I just want the spear back. For Jonah's mother."

God, I was laying it on thick. But the thing was, I was making myself sad. It wasn't all fake. And the words I was saying were technically true. Or mostly true anyway. Probably once I figured out who the thief was I would pepper them with follow-up questions and then report it all back to Emily Swenson, so I guess I was a little bit interested in placing blame. But globally, I meant what I was saying.

Perhaps it was all the loot that Jonah had foisted on them, or perhaps I was just more persuasive this time, but suddenly everyone was interested in what I was saying. I didn't know if I was going to get any clues, but at least it looked like Jonah's funeral was going to be a hot spot.

———————◆———————

You might have expected Jonah's posthumous largesse to prompt a lot of last-minute eulogy material, but this did not prove to be the case. It was only Chtusk—mic-less Chtusk—who had any material for me.

"he had nice teeth," she texted to me. "very clean."

I texted to her that this was not exactly the sort of material that made for a thrilling eulogy. I asked her if she had any more personal details about Jonah.

"his breath was nice also. i can't help much with personal details. i did not know him very well."

Generally speaking, when I have positive opinions of someone's breath, I know them pretty well. I suggested this to Chtusk, who typed:

"no sorry. didn't know him. just nice teeth is all."

So, a Shakespeare quote, some platitudes, and nice teeth. This eulogy was shaping up to be awesome. At this rate, I was going to have to crib from Jonah's real-life funeral tomorrow to get material, which seemed reasonable but tacky. Let's face it, you don't want to be the girl taking notes at a funeral.

In any narrative such as this, there are a lot of things left out. Bathroom breaks, mostly, and I've probably said "er," and "um" hundreds of times up to this point, but if I were completely faithful to the record, it will make me look like an idiot. *You already look like an idiot*, I can hear you saying. You're probably right.

But among the more substantive things I'm excluding were my brief interviews with the other Horizons. The guild had about ten members, and I tried to at least touch base with everyone, even though these other members couldn't use the spear and were almost certainly not involved. Not much came of this, but for the record, I did interview a fire mage who was almost certainly drunk, a dwarven tinker with a syrupy Southern accent, and a human pugilist who I think might have been a twelve-year-old girl.

But I will mention part of my interview with Oatcake, the Horizons' guild leader. Oatcake, of everyone I had spoken to thus far, seemed the least interested in anything I had to say. I learned the basics of his biography—his name was Owen; he lived in Halifax, Nova Scotia; and he owned a small business that made high-end handcrafted furniture. It had been mostly a side project in his early twenties, but now that he was cresting thirty, it was really taking off.

He could speak with a terrifying enthusiasm about wood-carved furniture, but for everything else he sounded bored. He clearly was elsewhere, and these questions were just a to-do to him. With the other interviews, I felt guilty for being pushy or judgmental; with Oatcake, I just felt like I was wasting his time.

"You seem very distant right now, I have to say."

"I'm sorry," he said after a damning pause. "I'm just trying to multitask. What was your question again?"

But then it was my turn to multitask, because I got an in-game email, with a flashing crow icon tucked away in the corner of the screen. To check it, I'd have to go to a mailbox, but since I was hanging around that same damned bar, there was one right next to me.

Maybe it was rude of me to check my mail during an interview, but it seemed clear that a talk with Oatcake was going nowhere. He was a guy who was getting too busy for *Zoth*, and he was without question too busy for me. He was definitely not a suspect: Here was a guy who did not care about the game enough to commit digital theft. Particularly for a weapon that his character couldn't use in the first place.

So I checked my email. I was intrigued—no one knew me aside from the Horizons and, okay, Erik. I was put out by the idea of another email from Erik—not emotionally devastated this time, just put out. I was never going to get anywhere if he kept interrupting me with undecipherable koans.

It was from a character named Apologia.

I didn't know much about her except that she was a level-one human thief. Never heard from her before.

There was no text in the letter, just a subject heading. It read:

SORRY 'BOUT IT

At first I thought the whole thing was some kind of performance art. Apologizing to people you've never met; this was the *Zoth* version of a twelve-step program. Or a cult. But then I noticed that there was an attachment. A rather spectacular attachment.

In the letter was the Bejeweled Spear of Infinite Piercing.

There it was, the most powerful weapon in the game. It was something that men stole for, perhaps even killed for. And it had landed in the hands of a rookie fairy with a harp.

Getting the spear made me feel electric, in part because I had a secret. I wasn't ready to tell anyone that I had it—or at least, I wasn't ready to tell Kurt, and the walls were awfully thin at Nathan's. Assuming I wanted to tell Nathan anyway, which I wasn't sure I did.

I markedly considered spending the night at Nathan's apartment, but my head was full of ideas and I wanted to get out. And deranged laughter or not, I was still wary about getting too emotionally involved with him just yet. Was he a murderer—okay, probably not. But I couldn't say for sure that he wasn't involved. Yes, okay, that's probably a flimsy excuse to avoid emotional connection, but I had gone fast with Erik. And with the next guy, I was going to take it slow.

My apartment was still inaccessible, so I chilled at a coffee place near Nathan's that I used to frequent in my carefree days.

I recognized no one there, not a soul—not even a barista—and this made me consider that my carefree days were a lot further in the past than I had immediately remembered. I sipped steamed milk with hazelnut and waited for the allotted hour to return to my home.

If I had known that Detective Shuler would have been waiting for me at my building, I would have lingered at the coffee shop. Hell, I might have slept with Nathan. But I didn't, and when I walked up to my building from the street, Shuler surprised me so much that I nearly jumped into traffic.

"Jesus!" I told him when he showed up behind me.

"Dahlia Moss," he said, smiling. "I see you've still got those gimlet eyes of yours."

"I'm full of steamed milk right now, and I don't need to be frightened like that! You're lucky I didn't vomit."

"As concerned as I am about that," said Shuler, following me into the building and actually getting into the elevator after I pressed the button, "I'm actually here to ask if you bugged me."

Damn Charice. Why am I always the fall girl for her exploits?

"It wasn't me?" I said, managing to end the sentence on a question mark, despite my intentions. And it actually wasn't me, which is, of course, what everyone says in prison.

"It's a really bad thing to do, Dahlia. If that had been Maddocks, you would be in a lot of trouble."

"And I'm not in a lot of trouble?"

"No," said Shuler, his voice sad, as if acknowledging a deep character flaw, "I suppose you're not. Although I have another question for you."

I was being as kind as I could to Detective Shuler, because I did not want to go to jail. "And I have another answer."

"Did you hire photography students to monitor Jonah's parents?"

"Not the parents, the apartment. And, no, I didn't."

Detective Shuler gave me a look that I would describe as "sister, please." I noticed that he had permanent creases on his face from this expression, so I'm guessing that it was a go-to look for him.

"I didn't hire them. They're working for free. It takes a village." This was maybe a little snarky, but I was flying high with the spear in my possession.

"No," said Detective Shuler. "It doesn't take a village. It takes the police. *The Lottery* takes a village. Solving crimes takes the police."

"Right," I said, suddenly anxious about that damned trash from Kurt's car again, even though it wasn't being talked about. "I get those two things confused sometimes."

Shuler smiled again at me. He's a very smiley guy, honestly. Probably in the wrong line of work.

"Listen, Dahlia. I like you."

I wasn't sure where Detective Shuler was going with this. I felt equally perched on the precipice of being vaguely threatened and awkwardly asked out. Shuler must have sensed my uneasiness, because he tried to fill in the space. Although I'm not sure that he knew where we were landing either.

"I'm just saying that I like you—in a broad sense—and I would hate to see something bad happen to you."

"Bad like getting arrested?"

Shuler gave me a look of concern.

"Or bad like getting killed."

We were at my door now, and I wasn't sure what Shuler wanted from me. Plus, I had gotten here too early and we couldn't really go inside.

Shuler looked sad now. "I shouldn't be sharing any information with you at all, but I just think you ought to know something. Is there somewhere where we can be private for a moment?"

"More private than the hall?"

"Preferably."

I coughed. "Not exactly. There's a production of *Godspell* going on in my apartment at the moment."

This momentarily broke the spell of whatever confession Shuler wanted to make. He cocked his head at me.

"Is that some sort of post-apocalyptic musical?"

"I'm actually not sure. I usually try to stay out of the way of theater people. They're not like us."

I opened the door and was instantly booed for flooding light into the room. There must have been thirty people crowded into cushions on the floor. From what I could glimpse of the production, there was a half-naked man draped across the television with a spotlight on him. I closed the door.

"I think maybe the naked man is supposed to be Jesus?"

"That's surely in violation of some kind of fire code."

"You would know better than me. But I'm not opening the door again. I don't want to get catcalled. Just—what's your advice?"

Shuler looked less like a detective and more like the guy a detective would grill. He was nervous and seemed a little cornered. He obviously had something that he couldn't bring himself to spit out. He behaved a lot like me, ultimately, when cornered because he changed the subject.

"What do you say we go out somewhere?"

"Wait, what, right now?"

"Yeah," said Shuler. "For frozen custard."

If Anson Shuler had finished that sentence in any other way, I would have unquestionably turned him down. But he didn't.

"Fine," I said. "But I can't be out too late. My client's funeral is tomorrow."

If you're not a Saint Louisan, you probably don't understand the unquestionable awesomeness that is frozen custard. You're probably thinking that it's some sort of weird acquired taste like chitlins or Moxie.

You'd also probably think that Ted Drewes—legendary frozen custard vendor—doesn't look like much. And okay, maybe it is sort of a giant hot dog stand—but looks are deceiving, auslander. To a trained Saint Louisian eye, the place looks like heaven. Anson Shuler and I were there, late at night, on a Wednesday, and there was an enormous freaking line. A custard line. Because it is awesome.

Conversation in the car with Shuler had been awkward, particularly because he insisted on playing King Crimson, which I don't want to talk about, and I don't have words for. But in line for custard, I was feeling much more amenable toward him.

"So," I said. "You don't seem like someone who would be a detective."

"Neither do you," said Shuler, who had a point.

"I asked first. How did that happen?"

Shuler sighed, and it was such a sad little sigh—a middle-aged sigh, if you will—that it seemed not quite to fit on him. "It seemed like the right thing to do at the time?"

I liked wistful Shuler more than chipper Shuler, or at least more than let's-listen-to-King-Crimson Shuler.

"But not now?"

"I haven't completely decided yet."

And then it got sort of awkward. It was strange, because it was fun and, I don't know, slightly charging to talk about detective stuff with Shuler, but the moment we hit upon anything personal, it was weird. So I stuck with the case.

"So how's it going with that whole murder investigation?"

So brazen was the question that Shuler broke from his usual brow furrowing and actually bugged his eyes at me, a little.

"I can't discuss that with you."

"I could share with you details about the spear theft online," I said, sounding a lot more coquettish than I had originally intended.

It got his attention. Oh, he tried lobbing it off, as if he didn't care, but I saw the flash of interest.

"I cannot discuss the case with you."

"I see," I said. And I did. But then it was awkward again. I think that's what pushed Shuler into talking—not any particular powers of persuasion on my part. He just didn't want things to feel weird. Neither did I.

"So," he began. "I was watching this really great show on Netflix."

"Oh? What was it?"

"A mystery," he said with a conspiratorial tone in his voice that I didn't notice until later. "A police procedural, actually."

"What's it called?"

Shuler seemed irritated that I kept peppering him with questions.

"It's called *Interrupted Cop*, Dahlia."

"Oh, right!" I said, suddenly seeing where this was going. "I think I might have seen that one. Handsome lead?"

Shuler raised his brow at me. He had great brow action.

"You tell me."

"In an unconventional way."

This got more brow action. Peter Capaldi would have been impressed.

"So, on the show—"

"*Interrupted Cop*," I said, interrupting him.

"Yes," he said, "*Interrupted Cop*. There's this investigation of a murder. At first the police think that it's a break-in, but the deeper they get into it the more they wonder if the thief didn't have a key."

"Ooh, intriguing. What happens next?"

"I don't know, I'm only on episode one," said Shuler. "What about you? You seen anything good?"

"Yeah," I said. "I've been really getting into a mystery series myself. More of a cozy. It's, uh, called *Glamorous-Looking and Extremely Competent Amateur Detective*."

"*GLECAD?*"

Shuler was faster with acroynms than I was, because by the time I figured out what he had done, he'd gotten in another line.

"Doesn't seem like something that you would be into."

"Are you kidding me? It's like it's my life."

Shuler gave me more brow.

"I haven't been keeping up with that show. What's happened on it lately?"

"The GLECAD had been after this, uh, stolen pole that a bunch of people wanted, and, just in this most recent episode I saw—she found it."

Now, this got a reaction.

"Really?" Shuler was floored. I should honestly have been

insulted by how shocked he was, but I was too busy with my metaphor to notice.

"Well, sure. I mean the 'C' stands for 'Competent,' right?"

"Who took the pole?"

"Well," I said, "the GLECAD hadn't figured that out yet. It was returned anonymously. But she's working on it."

"What's the GLECAD going to do with the pole?"

"She was thinking of using it as a trap to discover the identity of the thief."

Whatever the correct answer was, this was not it. Anson Shuler's face practically doubled over at me with disapproval.

"GLECAD's gonna get canceled, if she doesn't watch herself."

"Pshaw. This glamorous detective has also acquired a replica of the murder weapon. It's all under control."

"Dahlia, you really need to pull back from this."

"Incidentally, how much strength does it take to spear someone to death? Could a woman do it? Would you have to be in great shape?"

Shuler sighed at me. "You've got the strength to do it. And the brazenness."

I wasn't so sure. For all its bling, the spear wasn't actually all that sharp. You could bludgeon someone with it for sure, but to gore someone to death? It'd take some force.

Shuler wasn't such a bad detective after all, because he answered my question without me ever voicing it.

"The replica you have is a revision of the original. It's duller. It also has less gems on it."

I was impressed by his reading of me but mostly floored by the notion of something with more gems on it than the spear I had. "How many more gems could it possibly have?"

"I don't know; I'd have to see yours," said Shuler.

I nearly invited him to my room for a comparison, but I felt it was bit too much like inviting someone to look at a collection of etchings.

Marshmallow. That's the flavor I got. Shuler went in for something fruity. Banana? Big Apple? I got a Concrete—a custard confection named for its legendary consistency—so I wasn't paying that much attention. It was a little cold out, and so we adjourned to his car. It was a slow walk because I was feeling happy and increasingly sated. Mostly with custard, but maybe with life too.

"So what's this big confession you were going to make to me?"

"You should be cautious around Jonah's friends."

I gave him some skeptical brow work of my own. "That was the big tip you were going to give me?"

"Not originally, no," said Shuler. "But it's the tip I've decided to give you now."

I was playing it off like it was nothing, but it did make me a bit nervous. Who was he trying to warn me against? Was Kurt not the benign panda I had taken him for?

"You know Jonah's sending all the Horizons to a convention in Phoenix, right?"

Shuler looked surprised, but I soon realized he wasn't surprised about Jonah's plan—he was surprised that I told him.

"We have his credit card receipts, and it's something we worked out."

"Are you going out there?"

"Why would I do that?"

I felt like this was a question that should have a solid answer. Maybe not Marshmallow Concrete solid, but I should at least be able to turn it upside down without it falling out. But I couldn't muster up a single reason that wouldn't sound ridiculous out loud. And I didn't have time to consider it much, because we got to his car then. Shuler picked up a flyer that had been placed under his windshield.

He glanced at it and smiled.

"Maybe your string of unemployment is over," he said, handing me the flyer. It was written in black Magic Marker on Astrobrights-red Xerox paper: JOB FAIR—SATURDAY 3 PM.

Ugh, gainful employment. The fantasy was broken. "Oh, thanks," I said.

But as we got back in the car and drove away, I noticed a curious thing. Not a single other car had a flyer placed on it.

CHAPTER FIFTEEN

The next morning was Jonah's honest-to-gosh, real-life funeral. I probably should have been more focused on that, but my head was still in the events of the previous day. Don't laugh, but I couldn't shake the feeling that someone had left that job-fair note just for me—which I know sounds like crazy paranoia. And yet. Did I have some fairy godmother who was trying to find me a job? If so, she should have shown up several months earlier, when my life was falling apart. Why now, when I actually sort of, kind of had something going? I wasn't just being paranoid, was I? It was weird. I mean, who distributes flyers late on a weeknight at a custard joint? To a single car? Still, maybe it was paranoia, because Anson Shuler, Interrupted Cop, didn't think it worth commenting on. Maybe he had left the flyer for me.

That little mystery was troubling enough. I didn't even know what to say about the slightly cheeky vibe I had picked up around Anson. It was like the pseudo-flirting you can do around gay guys: fun and brazen and, because you know there's zero chance of a relationship starting, totally risk-free. I was doing it around Shuler, without the fail-safe. Dangerous waters, Dahlia. Canceled? *GLECAD*'s cast was expanding like it was working toward a spin-off.

I found myself wishing that I had asked more questions of Shuler when he had made his vague little proclamation. Which friends? I should have asked him. Biology friends? Gamer friends? Nathan and company? Technically speaking, Jonah was someone who didn't really have friends. He had people, acquaintances of varying degrees, whom he probably referred to as friends. But they weren't friends, at least not as I understood the word. They were, well, a politician's idea of friends. People who Jonah had a little history with, and who perhaps might prove useful down the road, career-wise, or for tanking aggro off a raid boss. If he had lived, he'd probably be describing me as one of his "friends," eventually.

The trick was, with Jonah's broad definition of friendship, an edict to avoid friends of Jonah Long was not practical. Jonah was one of those souls who just went around collecting people. He wasn't the head of the Event Horizons, he wasn't the heart of the Horizons, but he was definitely its fingers. More than half the guild seemed to know him personally. He interacted with everyone, however facilely. So the question of avoiding his friends was not very constructive. Doing it properly would probably entail avoiding wide swaths of Saint Louis.

Of course, Charice was nowhere to be found. I took this to mean that she went home with one of the actors, which was a very safe bet. My money was on the half-naked man I saw who was playing Jesus. From what I saw, Jesus had abs. Plus, it would play to Charice's sense of the grand.

But it was just like her to not be around when I actually wanted to speak to her. Hot and cold, that Charice. Instead, I spent the rest of the morning in solitude. A quick trip to the library, a little mulling around the mall. I took Shuler's advice, but that meant making no progress on the case at all. It worried me that this was perhaps the intended result of his warning.

———————◆———————

I still hadn't told Charice about the spear. By the time I made it to Jonah's funeral, I was ready to shout it from the rooftops. If Jehovah's Witnesses had wanted to enter my home to go over the wonderful appeal of eternal life, I would have more than happily entertained them, provided I also got to bounce off my own exploits.

It was certainly not the attitude I should have entered the scene with. I should have been solemn, respectful, and most of all observant. I was none of these. "Peevish" was a good word to describe my mood. And the only person I was looking for was Charice, who, goddamn it, really should sit and listen to how amazing I was for a minute. Or so I felt at the time.

I didn't have a lot of experience with funerals. The only one I had ever attended, at least that I was old enough to remember, was for my uncle Kyle's grandmother, who died at 103. The entire family went, because my aunt Lorraine had been cheating on Kyle for some time, which my parents knew about, and they felt guilty. So we went to the funeral of this strange unknown woman to compensate. I realize that doesn't make any sense, but it's how we Mosses operate.

It was basically a kind of nightmare. Kyle cried constantly. Lorraine glowered at us for coming. Alden hit on a pallbearer and disappeared with him behind the church while the rest of us sang "Amazing Grace." Me, I just sat there and squirmed. At fourteen, I could notice the details, but I didn't have any of the subtext. The only clue I had was what all fourteen-year-olds have: Grown-ups are weird.

It was an insight that, while still true, didn't help me now. Surely this funeral would go better. Even if I didn't get any clues, it had to go better. Right?

I got there early for the purpose of speaking to Charice before the funeral began and because I took a chance and drove my jalopy, which you always need to allot extra time for. But she was not there, still. My other purpose was to figure out where these alleged photographers were, which I found was not hard at all. There were just photographers around, taking pictures of things. They made no particular effort to hide themselves. It looked like three people to me. But they weren't being a burden—it wasn't as if they had flashbulbs that they were irritating everyone with or were forcing people to stand awkwardly together.

The funeral was taking place outdoors, at a cemetery I had never visited or even heard of. This was probably because it was not a cemetery for poor people. It was very old—at least for Saint Louis—and had the lavish sort of mausoleums that one expects in the Northeast. Jonah's gravestone, by contrast, was pretty modest. A crowd, smaller than I would have guessed— perhaps sixty people or so—sort of muddled about in folding chairs, most of them not sitting down just yet, as if they weren't ready to commit to the thing. From the uneasiness and uncertainty in the air, I guessed that Jonah's parents hadn't shown up yet. Perhaps they were making an entrance with the priest. The thing wasn't going to start without them.

I was scanning the crowd for Charice but instead found Jennifer Ebel. She was dressed as soberly as she had been when we first met, but then it struck me that she was probably perpetually dressed for a funeral. She took my polite nod for a suggestion to come over and talk; that, or she was bored. I couldn't blame her—for someone so young, it seemed that most of the mourners here were rather advanced in age. It was hard to guess how they could have known Jonah, except for the obvious guess that they were all friends of his parents.

Jennifer was upon me faster than one would have thought possible to move in a getup as highly starched as the one she was wearing. As she got near to me, I realized that she was also wearing tiny skull earrings, which, while subtle, had to be said to be unspeakably tacky. At least it answered my earlier question about her. Jennifer was a humorless girl who had somehow acquired an inexplicable penchant for novelty jewelry. No one, as Christopher Durang says, is all one thing.

"How's your case coming?" asked Jennifer.

Had I said that I would have confessed details of my case to Jehovah's Witnesses earlier? I meant it then, and damn if I didn't want to spill the beans now, but there was something in Jennifer's fake casualness that made the hair on my not-recently-enough-shaved legs stand on end. Who did she think she was fooling?

"So far," I told her, "he's still dead. Nothing I've accomplished seems to have brought him back."

As comments go, this was a little like fetid air. It meant nothing, signified nothing, and was vaguely distasteful. It was just the first thing I had thought to say. It did not deter Jennifer in the slightest, however. Why would it? She was wearing skull earrings to a funeral.

"I heard that Jonah was murdered," she told me. She could not have achieved a more fake version of a casually lobbed-off comment if she worked on it. Maybe if she had thrown in a "girlfriend" to preface the phrase—as in "Girlfriend, I heard that Jonah was murdered." Maybe then. But then again, it was all so forced and fake that I'm not sure it would have made a difference. This second query didn't irritate me as much as the first. Mostly it just left me embarrassed at Jennifer's terrible social skills.

"I don't know that a funeral service is the best place to discuss this, Jennifer."

"That's why I thought I'd ask you before it starts. You're the detective. Who do you think killed him?"

At least she had had the good graces to keep her voice low, although apparently the gentleman behind me had heard her mindless theory-mongering, because he was graceful enough to give me a chance to escape.

"A detective?" he said, in a faux British-y voice that I realized instantly had to be Threadwork's. "You must be the unstoppable Dahlia Moss. A pleasure to meet you."

I don't know why I was so shocked to see a Horizon at Jonah's funeral. I suppose I thought of Zoth, however irrationally, as a distant land only reachable by modem. Of course, it wasn't. And here was living proof.

"Good grief," I said. "I didn't realize you were a local."

"I'm not a local," said Threadwork, just as puffily as you would imagine it. "I hail from the fabled city of Baltimore, glimmering city of glassphalt."

It was a ridiculous delivery of what was already a very silly line, and I regarded the man in front of me with what must have been too long a stare. Jennifer seemed to be doing it too. It was just that I was checking to see if he were some sort of hologram or ventriloquist's doll. The voice that was emanating from him—this fey, wispy British thing—seemed to belong in a completely different body.

The gentleman—Threadwork—was African American (or I supposed, possibly African English—but really, who in Britain actually spoke like that?) and must have been close to seven feet tall. Or would have been, if he were standing. But he wasn't standing—he was sitting in a wheelchair. Despite this, he seemed to sort of loom over me and Jennifer both. I'd generally never describe someone in a wheelchair as being menacing, but I had to admit that Threadwork was indeed very large. His muscles had muscles. If his legs were inoperable, it seemed as though his arms and chest were going to pick up the slack. And when they were done picking up slack, they might just rip a tree out of the ground and throw it.

It was not the man I had imagined, to say the least.

But it was definitely Threadwork—you could tell that from how he expanded to fill the conversation.

"There's no good weather for a funeral, don't you think? Either it's dreary and cold, and makes everyone miserable, or it's sunny and beautiful and seems as though God isn't actually all that sad about you being dead."

He looked up at the sky, which was indeed sunny and beautiful. "Still, I suppose. Better this than hail."

Threadwork went on for a bit more while I gaped at him, and Jennifer quickly made her escape.

"What a detestable woman," he said after she left. "Asking you who you thought murdered Jonah. Oh, by the way, I'm Threadwork."

Incidentally, just so he doesn't come off as a complete crazy person—Threadwork did tell me his real name. But to keep things simpler, I'm sticking with Threadwork. It suits him better anyway. And less hyphens.

"Yes," I said. "I gleaned that. Thank you for driving her off. Although I don't think that she's detestable so much as awkward."

"Awkward or not, there are things that we do not do."

It was such a puffy thing to say that it prompted my next question with almost no thought at all.

"Is that your real voice?"

"Not in the slightest, no. But I've decided that I'm going to use it for my adventures today, and at the convention. Are you going, by the way?"

"I hadn't planned on it."

"You should. You'd have a lovely time, and perhaps you would solve your case. Besides, I'm going to go, and you would be another interesting person to talk with."

Crowds were beginning to gather, and I found myself thinking that we should move toward the chairs. But I was still slightly hypnotized by the improbable figure in front of me.

"Why don't you use your real voice?"

Threadwork paused for a moment, as if deciding to answer my question cleverly or truthfully. "I don't much care for the way people react to me when I use my 'real voice.'"

"Is this some kind of race thing?" I asked him. Apparently the wake of Jennifer had left me with a surprising directness.

"Partially," he said. "But mostly it's that when I speak in my regular voice, people regard me as some sort of walking tragedy. 'That poor man.' I've actually heard someone say that when they thought I was out of earshot. But when I'm Threadwork, they regard me as a curiosity. Have you met that strange fellow in the wheelchair? What a curious gentleman he is."

I wasn't sure what to make of any of this. Frankly, I thought using a false voice all the time seemed a little tragic myself. But it was as if Threadwork had read my mind and answered this unspoken thought at once.

"I don't use this voice in my regular life, please understand. It was just for the character. Just for Threadwork. But now that I'm being dragged into the light, as it were, I don't want to be recontextualized. I am not a tragedy."

"Do you want to tell me your story?"

"Most definitely not, no. Although I fear you'll just look it up anyway."

"Probably so. I'm not very good at leaving unanswered mysteries alone."

"I'll give it to you in six words, then. I played college basketball," said Threadwork, then gestured at his legs. "Very briefly."

"Car crash?"

"A horse."

"It's nice to meet you, Threadwork. I'm sorry to force you out of your comfort zone."

"Well, you didn't murder Jonah Long and steal the Bejeweled Spear of Infinite Piercing. You're not the cause of any of this, just another thing to be endured."

And his tone had gotten shorter with me. It was a mistake to force the story out of him. It wasn't relevant to the case; it wasn't relevant to anything. Being a detective, if you're not careful, can give you false license to get into everyone's business. Like one of those horrible people at dinner parties who consider themselves "truth tellers"—and yet only seem to offer truths that are critical. Any virtue can be taken too far.

"Did Clemency come with you?"

It was an unjustified question, honestly—but something about Clem and Threadwork struck me as a pairing. Not a romantic pairing, just a pairing. Like Laurel and Hardy, or Tycho and Gabe.

"I met her at the airport. She's with Jonah's parents now, I believe. I assume they're going to all arrive together."

This surprised me more than Threadwork's backstory. "How does she know Jonah's parents?"

"I don't believe she does. But she went to meet them this morning with food she had made, and I haven't heard from her since. But you know Clemency. She's so good at feelings."

The funeral started late, because no one was willing to begin without Jonah's parents there, although at twenty minutes after its start time, doubts began to foment that they were going to make the event at all. On the one hand, it should be inexcusable to miss the funeral of your son, but on the other, it really feels like an event that you shouldn't witness. Getting there very late, and looking dazed and beleaguered, as Sylvia and Harvey Long did, was perhaps the most socially acceptable way to deal with the situation.

The funeral was more secular than I had imagined. The priest spoke only in generalities and never mentioned God or any particular religion. Rather, he focused on how much Jonah would be missed, all the holes he would leave behind, and how it was up to us to honor his memory.

It was depressing as hell.

After the funeral, I had had a vague hope of speaking with Sylvia or Harvey Long, but they were swarmed with well-wishers, and they clearly didn't want to deal with the ones they had. Sylvia, it had to be said, looked remarkably like her son. Same facial structure, same body type. Harvey, on the other hand...If I had to describe him quickly on a Ouija board, I'd go with LLWBRIMLEY. Regardless, they bolted out of the funeral as if they expected the coffin to explode in a rain of fire, mowing through friends and family as they headed toward the limo that had brought them here. Stopping them would have required an elemental force, such as lightning, or a wall of plague rats. And frankly, I wasn't sure the rats would do it.

I still hadn't seen Charice, but I could just feel that she was here. She was waiting for me to let down my guard so she could pop out at me from behind a tombstone, or leap out from a casket. I was not having it.

I made small talk, but it was clear that this was a work obligation, not some terrarium of suspects, which was what Charice had hoped for. I did notice the pretty brunette that was talking to Threadwork. She was as unsurprising as he had been revelatory. Clemency was exactly as I had imagined she might look.

She looked to be about thirty, with the short, straight plain hair that one expects a kindergarten teacher to have. Her face was small but expressive, and she had—I could tell, even from a distance—a teacher's way of talking with her hands. When she spotted me, she brightened visibly.

"Dahlia!" she said, hugging me. "Thank you for coming out for this."

At least from outward appearances, Clemency had the sort of pregnancy that women's magazines yearn for. She was pregnant but otherwise rail thin, a cute little baby bump showing at her waist, while the rest of her looked ready for a trip to the beach. "Glowing" is the word my mother likes to use for the phenomenon.

"It's nothing," I said. "How are Jonah's parents?"

"As well as can be expected. So, lousy, really. They're very impressed with you—I guess their lawyer is sending them good reports."

I think I preened a bit at the line, which probably wasn't wise or appropriate given that Clemency was a suspect herself. Perhaps not a very likely suspect, but a suspect nonetheless—and I should accept her secondhand assessments of me with Bogart indifference. That's in retrospect, however. In the moment, I preened. I don't even think she noticed, though—she had her own problems on her mind.

"I went over to see them this morning with cinnamon buns. Which seems like a ridiculous offering, I know. Your son was murdered, here are some cinnamon buns. But you know, people die and you bring food. That's what you do."

"You came with them, so I guess the cinnamon buns worked out."

"I suppose," she said, looking sad and far away. "They were all alone. I had expected that there would be family and well-wishers, but it was just them, hanging around in their son's apartment. I barely explained who I was before they just sort of melted into me. I think it might have been the first food they have had in days."

And now I felt guilty. Clemency was worried about their well-being. I had been worried about my prime position as fake detective, and evidence. Touchy-feely bits weren't really part of my wheelhouse.

"So, Dahlia," said Clemency in a tone of voice that suggested she was putting the unpleasantness of the morning behind her. "What would you recommend one do with two days in Saint Louis?"

"Keeping ADA compliance in mind," added Threadwork.

It was, of course, at this point that Charice popped out from behind a tombstone. Well, not exactly. More that she just came into my field of view—she had been sitting modestly in the back, mostly out of sight. Probably she had been supervising the photographers, which is why I hadn't noticed her before. The other reason I might not have noticed her was that she was wearing a disguise. Charice was standing there in a little gray hat, with luxurious brown curls coming down her shoulders. I realized, with dawning horror as she drew closer, that this had been Jesus's hair.

Her sudden appearance shouldn't have surprised me, at any rate. The question "What would you recommend to do in Saint Louis?" was practically an invocation of Charice—the way saying "Bloody Mary" three times in the mirror brings forth evil spirits.

"Dahlia," she said, smiling broadly, all but daring me to ask about the wig. "Are these friends of yours looking for a diversion?"

It had barely been twelve hours since Detective Shuler had given me explicit instructions not to hang around with Jonah's friends, and so I started to say, no, Charice, let's let them find their own way. But I stopped myself because I was momentarily confused if I should call her Charice or not. Given her getup, she may have already introduced herself as Dorothy von Higgenbottom, and I would be giving her away.

Charice took my confusion and ran off with it. Also, she ran off with the suspects, telling them, "I'm Dahlia's roommate. I'd be happy to show you around town. How do you feel about cheap sushi?"

I would have been irritated, but I had business inside.

———————◆———————

I knew what William Chetwood looked like from the funeral home's website. He wasn't quite the man I would have imagined for the job—that guy would have been tall, thin, and cadaverous. A nice character-actor type. Actual William Chetwood was more of a fuddy-duddy; bald and pear-shaped, always futzing with his bifocals. Still sort of a character actor, but less Hitchock and more Dickensian countinghouse. Probably it was the suit.

"Mr. Chetwood!" I said, drawing his attention as he headed back toward his car.

He turned to look at me, and his face lit up with a kind of illumination. It was exceedingly grandfatherly, and despite not knowing him, I felt an unexpected rush of warmness toward the man. I presumed it was this sort of thing that made him good at dealing with the bereaved.

The illumination wasn't an affect, though. He recognized me.

"Dahlia Moss, isn't it? Are you Dahlia Moss?"

Jesus, had I applied for a job at a funeral home in the past thirteen months? I couldn't remember doing so, but it wasn't strictly impossible.

"Yes, that's me. How do you know who I am?"

"I didn't," said Mr. Chetwood with a lot of cheer for a funeral director. "I was just sort of hoping."

The obvious question to ask was: Why would you hope this? But I felt this all had the influence of Charice about it, and so I saved the question for the end of the conversation. I never liked giving Charice her treats right away, even if she wasn't around. Besides, she was probably listening in.

Instead I got to my point: "You didn't make my announcement."

"Announcement?"

"For a funeral for Jonah Long?"

Mr. Chetwood smacked his lips in a gesture of confusion.

"We just had the funeral for Mr. Long. You missed it, my dear. Dead and buried."

"No," I said. "For another one. An online funeral."

"Another funeral? No, I don't think so. Usually our patrons die just the one time."

I think perhaps this was a joke, but it was very dry.

"An online funeral. More a remembrance, really."

Mr. Chetwood looked at me with confusion. "Online? Like Facebook?"

"This is to be in the online world of Zoth. In the Sunsalt Marshes?"

And his face lit right up again. Clowns had less buoyant smiles.

"Oh yes, right! I do remember that now. No, I didn't announce it. I thought that was a joke." Then he seemed to suddenly realize that this was some sort of faux pas, and his face transformed into the very picture of contrition. He was good at faces; he seemed to have quite a tableau of them.

"I'm quite sorry."

I frowned. "It wasn't a joke. I really wanted to invite everyone to Zoth."

"Is that a bar?"

"No, an online world. With dragons, and ogres, and there's this talking crab that wants you to kill fish for him."

Mr. Chetwood gave me an appraising look. He may have been slightly bumbling, but the guy oozed empathy. Mentioning the talking crab wasn't the smartest thing to say, and there were plenty of openings for snark. He avoided them all. "I apologize, Miss Moss. I'm really not very up-to-date on the hobbies of young people. I gave up somewhere around Go-bots. I thought it was a joke. Mea culpa."

"Is there some way to get the announcement out after the fact?"

Mr. Chetwood made a sort of a thoughtful clucking noise. "Tell me. Do you think that very many of those people who attended the funeral today will visit an online world with dragons and ogres and a talking crab? I'm not up-to-date, but I do have a good sense for people. The crowd I saw looked a bit on the, hmm, august side. I don't they would be interested in talking crustaceans, unless they were mascots for a seafood restaurant. Even then, many of them would have questions about heartburn."

"That's not the point."

"What was the point?"

I suppose the point was to show Jonah's parents that I had been trying. Then again, based on their dazed and beleaguered (and entirely natural) behavior at the funeral, they probably wouldn't have noticed anyway. Easy come, easy go? But I suddenly had a second thought.

"I don't suppose I could pick your brain about a slightly related matter?"

"My brain, my dear," fluttered Mr. Chetwood, "is always ripe for picking. Even for matters less than slightly related. Sometimes ideas fall out of it without any picking at all."

"If you had to deliver a eulogy for someone you didn't know," I began. "Let's say, in a fantasy world. How would you go about it?"

Mr. Chetwood rapped his fingers along his face. "I would avoid doing that. And not just the fantasy world. A eulogy ought to be personal. If you really must have it delivered by someone who didn't know the deceased, you should get a priest."

My face must have sagged, because Chetwood instantly asked, "Can't find a priest?"

"I can, but he's a war-priest, and I don't think it means the same thing. Any other advice?"

"Platitudes and quotes from the Bible. Shakespeare, if they're not religious."

This was less encouraging than I might have hoped. Sensible, but not encouraging.

"Thank you. Incidentally, why did you hope I was Dahlia Moss?"

Mr. Chetwood looked at me blankly, as if he had forgotten this portion of the conversation, then lit up again with recognition. It was like dealing with Kurt Campell's senile grandfather. "Right, oh yes," said Chetwood, fishing into his pocket for a plain white envelope. "I was supposed to give this to you."

I looked at the envelope, which had my name on it.

"Who is this from?"

"From?"

"Yes, who gave it to you?"

"Samantha?" suggested Chetwood with very little commitment.

"I don't know anyone named Samantha."

"Perhaps it was a Julie. Or a Linda?"

"I don't know anyone with any of those names." And they aren't even related names, I thought, although I wasn't going to badger Chetwood on this point. He obviously dealt with a lot of names and faces. "What did she look like?"

Chetwood was giving me a face—a tableaued one this time, from his bank of expressions—that quite clearly said: I'm very busy and why don't you just take your envelope and leave? With his lips, however, he said: "I must confess that I'm not entirely sure. Someone tallish? Or perhaps medium height. Definitely not short."

"White? Black?"

"Probably one of those, yes. But not short."

"How are you sure not short?"

"I have a smallish coffin I'm trying to get rid of. So short people are on my brain."

There was a little more small talk, and I thanked Chetwood again for his advice. I was back in my jalopy when I opened the envelope, which was white, and unassuming, and unlabeled. It was an article, clipped from the *Cadenza*, about gaming addiction. The headline read: "How I Overcame My Gaming Addiction and Found My Life." I didn't read it because even starting the article made my blood boil. I did see one passage that had been helpfully highlighted for me: "Players of MMORPGS are three times more likely to be unemployed than nonplayers." Very helpfully highlighted. At the bottom of the article, written in the same block-lettered handwriting from the job-fair flyer were the words: "Just worried about you, Dahlia. —An anonymous friend."

I wanted to storm away, but my car wouldn't start. It'd been doing this thing where its anti-theft mechanism randomly kicks in, so I had to wait a half hour in my car, reading the article over and over and considering: Who is this really from? I don't have any friends.

CHAPTER SIXTEEN

I really didn't have friends. Usually when people say things like that, they're angling for some kind of hug, and believe me, I'm not. But let's be honest—I did not have people in my corner. I had Charice, obviously, but she was less a friend and more an elemental force, like fractals, or entropy. My friends had just sort of evaporated away with the end of college. They had moved away, or gotten jobs, or gotten married, or done all of these. And even before they'd wandered off into whatever brave new world was supposed to await you in your twenties, they were direct. Charice, insane as she was, was a decent model for what my friends used to look like.

They were not writing anonymous concerned notes about my "gaming addiction."

When I had finally gotten my car safely ensconced back in its traditional parking place, I headed over to Nathan's. Charice was out—always out—and whatever proto-thing this was becoming, it was what I needed.

Thanks to an extremely unfriendly iPhone upgrade, my phone was powered down. Whenever I attached it to my car charger, I now received a scolding, telling me that my iPhone was "no longer compatible with this [antediluvian] device and may not work reliably." You have to love that language: "may not work reliably." Although it was completely accurate—the phone seemed to charge on a schema vaguely akin to a d20 table for "Wild Magic." One of these days I was going to plug it in and get, I don't know, a swarm of rats or a Limited Wish. But today I got nothing. If anything, I seemed to lose power at a quicker rate.

So I showed up at Nathan's without texting first. I didn't think he would mind, and I was probably correct about that. But when I knocked on his door, I found that he too was out. Masako was there, looking dark and radiant all at once, and I decided, on the spot, that hanging out with her was what I had wanted all along anyway.

"Let's lunch together in secret," I told her when I knocked on the door. Masako, for her stake in the matter, seemed utterly unsurprised by my appearance, or the request.

"If you like," she told me. "But let's not go to that awful Thai place you took Nate. It's…" And she searched for a word that appropriately expressed her unspeakable venom and, not finding one, settled on "inauthentic."

We ended up at another Thai restaurant, a much more expensive one, but what did I care? I had money. Masako regarded her silver noodles with squid with something akin to reverence, but as for me, I felt like the same green curry I always got was about the same as usual. They were a little stingy on the rice.

"I've brought you here for a solemn purpose," I told Masako, who just looked at me blankly, eating noodles.

After an entirely too long pause, she asked, "Fine. What?"

"I have recovered the Bejeweled Spear of Infinite Piercing."

I explained the story to her, how it had been emailed to me

anonymously after Jonah's largesse guilted the group. I had mostly expected her to be unfazed, because this was her thing. But instead she brightened.

"So you have the digital version of the spear that Jonah was murdered with?"

I told her yes.

"Who else have you told?"

"A police detective, through the veil of metaphor," I told her. "I only got it last night."

Masako considered this with what struck me as a dawning happiness. "Who else do you intend to tell?"

"No one, immediately. Eventually Charice, if I ever see her again."

"I am your trusted confidant."

"So it would seem. I can't tell Nathan; he would tell Kurt."

"He would tell everyone."

"What do you think? Is it a reasonable plan to keep the spear secret?"

Masako considered this as she sipped on her iced coffee. "It's reasonable, yes. But I'm doubtful that keeping it secret will immediately do anything. If the thief is that broken up about it, they'll probably just communicate with you in the same way as before. You'll get threatening anonymous emails in-game."

"Maybe they will leave incriminating clues as to their identity," I said a tad too hopefully.

"Possibly. But it's also possible that by returning the spear to you, the thief has solved the problem. They didn't feel guilty because they had stolen the spear; they felt guilty because they had it. Now that they've sent it to you, it's your problem. If you want to really leverage this into something, you're going to have to twist the knife."

———————◆——————

Generally speaking, I was on an upswing. Things were going my way—powerfully so. Clues were appearing, romance was vaguely slumping around in the background, and I'd actually made a little coin. However, in the grand tradition of Mosses, I did find something to be grouchy about. My apartment—once impregnable to outsiders—had been seriously impregnated.

Okay, not the best word choice. The sanctum sanctorum wasn't what it used to be. It wasn't even a sanctum anymore. It was practically a hotel. The Swing-by-um Swing-borium, which even Chris Claremont's Doctor Strange wouldn't have put up with. But I digress.

It was probably because of this general sense of edginess that I was noticing the door. In previous incarnations of Dahlia, the door was simply a piece of wall that could swivel. I didn't concern myself with it. Should anyone be there, they were certainly not there to see me.

But now the door was a point of interest. I had been surprised twice now—three times if you count the cops—and I felt like it would be prudent to keep an eye on it. Even if I wasn't a detective, it's no fun to be constantly surprised by strangers.

So that's probably why I noticed it. It wasn't a loud sound. It was just a rustling. The sound that you would make if you wanted to keep quiet. Someone was out there.

The door was unlocked, and it wasn't as if I was expecting an ambush, so I took the opportunity to make a good first impression. I glanced at a mirror, sat down at the sofa, and grabbed a copy of a book that I thought would make me look studious.

I was hoping for *Ulysses*, or Malcolm Gladwell. I did not have these handy, and by "handy" I mean that I did not own copies of either of them and would probably physically recoil at their presence. What I found was a copy of the writings of the Marquis de Sade, Charice's, obviously—which was smuttier than I would have hoped for but was at least classy smutty. I arranged myself in a pensive and thoughtful-looking position, readied my "Come in—oh, excuse me, I was just doing a little light reading," look and waited for the knock.

No knock.

Someone was out there, I was sure of it. Nathan again? We really would have to have a conversation about this door-crouching predilection of his.

I quietly got up from the sofa and, as soundlessly as I could, crept over to the door. I peeked out of the peephole, and there, in fish-eye lens, was the most nervous-looking woman I had ever seen.

No one is flattered by a fish-eye lens, but the girl in front of me was especially maligned. Probably, she was an okay-looking gal, but the bent view through the peephole gave her the Innsmouth look. It was a woman, about my age, who could be described as exceedingly flat. Not just her chest—everything. Long, flat brown hair, flat little nose, flat little hands. She was dressed in flat clothes too, lavender heather sweatpants and a white T-shirt.

She looked nervous. Not "I hope I don't turn into a Deep One" nervous, but in a similar neighborhood. She had big eyes, and she seemed to be in some sort of internal battle over whether to knock on the door. She lifted her hands twice to knock, but then those big Innsmouth-y eyes would flicker, and the hand would come right back down.

Who was this gal? There was a chance, of course, that she was somehow involved with Charice. But she looked tightly wound, and no one involved with Charice was tightly wound. Charice's visitors usually didn't knock at all; they just came in. Often with props. She was here to see me.

Hell with it. I just opened the door, but Miss Innsmouth was gone. She apparently moved quickly—she was practically all the way down the hall, heading toward the elevator.

"Come back," I yelled. "What were you doing at my door?"

I then ran after her, barefoot, still holding the Marquis de Sade. Perhaps processing me as a crazy person, she hastened her way to the elevator, got in, and pointedly did not hold the door for me. The doors closed and Miss Innsmouth was gone.

First-class detective work, Dahlia.

———————◆———————

Only so much time could be allotted for vanishing strangers. I brooded a bit and tried to find some less trashy reading material for our common room. But that was it.

Five hours later and I was, again, a little pink fairy named RedRasish. I'd been in Zoth for only a few days, but I could see how it could easily become addicting. RedRasish's life was simultaneously more exciting and more predictable than mine, and this was proving to be a comforting combination.

I was due at the Sunsalt Marshes in an hour. I had picked out this zone because the site WikiZoth had noted that it was known for "beautiful sunsets and sunrises" and because all these dawns and dusks inexplicably occurred there more frequently than in the rest of the world. Clemency had offered to teleport me there yesterday, but I felt like this was a little like Skyping in to someone's wake. "Can you hold the camera up to his face, Herb? I can't see him! Oh, wait, yes, he looks very lifelike!"

It was half-assing it, is what I am saying. This had been mine to run, and run it I would. The least I could was to actually walk to the funeral myself.

And there was plenty to do. I'd been reading a very lovely book on funeral planning titled *Funerals—Step by Step Planning: A Death has Occurred, What Now?* by M. L. Veres, which has a lot of practical advice, although nothing specifically on planning the online fantasy funeral of someone you barely knew. Frankly, I think if M. L. Veres had to be forced into a position on the matter, his advice would be to escape. But no matter. I focused on the practical things I could control. The locale. The time. The ambiance.

Plus, I had real-world money to spend, and real-world money buys you a lot in Zoth. I had hired two trolls and one two-headed ogre, who were sprinkling black and pink flowers on the ground. I know that sounds tacky in the real world, but in Zoth it was a nice touch. Also classy: They were wearing tuxedos, although this made me feel underdressed and retroactively made me worried that I had underdressed for Jonah's analog funeral too. Clemency was also dressed in black, which further made my orange gauze outfit seem a little tasteless. I also had a wizard on hand—not in a tuxedo but more of a nice dinner jacket—to help with visibility and for teleporting guests. Some woodworkers had made pews and laid them out. I was supposed to plug their services at the end of the funeral, which also struck me as a little tacky, but I suspect different rules apply in *Zoth*. When it was all said and done, it was really pretty picturesque. Maybe it looked more like a destination wedding than funeral, but at least there were no flame pits.

After twenty minutes of putting things together, I got a message from someone who was rather unimaginatively named "Detshuler," which read:

"Can you port me there?"

God, Shuler was such a closet geek. "Port me there"? Please. This was clearly not his first time at the rodeo.

"Sure," I messaged him. "The port will come from a wizard named Grisgris."

A bit later, and "Detshuler"—a dark-skinned human who looked an awful lot like the real-world version, assuming Detective Shuler had the upper-body strength of an Olympian and liked wearing very tight shirts—was milling around the place too. I was afraid that he would want to make small talk, but apparently not. He was just here for the event, I guess.

The Horizons were amassing now—Clemency, tall and wispy, in her black dress. Tambras—who I knew to be a black female violist—appeared as a roguish white male troubadour, sexy and thin, with a lute in one hand and a perpetual grin on his face. He was playing a dirge, which ought to be appropriate for a funeral, but let's face it, is dirgelike and unappealing even in this most appropriate of circumstances. Orchardary was here, an enormous tree-person, twice the size and mass of anyone else, carrying a Templar Knight's shield. She (it?) looked very dignified, except for the shield, which seemed like something a tree ought not to be carrying. Kurt's wise kung-fu master was sitting on the ground meditating. Oatcake's golem was sitting off to the side, looking as if it had been depowered.

Not everyone was there. We were still missing a few Horizons. But it was still a little early. Although, at this point it was getting a little crowded—all manner of people and things were amassing here. Maybe seventy-five? This would mean that

Jonah's funeral in Zoth was better attended than his one in real life, which was either a good or bad thing, depending on how you considered it.

At five minutes of, there was getting to be quite a crowd, maybe a hundred folks. Wayne, a dwarf tinkerer with a Southern accent showed up, looking harried as he rode in on a clockwork horse. Chtusk came skittering in, literally, from a hole in the ground. And Oraova, the drunken fire mage, apparently wanted a good crowd before he made his entrance—in a flaming chariot that came from the sky, which arrived with fireworks. I was mightily impressed by the chariot, but if anyone else was, they didn't register it. Black flowers and pink flowers now littered the ground, and my wizard-for-hire conjured up a podium.

Also at that time, I got a message from someone named "Mandarina":

"This is Emily. Can you bring me to the funeral?"

Yegads. Speaking of funeral invitations I didn't expect to be cashed in. I told "Mandarina" that Clemency would teleport her here, and that it would be just a moment. When she arrived, I could see that Emily had spent some time and money in the cosmetics shop before logging in. There was a little geek in her yet. Although she was merely a level-one elf, Emily had taken the trouble to create a dignified character of mature years. She was tall and thin and had an impeccably made-up face. Her hair was tied back in a bun, and she was wearing an elaborate white gown with complicated patterns embroidered lightly in orange. Pastels for Emily, as ever.

"Welcome to Zoth," I told Mandarina when she arrived.

"Wow," she typed to me. "There are a lot of people here."

And there were. I was glad I had noticed everyone from the Horizons already, because the crowd was getting large enough that it was hard to immediately see anyone. It was time to start, and so I signaled my wizard-for-hire to levitate me so that everyone could get a nice view of me.

The beautiful sunset was fading on cue—sheer luck, incidentally, and the sky was growing solemn and dark. Players lit candles, and I floated high into the sky to speak.

"Greetings, everyone—humans, trolls, ogres, golems, scarbati, dwarves, treants, undead, elves, mummies, harpies, and other—we have all come here today to honor the passing of Kristo Krispoint, the human thief we knew in real life as Jonah Long. Kristo, as he was known to most of us, was a great friend and a wonderful human being."

It wasn't a terrible introduction, but I had the distinct feeling that people weren't listening to me. Maybe Chetwood was wrong. Platitudes weren't the right way to go after all. I had planned a few more paragraphs of this, but I got nervous and skipped ahead to the literary quotes.

"If our great poet Shakespeare had played *Zoth*, I think we can all agree that he would have rolled a bard." Pause, wait for laugh. No laughs. The crowd seemed to be scattering, actually. Would a quote from *Henry VIII* stanch the bleeding? "Said Shakespeare of death: 'He gave his honours to the world again, his blessed part to heaven, and slept in peace.'"

But no, people seemed to be speeding away now.

"The one thing we will all miss about Jonah is his clean, clean teeth?"

And then things went to hell. It was comforting, however, because it was at just that point that I realized that it wasn't me. The sky was getting dark. Beyond nightfall dark. It was starting to look a bit creepy. I also was wondering if I wasn't hearing some sort of whispering noises—like, the darkness was whispering to me. It's just horror-movie stock stuff, but when you're wearing headphones, things like that can wig you out.

Also, there were pirates.

Circular glowing runes began to appear on the ground all around us, and it appeared that pirates were magically teleporting in. They were all yelling things at the same time, as pirates do.

"KRISTO WAS A SCALAWAG AND THIEF AND ZOTH IS BETTER WITHOUT HIM!" and "ANYONE WHO'S HERE TO HONOR THAT DO-NOTHING HAS BEEF WITH ME" and "MURDER! PILLAGE! RAPE!"

was the sort of thing they were typing.

There was a moment or two of stunned silence while everyone processed what was happening, and then hell, as the proverb goes, broke loose.

I was pleased to see that Detshuler was instantly incinerated. A great wall of flame swept up from the ground, and this meant that I did not have to worry about his scowling visage. My primary concern was for Mandarina, who was also in that wall of flame but seemed unconcerned by it. She was ethereal, I had now noticed, and the flames just sort of passed through her. A resourceful woman, that Emily.

And then I was dead. I wish I could tell you what happened— I was probably knifed in the back—but who knows? Being dead in *Zoth* is not such a bad thing—you can still watch what's happening, which is all I wanted to do in the first place.

My ghost sat motionless, watching the fight but unable to do anything to contribute to it. Frankly, I couldn't contribute to it much regardless.

"Why are we losing?" I yelled out. This was not a rhetorical question—it was directed, loudly, to Clemency, who was huddled on the sofa with what she had ironically referred to as a gaming laptop. Threadwork, meanwhile, had been stationed in Charice's room.

It goes without saying that I did not, by the way, mention Detective Shuler's warning to Charice. If I had warned her that Shuler was speculating that one of them might have been involved in Jonah's murder, she would have viewed the warning as an open challenge, and not only would they be staying with us, Charice would also have them armed.

"We're losing," Clemency said plainly, "because they are dressed for battle, and we are dressed for a funeral."

And yet, we were only mostly losing. Not everyone had come dressed in flimsy black silk. Tambras wore the same battle gear that she always did, and she was now nimbly taking out pirates with a crossbow. Chtusk, who was basically a large beetle and wore no clothes that I could make out, was picking up some of the smaller pirates with her mandibles and hurling them around, like a terrifying insectoid dog playing with a stick. Or a small animal's corpse. Likewise, Orchardary and Oatcake—the treant and golem—seemed perfectly prepared for battle. Orchardary was throwing up some kind of force field while she swung that silly-looking shield of hers around, and Oatcake was walking around drawing runes on the ground in pink chalk. Granted, that didn't look like an especially helpful thing to do when one is attacked by pirates, but what did I know? Presumably, it was somehow useful.

And so it was, after an initial wave of beheadings and incinerations, that the two factions started to seem more or less equal in power. I don't want to imply that there was an actual break in the fighting, because there certainly wasn't, but there was a kind of slowdown, in which people apparently took to typing at one another.

"For Kristo!"

"For Jonah!"

"Avenge Jonah's passing!"

typed the survivors of the now half-dead funeral party. While the pirates typed:

"Vengeance shall be ours!" followed by

"BLOOD FOR THE BLOOD GOD!"

To which one of the pirates asked, /shouting,

"What does that mean?"

And was answered by another, drenched in blood,

"IT'S A MEME!"

If you will recall earlier, I had commented that the sky had grown unusually, you might say disturbingly, dark. For those in the fray, this was easy to overlook, as there were bands of angry pirates or mourners actively trying to kill them, depending upon their goals and persuasions. But for the freshly dead—our ghastly white spirits sitting comfortably on the ground, watching the action through a pleasant ethereal haze—it looked awfully obvious. As entertaining as it was to watch a tree pick up and throw a pirate, and as curious as I was about the pink chalk the team's leader was putting everywhere, I couldn't help but look away from the fight to survey the sky.

Things were happening up there. Unpleasant things. And even though I was dead, I could still hear through my headphones these terrible skittering and hatching sounds. It was all very disturbing, really. I felt as though I should yell and warn Clemency, who was still, improbably, alive—even if she were wearing a black dress to a knife fight. But I was worried I would look stupid, like a little kid complaining about a noise in a horror movie. If I brought the terrible noise to someone's attention it would invariably just be a cat, which would jump out and scare me anyway.

It was not a cat. The sky burst open—no longer black, but silver and gray. The sky was covered in webs. Infinitely many webs. And the webs were not empty—they were filled with infinitely many spiders, whose eyes gleamed at me, little red dots glowing in the sky like angry stars.

A terrible wispy voice rang through my headphones. It was female but sounded old and scarred and not at all human.

"Worldlings of Zoth. It is I, Zxlyphxix"—I had to look this spelling up later—"whom you thought you had defeated ten thousand years before. I come to you now, my resolve restrengthened. Your world shall be sundered and cast into the eternal web. Bring your strongest to me, and prepare to feel the wrath of my spider-guard!"

This speech is, in fact, quite truncated. Zxlyphxix went on for a great many minutes that I will spare you, detailing her history, her banishment from Zoth, and, like a good Bond villain, strong clues as to how one should eventually go about defeating her. I see no reason to include those here, but if you are interested, I'm sure you could google them. Suffice it to say that she was a lady who took things very personally.

This completely stopped all the fighting, by the way. I'm guessing the game somehow ordered everyone to sit still for Zxl's monologue. It would destroy the sense of drama if folks wandered off or simply went about their business—picking herbs or sewing pants—during it. However, when she was finished, there was a universal euphoria. I was altogether displaced by it. I had expected alarm, or distress. Instead everyone was all-capsing:

"IT'S A SERVER WIDE EVENT!1!!"

"THE EXPANSION MUST ALMOST BE HERE!"

Even Threadwork was burbling with happiness from Charice's room.

Tiny spiders riding what seemed to be angry-looking,

demonic sea horses descended from the sky and began slaughtering everyone. Few words were typed on the matter, but it was a matter universally understood that this little fracas vis à vis the matter of Jonah's death was now on the back burner, and that the pirates and mourners should put the matter of the funeral behind them and focus on the death-spiders riding the demonic sea horses. The whole thing really was quite a spectacle. The number of combatants continued to swell, despite a generally alarming number of casualties, because it seemed that most of the world of Zoth were coming to the zone to check things out. I saw about twenty guilds, a woman riding a giant squid, and what seemed to be a queen's royal guard, although I wasn't aware of Zoth actually having a queen. At any rate, everyone was eventually killed by spiders.

It was agreed by all that it was an excellent funeral. The only regret that anyone expressed, pirates included, was that Jonah had not been alive to see it.

Emily, having eventually been killed herself, and being unable to figure out how to return to life (Just walk to a spirit fountain, come on, Emily!), decided to simply turn off her computer and call me directly. I had expected some sort of chewing out, but Emily sounded almost pleased, saying the same thing that people were saying in-game.

"I'd only met Jonah a few times, but I think that might have been the perfect send-off for him. It was completely ridiculous, and he would have adored it."

I did eventually correct Emily's assumption that I had arranged for the Spider-God to crash the event. (I don't know what power she must have assumed I had over Zoth, but that's non-geeks for you.) "Ah, well," she said, just as easily, "it was a happy serendipity."

I'm not sure that spider demons eating everyone at a funeral would be something I would casually characterize as a "happy serendipity," but you know, the client is always right. Even Detective Shuler messaged me:

"Highlight of my week. Thank you for inviting me to this bloodbath."

Which I took to be partly—but not entirely—ironic.

The one person who did not message me, however, was Chtusk, the green-and-black beetle who seemed to always have mic problems. First she had dipped her microphone into a fluted champagne glass, which was so dopey that it sounded completely true, and then she had a new mic that also wasn't working. The second instance of her mic not working was a little less plausible. Regardless, I knew her mic was working now, because she had been yelling out commands in the funeral battle. Mostly "run!" and "spiders!" but her name lit up, even so. I was getting increasingly suspicious about her mic never seeming to work when I was around, so I jumped at the chance to speak to her "in person."

"Glad to see your mic problems are resolved! Are you available to chat for a moment?" I asked her.

But there was no response. I knew she had gotten it because she was online. A little green dot next to her name made it abundantly clear. I sent her a second message, which was a little more forceful.

"I really need to speak with you."

And I watched the green dot turn red. The little bug had fled the Internet entirely.

CHAPTER SEVENTEEN

Walking late at night—and here, past nine PM qualifies as late at night—is never an exceptional idea for a girl of my station and age in Saint Louis, and so my anger more or less evaporated after a few blocks. One needs to keep an eye on other pedestrians, and for that, one needs to keep one's temper in check. Also, I wasn't entirely unsure that Shuler wasn't going to pop out and interrogate me on the street.

It was for this reason, probably, that I ended up back at that same coffee shop, sipping on the same steamed milk I had had only yesterday. It was strange—I hadn't been in the place for months, and now twice in a week. I supposed I had been keeping myself away as some kind of penance for career failure, but as I licked the last bits of foam out of the cream porcelain cup they had given me, I began thinking that this had been pretty lousy penance.

This was my kind of place. Geeks, drunks, hipsters, and delicious-flavored milk. Even if I didn't get another job again, I shouldn't deprive myself of the things that I like. What was the point?

It was probably for the best that I was in lifted spirits when I came back to my apartment. The online funeral had put me in a bad mood, and I needed some air. When I had left, Charice, Threadwork, and Clemency—I could never get the hang of calling her Ann—were sitting in the living room talking about *Zoth*. From the conversation, you would have thought that Charice had been quite an expert, which I knew was utterly untrue. But she was good at faking things, you had to grant her that.

I really hadn't been gone long, but when I came back in, Threadwork and Clemency were both asleep, each on a sofa. I don't know where the other sofa had come from. When I entered the room, Charice mimed an enormous shhing at me, as though if I hadn't seen this gesture my reflex would have been to run into the room and start screaming.

"Why are the lights on?" I whispered. "Just turn them off and let everyone go to sleep."

I was still irritated that Charice had invited them to stay with us. Threadwork had been resistant to the idea, but Charice just wore him down, the way that I knew that she would. It's hard to say what irritated me, really. I suppose I was still just fearing the judgment of Shuler.

"We need the lights on," whispered Charice, "because we have business to discuss."

Well, a moment at last. I started to tell Charice about my recovery of the spear, but then I made an overly skeptical look at the sleeping forms of our new flatmates.

"I've got some news for you, but they might overhear."

"They won't overhear."

And there was something about her confident finality that I found deeply distressing. I should have asked her then and there, but I went on with my worry at first.

"It's good news, but I really don't want them to overhear it."

"Trust me," said Charice. "They won't overhear it."

This made me very nervous indeed. With the lights on, I could at least see that Clemency's chest was rising and falling, so at least Charice hadn't strangled them to death.

"You've drugged them," I said as another one of Charice's horrors made itself known to me.

"Of course," said Charice.

"That's the most horrible thing I've ever heard. And besides, I think Clemency is pregnant."

Charice was undaunted. "I thought about that. She's fine. I googled 'drugging a pregnant woman' before I brewed their tea."

I did stop to wonder at the wisdom at this. A brief vision of a Yahoo! Answers page that said "How much Amytl can i give to pregnent woman before dies?" flashed in my head, but it was too troubling to consider very deeply.

"You've all but forced them to stay with us, and then you drug them."

"Relax. The drugs are all-natural," said Charice.

"Hemlock is natural."

"We're fine. I've done due diligence. Just a swatch of Sleepy-time is all."

The worst of this is that Charice was always fine; she was undoubtedly fine here. She just seemed charmed that way. If I tried drugging a pregnant woman, I'd end up on death row twice over. With Charice, it was just another evening.

She could probably tell that I was internally grousing at her, but she had other things on her mind.

"We need to go over the pictures I got," she said solemnly, tugging me into the kitchen as she spoke. There, sprawled out over the table, were maybe a hundred and eighty photographs, printed out in black-and-white, on glossy white paper squares. Charice had been making notes on the photos in pink

Sharpie and putting some of the photos on our refrigerator with strawberry- and watermelon-shaped magnets. The effect of the whole thing was like walking into some massive police search from *Prime Suspect*, except that it was in our kitchen and involved fruit magnets. And instead of Helen Mirren, there was Charice, who had thankfully shed her Jesus wig.

"How was Jesus, by the way?"

"Divine. And you're missing the point."

I looked at all of the photos, casually. It was a staggering amount of information—countless shots of people entering the apartment building where Sylvia and Harvey were staying. It was so much information as to nearly be meaningless. I didn't know any of these people. This was the problem with casting a wide net.

"Charice, this is just too much. Is there some way to screen the people who were actually visiting Sylvia and Harvey?"

Charice frowned. "I realized that at the end. We probably could have arranged something, but I didn't fully understand how many people this would be. Next time we stake something out, I'll have a better system in place. But you're missing the interesting bit."

Charice pointed to a picture. It was Clemency in a tailored white shirt and jeans, buzzing the apartment, with an expression of boredom on her face.

"Yeah? We know that she went over there before the funeral. She brought cinnamon buns."

But as I said this, I realized that Clemency wasn't carrying anything. If she had cinnamon buns with her, they would have had to fit in her purse. Which was stylish and small in the first place.

"I have pictures of her doing that. She did go over there

before the funeral, and she did bring baked goods. I thought they were cookies, but they were in a translucent container."

Charice started pawing through photos, looking for the other Clemency shot, as if the cookie vs. cinnamon bun theory were the crux of what we were investigating.

"Forget that," I told her. "When was this taken?"

"The night before the funeral, right after Threadwork and she arrived in town. I made small talk with them before I gave them their tea and learned that Threadwork knew nothing about it. He thinks that Clemency went out to the grocery store."

"That's very curious."

"Are you going to ask her about it?"

I was less than convinced that this was a massive revelation, but then I hadn't supervised photographers to get this information, and so I wasn't vested. Still, I'd do my due diligence.

"A secret meeting with my client. I suppose I should. Maybe I'll ask Emily first."

Even so, it was strange how I had moved from having no real suspects, save for an imagined foreign hacker, to a world where everyone was behaving suspiciously. Chtusk was fleeing from inquiries. Threadwork refused to speak with me in his normal voice and wouldn't give me enough biographical information to fill a haiku. Clemency was holding secret meetings with the mother of my murdered client. And even Kurt and Nathan were under the pall cast by Detective Shuler's suggestion that I should avoid Jonah's friends.

"Anyway, I've got news for you. I've got the spear."

I had expected some sort of shock, or one of Charice's ridiculous revelatory faces, or something. But what she did instead alarmed me even more.

She hugged me.

As I've said earlier, I am not a hugging person in general circumstances, but despite my writhing, Charice just squeezed the hell out of me.

"I knew you would do it," she said as buoyant as I'd ever heard her.

I explained the story to her, how I hadn't figured out the identity of the thief but that I knew it was someone in the guild.

"Why?" asked Charice, less with skepticism and more with a Nigel Bruce chumminess. She was asking only so that I could show off.

"We know it couldn't be a gold farmer or hacker now—because only someone from inside the guild would have known that I existed, much less have my username to mail it to me. And they didn't just return it to me—they apologized."

"Someone from the guild couldn't have just blabbed to a hacker?"

"Why would they? And even if they did, why would a hacker return it in the first place? The thief returned the spear after Jonah's posthumous gift-giving. A hacker wouldn't have cared about that. The thief is a Horizon. I just don't know which one."

The fact that the mystery wasn't completely solved did nothing to dim her enthusiasm. It seemed to gird her, actually. "You'll figure it out," said Charice.

I tested my second theory on her.

"All I can say is that whoever stole the spear definitely didn't commit the murder."

Charice liked this, and said "Oh?" in such an overly intrigued tone that an onlooker might have thought that she was the killer. "Why is that?"

"Think about it. A Horizon stole the spear and then returned it because they felt guilty. What do they risk by doing that?

214

Getting kicked out of *Zoth*. And probably not even that—they'd just have to create a new account and start from zero. Which would be a pain, certainly, but as risks goes, it's nothing special. A murderer returning the spear risks being uncovered—they risk jail time, or death even. Is a ticket to a con going to make you feel so guilty that you're willing to risk a lifetime in prison? It's not. The only Horizon I can say for sure didn't do it is the thief."

"Are you trying to catch the murderer, Dahlia? Or just the thief?"

"Just the thief," I said, trying to laugh, but it came out a bit hollow. I was not going to try to catch a murderer. I didn't even know that the murderer was a Horizon. Did I? I felt like there was some little piece of information niggling at me. I had a terrible feeling that my subconscious brain had worked something out that it wasn't telling the rest of me. Detectives usually live for these sorts of moments, but in practice it's not a lot of fun. I felt like I was having a combination of an earworm and heartburn. My best option was to change the subject.

"Listen," I said, lowering my voice even further. "You haven't been concerned lately about my unemployment?"

"You haven't been unemployed lately," said Charice. "You've been doing this."

"So you haven't been leaving me notes about online gaming being unhealthy, or, say, flyers about a job fair?"

"No," said Charice—slowly. And with a look of guilt.

"Spill it," I said. "What do you know?"

"I haven't been leaving them," said Charice. "I've been taking them. Someone keeps stuffing flyers about a job fair under our door. I didn't want you to see them."

Now this surprised me. Charice protecting me for a change?

215

"I'm a big girl. I can take it. What, do they have mean little marginalia on them?"

"No," said Charice. "I just didn't think you should get distracted." This was genuine, honest Charice, who was quickly replaced with a more familiar model. "Who do you think is leaving them? Maybe this job fair is a trap!"

"It's not a trap," I told her.

"Maybe you're getting too close to something. The killer wants to lure you to the job fair and bump you off. Maybe there is no job fair! Maybe it's a dark alley."

This would sound completely crazy, except for the fact that I had considered it—briefly—myself. "It's a real job fair," I said. "I googled it."

"Hmm," said Charice, deep in thought as to how to spin this back into something sinister. But I already had the answer.

"I don't think the flyers are from a friend. And I don't think anyone means to 'bump me off.' The job fair coincides exactly with the Games Summit. I think that whoever sent the flyer doesn't want me at the summit."

"Why?" asked Charice, with as little skepticism as could possibly be put into the question. She was loving this.

"I don't know," I said. "I really don't."

There was a beat, and for once Charice said nothing. She was going to make me volunteer the craziness myself.

"What do you think," I asked, "about going to the Games Summit with me?"

"I think it's too late. The tickets are sold out."

"Would it be crazy to fly there and just try to scalp one? Or sneak in?"

Yes, I had been living with Charice too long now. The fact that a plan that could have been conceived by vintage-era

Lucille Ball could roll so effortlessly off my tongue was damning evidence indeed.

Charice lit up like her hair had been set on fire.

"That is a wonderful plan. We'll sneak in! Or maybe we can drug someone and take their badge."

A lot of Charice's plans, I realize, involve drugging someone. Frequently me. But her enthusiasm gave me pause; she's not one of those people you necessarily want a positive endorsement from. It's like introducing your new boyfriend to V. C. Andrews and getting a thumbs-up and a wink from her. You don't want the thumbs-up, and the wink makes you outright nervous.

But I did want to go to the Games Summit.

"Maybe," I said, "we can find something from a scalper online."

The nice thing about Charice is that she could let go of ideas easily, largely because her next caper was around the corner regardless.

"If we must," said Charice. "But we'll pay an outrageous markup."

I did pay an outrageous markup. The Buy It Now button on eBay had rarely proven so treacherous. But I'd been paid a good sum of money for this investigation, and for once, I was all in.

CHAPTER EIGHTEEN

The next day passed without much interest, these things being relative, of course. Clemency and Threadwork woke up from their slumber perfectly fine and did not ask any probing questions about how they had gotten to be so very and suddenly tired after Charice gave them some herbal tea. Threadwork did remark a few times that "travel can take it out of you," but aside from that, it all passed without comment.

Clemency and Threadwork cleared out of the apartment by midmorning and were going on to Phoenix early, because they had not imagined that they would have Charice to guide them around the city. Charice could make Detroit compelling. There was some talk about trying to shift around their travel arrangements to stay an extra day in Saint Louis—the cost in airfare would be balanced by their free lodgings, so they reasoned—but nothing came of it. And of course, Charice had told them—before she had told me, even, that we were going on to the Left Field Games Summit. So they cleared out their things, were trundled to the airport by Charice, and that was that.

I spent the morning in solitude, sipping what I hoped was non-drugged tea and trying to make sense of everything that had happened so far. I had left a message with Emily to call me as soon as I'd woken up, but there was still no response. Charice and I were only a day away from flying out to Phoenix ourselves—and I felt like I was suddenly left with a very awkward unit of time. I wanted to chase down Chtusk, and I wanted to chase down Orchardary, but there wasn't much to do until then.

I was trying to avoid Nathan as well, mostly because I was thinking about him much more frequently than I should, and I had learned from my lost years with Erik that this was a Very Bad Thing. My relationship with boys ought to be more like Charice's—things that just happen around you. Instead, I brood over them and relive conversations and basically reengineer myself into an awkward, pouting mess. Because, clearly, that's what fellas want. I probably should have just called him or texted him, but I could feel myself shifting into "nervous Dahlia," which is a version of me that pores over word choices in texts with a dangerous and laser-like acuity. "What does it mean that he thought I looked 'cute'? Cute like a dog? Cute like a little girl? Is this some kind of fetish? *Merriam-Webster*'s third definition for cute is 'obviously straining for effect.'" Is that what he meant?

This ultra-neurotic version of me doesn't show up frequently, thankfully, and her appearance generally coincides with periods of too much coffee. But I could tell that Neurotic Dahlia was thinking of swinging by the sanctum sanctorum herself, and so I decided it would be best to meet with Nathan in person. It left less evidence that way.

By the time I had hoofed it over to the apartment building, I regretted the idea, but having made the walk I was unwilling to turn back.

Nathan answered the door with wet hair.

"The detective reappears," he said. "Has the plot thickened?"

"It has," I told him. "Next I'm going to knead it into a nice dough and bake it."

"Sounds delicious. As it happens, I'm going to have lunch now anyway. Would you like to join me? How do you feel about swordfish with a red-wine-reduction butter?"

I told him I felt quite fine about it.

"Well, tough, because I don't have that. I have cucumbers."

Nathan looked extremely pleased with himself. I was beginning to feel that I should keep him away from Charice, not because I was worried that they would date each other but more that they might create some sort of self-amusedness singularity that could destroy the world with its terrible smugness. Although this was a meeting I could forestall for only so long.

"You're making cucumber sandwiches?" I asked. As with Charice, the trick was to never acknowledge the joke.

"If you like."

Which is what we did. If Nathan had noticed that I had avoided him, he didn't say. To be fair, it had been only a day since I had seen him last. It just felt like longer.

"You weren't at Jonah's funeral."

"What, online?"

"At either of them."

"I had a class to teach, and I find funerals uncomfortable."

"Anyway, here's my thing," I said. "The police have told me not to spend time with his friends."

"I was never exactly his friend."

"I'm not going to debate you on that point. I think it's probably pretty unlikely that you had anything to do with it, but you know, I do what the police tell me."

"So, is this good-bye?"

"I just think that we should not hang out until the case is solved."

"Oh," said Nathan, brightening, "then you just need to solve the case."

Yes, that was all I needed to do. Child's play.

"If I tell you something, can you promise that you absolutely will not, absolutely will not tell anyone?"

"Hmm," said Nathan. "It would depend upon what it is."

"Just say yes."

"No. What if it makes me an accessory to a crime? What if you tell me that you've kidnapped an eight-year-old and are feeding him cheese and Shiraz in your basement until his parents pay your ransom?"

"Is this about my 'you killing me' theory?"

And then Nathan just started laughing again, just at the memory of it. "Ho, ho, ho." He actually laughed like that. He said "ho, ho, ho" like Santa Claus, except that his voice was very different, because he did not have a belly like a bowlful of jelly, but a tiny waist that was sustained seemingly only by unpopular vegetables.

"I'm sorry I thought you were going to murder me."

"Meh. Let me guess. You found the spear."

I just looked at him. My secrets always get away from me like this. I will go to the grave with nothing to hide.

"What else could it be? So who's the guilty party?"

I explained that I hadn't exactly recovered the spear, more that it had been mailed to me, probably the result of a guilty conscious crumbling at Jonah's posthumous largesse. I considered this to be something of an admission of failure, but Nathan, as with Charice, regarded the news with excitement.

"So you plan to tell no one, and you figure that the guilty party will get irritated at you and reveal themselves."

"That's the plan. I don't know if it will work. But it's something."

"You should do something to twist the knife."

"That's what Masako said."

I expected him to look shocked or surprised that I had told Masako about it, but he did not. Perhaps she kept counsel with everyone. Perhaps world leaders visited her with secrets of state, which she addressed with her special brand of emotionless candor. She was like a Japanese Angela Merkel.

"Anyway," I said after the lack of a visible response, "I'm going off to Phoenix for a few days, to spend time with more of Jonah's friends the police warned me to avoid."

"Well," said Nathan, smirking. "Try not to get murdered."

———————◆———————

I left Nathan's apartment in a chipper mood—as long as he hadn't murdered anyone, I seemed to be acquiring a sort of proto-boyfriend. And that was good, wasn't it? (That's not a rhetorical question. I really would appreciate a second opinion. Tweet at me.)

As I was walking out, I got a FaceTime message from Emily Swenson. She was wearing black, which called into question every idea I had ever had about her.

"So, Dahlia," she said, after I answered, "I've got an update for you."

As a rule of thumb, I'm wary of Lawyers with Updates, but something about Emily's creeping smile told me that this was going to be good news.

"What do you have for me?"

"Get this: A spear came back. Another one."

"What do you mean 'came back'?"

For something as supposedly unique as the Bejeweled Spear of Infinite Piercing, it certainly seemed to keep cropping up in unexpected places.

"Jonah shipped one to a fake address."

"To who?" I asked. This was a big deal. Every Horizon had a received a spear, or at least claimed to, and all the spears had been accounted for. So if one of them "bounced," then a Horizon was lying. But why?

"Aishwarya Patel. Her address is real, but no one by that name lives there. It came back to Jonah marked 'Return to Sender.'"

It wasn't hard to figure out who Aishwarya Patel was—the name was pretty obviously Indian and there was one heavily accented tree in the group. What was hard to figure out was why Orchardary would have told everyone she got a spear when she hadn't. Was she embarrassed about being left out?

"I've also got a complete list of names and addresses for all the guild members who were sent spears. I thought you'd appreciate that."

"I do." And I did, although I was still trying to wrap my mind around the last piece of information. Orchardary, huh?

"Check your email."

And here was my own bombshell.

"Some news from my end: I've been emailed my own copy of the spear. The digital one."

"The original? Who was the thief?"

Emily was not nearly as gobsmacked as Detective Shuler had been. She honestly didn't seem surprised at all, which managed to be simultaneously rewarding and deeply disappointing. I was glad she'd had the confidence in me, but there's something to be said for getting a visible reaction.

"I'm still working on that. It was mailed to me from a new account. I think the account was created because the thief wanted to hide his identity."

"Guilty conscience, you think?"

"Probably. What do you want me do with the thing, what is it, Spear Number Four now?"

"It's the original, Dahlia. It's Spear Number One. Email it to Jonah." And she smiled at me. It was a smile that was worth the entirety of having a iPhone contract with AT&T. So, a lot. "Good work."

I hadn't exactly done anything to get the spear back, but I preened at the good work anyway. "Incidentally, don't tell anyone that you've got the spear back. I've kind of got a plan to smoke the thief out."

Emily raised an eyebrow at me.

"You're full of surprises, Miss Moss."

———————◆━━━━

True to her word, Emily had forwarded me the billing and shipping info for the spears. Each one cost $2,000 dollars, which I found somewhat mind-blowing. It put Jonah's hiring me as a detective into a kind of perspective. I'd been second-guessing his motivations for that ever since it had happened, and judging from the invoice, it would seem I had given the matter way, way, *way* more thought than he had. Jonah was a filthy-rich person masquerading as someone in the upper-middle class.

Once I got past the sticker shock, I settled on the information that was actually useful. For one, there were names and addresses for everyone. Aishwarya Patel of 100 Ladybug Lane, Akron, Ohio, did not exist. Some google-searching revealed that there was such a place, but it was not a house; it was an outlet mall. Aishwarya was not a real person. It had crossed my mind that she was not even Indian—that accent sounded perfectly acceptable to me when I thought it was genuine—but now it seemed a little overdone. It was like a carefully executed joke.

Of even more interest was that there were only nine spears mailed out. Which meant that one person didn't get one at all. Matching names to what I knew of folks did a pretty good job of determining who the spearless Horizon had to be. The one mailed to Canada was Oatcake. Boston was Tambras. Kurt's was mailed here. The one to Madison was harder—but that was where Jonah did his undergraduate work, so it probably meant that drunken fire mage, who had told me he was an old college friend of Jonah's. The fictional address was Ochardary's. Everyone else, save for our bug-person, matched up.

This meant that Chtusk had never gotten a spear at all.

Later, when I thought about the conversations the Horizons were having when they had all gotten Jonah's early Christmas present, I would remember that Chtusk had never actually professed to receiving one, much less to copping, as Orchardary did, as to how breathtaking it was. She was just quiet, taking it all in, and keeping to herself.

But at the moment, I was thinking, *You skittering little bug. You're about to get squashed.*

CHAPTER NINETEEN

When I got home, Charice was being fitted for what seemed to be a hoop skirt that was covered in skulls. So, a typical evening in my apartment.

"Bad news about the case?"

"Not at all," I told her. My face must have been grim, though, and I was truthfully in a brooding mood. I had told Emily and Shuler both that I had a plan, and this wasn't true. I didn't have a plan; I had an *idea* of a plan. A vague sort of outline whose details needed to be filled in, and fast.

"What's with the hoop skirt?" I asked.

"We have to dress for the convention, obviously. I'm going to be Griselda, the Auctioneer."

I had no idea who this was.

"It will be amazing," said Charice, and this was probably true.

It would help that Charice had filled our apartment with flouncy gay men. The boys—three of them—were from the Fontbonne Drama Department—and while I did not know them, officially, to be gay, they were flouncy enough to make the question moot. They seemed to be making a dress for Charice that was constructed largely from bone.

There was also a man there named Syd, who, in contrast, I

knew was gay and yet could be described as resolutely unflouncy. Syd was possibly the least gay gay person I had ever met, and this came on top of his being a hairdresser. He was old, and exceedingly thin, and looked much like Keith Richards would awaking from a nap. He had a gruff, perpetually irritated manner about him that had suggested that he had spent some time—a bad time from the looks of it—in the military.

"All right, Princess," he said to me in a voice that made it seem like he was insulting me, "Charice has paid for the works, so just lie back and I'll work some goddamned miracles on you."

In my usual mood and demeanor, I would not surrender my hair over to an agent of Charice, even if it were Syd, who was pretty good with hair. What alarmed me was the phrase "the works"—Syd was the kind of hairdresser who would push to make a simple trim a little avant-garde, so when he was paid for "the works," it ought to at least give you pause.

But it didn't. I was tired, and I felt weird and guilty, and so I just sat down at our kitchen sink with him.

"Do you ever think you should do something sensible?"

"With hair? Not when I can help it."

"I meant more in life, really."

Syd regarded me cooly with the sort of savage stare down that I would expect from a DEA agent.

"Every day of my life, cupcake. But this is the only thing that I'm good at. And I'm very good." Syd's face clamped shut to suggest he was done with the sharing part of our conversation. "Now how do you think you'll look with pink hair?"

Why this didn't send me screaming from the sink, I'll never know. Instead I asked, "Neon pink or cotton candy?"

Syd showed me a picture that Charice had taken of Red-Rasish. Her cute little cotton-candy, apostrophe-shaped hair would have looked lovely on a very young drag queen. It was hard to imagine on my face, which was markedly rounder than the fairy's. I did not have a tiny nose or enormous eyes. And while it was fetching on her, it seemed a fair guess that it was going to be considerably less flattering on me. Requiring even more consideration was the alchemy involved in transmuting my hair into it. My hair, which was basically a tangled nest of brown straw, was a long way from my best feature. The best that could be said for it was that it was abundant.

But I didn't fight it. I was apparently giving up a real, normal-person job for what was basically an insane whim, and if that meant having the hair of a Manic Pixie Dream Girl, so be it.

Four hours later, Charice was being wired with neon lights, and I was RedRasish. It wasn't quite as bad as I had feared—oh, I looked like a crazy person, perhaps a cross between vintage Susan Powter and a trained yet rabid pink poodle—but it could have been worse. I guess what I'm saying is that while I looked ridiculous, neither was I ugly. In some culture, somewhere, I probably looked sexy. The culture was probably the outer boroughs of the Lollipop Guild, but what can you do?

The Fontbonne boys had made an outfit for me that I was politely praising while privately acknowledging that I would never wear anywhere. It *was* ugly. RedRasish was a level-two fairy, and let's face it, her starting digs were nothing to write home about. Orange gauze. I was not wrapping myself in orange gauze. It just was not going to happen.

But the hair I could live with.

Charice was terrifying, by the way. She was now a harpy— probably approaching seven feet tall with those platform heels of hers, and she had enormous black wings that were realistic enough to be a little alarming. No detail was overlooked; her fingers were now claws, she was wearing contacts that made her eyes into dead black orbs. But the killer was those neon lights. Floating above her head, just like it would have in *Zoth*, was her name: "Griselda the Auctioneer."

"Who is Griselda, anyway?" I asked her. Syd had set off, giving me a curt nod when the job was over. But the Fontbonne boys remained, futzing over Charice, adjusting bits of fabric and feather here and there.

"Beats me," said Charice, "but a straw poll of my geek friends told me that this would be received as a cool choice."

I was surprised when one of the Fontbonners answered the question. It was a bit like a mime speaking.

"She's an auctioneer at the Harpy Outpost. She's not really very interesting in herself—like, she doesn't have a backstory or anything—but everyone sees her a lot when they're level ten or so. So there's this kind of nostalgia for her. It's a very cool choice."

Charice gestured to the Fontebonne geek that she bowed to his superior knowledge.

"You've outdone yourself, Charice."

This was the sort of sentence that Charice liked to hear best. She liked it even when it was negative—I had said it the time that a poisonous Gila monster had been released in our apartment, and she basked then as well. And she basked now.

"You and I are going to be the queens of Zoth at this convention."

I somehow doubted this. Our costumes were pretty good, but cosplayers don't mess around. We might be a princess or a duchess, but queens we were not. But my answer was more practical.

"Where's my harp, by the way?"

"What harp?"

"RedRasish's harp. I'm a priestess of Usune."

"Forget it. You don't need it."

"I'm. A. Priestess. Of. Usune," I repeated, but the emphasis was entirely lost on her. She didn't even know who Usune was.

"You'll look great without it."

I had clearly passed over completely into a crazy woman, because it was clear to me that I did need it, especially since I wasn't wrapping myself in orange gauze.

I made a quick phone call to Stephen, who was an old friend of mine who worked at Gaylord Music Library. I had not spoken to him in two years, but he was still in my iPhone contacts list.

"Stephen, it's Dahlia Moss. I need a harp."

I expect that Stephen was a little surprised by the phone call. It would have made sense for him to be spending a few moments in confusion as to who I was. He didn't do that, however, but just responded as though I had been calling him all this time making requests of musical instruments.

"No one needs a harp. Just spend the money on an ice sculpture."

"How are those things equivalent?"

"Your guests will be equally happy. I assume this is a wedding we're talking about."

"What? No. I'm not getting married."

"Well, I haven't seen you in a while, and it's not as if it's a crazy thought. You're not getting any younger—"

"I don't need a harpist, I just need a harp."

"Well, that's good because the harpists I know hate doing weddings. Loathe them. Three hours of 'Ave Maria' while people get drunk and hit on the bridesmaids. What kind of harp do you need?"

"What? There are different kinds?"

"Lever, pedestal, hand. Why do you need the harp if you're not going to play it? And I assume you're not playing it, since you don't know the three kinds of harps."

I thought about RedRasish's harp. "Umm...what kind of a harp does an angel have?"

Stephen sighed. "Is this for a costume?" The question was petulant.

"Yes?"

"First, that's a lyre. And second, I'm not going to help you get a musical instrument for a Halloween costume. Just go to Amazon or something."

"I need it by tomorrow. Please, Stephen, I'll get you those coffee beans you like. With the maple syrup?"

"I haven't had a cup of coffee in over a year."

There was an awkward silence, in which it suddenly seemed that we were no longer talking about lyres and coffee habits. Stephen broke the silence.

"Where have you been for the past year?"

"Here, in Saint Louis," I answered meekly.

"I realize that, Dahlia. I mean, why have you been ignoring everyone?"

Why had I been ignoring everyone? No one had ever put the question to me before.

"Things have been a little shitty lately. Everyone's just been so successful, and I thought I'd just lay low a little until I got a job, and then months went by and I still didn't have a job, and it just sort of became this cycle of, I don't know, seclusion. Misery? Broad shittiness?"

"So you've found a job and you're just trying to return to your old haunts, is that it?"

"Um, no. I still haven't found a job. Well, sort of. My job vaguely involves dressing up as a fairy with a harp."

"A lyre."

"Right. So, I'll tell you all about it if you can bring me a lyre? Pretty please."

Forty-five minutes later, Stephen came in just as the Font-bonne boys were leaving, which was serendipity to him, undoubtedly. He gave me the lyre in a deadly earnest voice:

"Don't break this."

Stephen took a moment before commenting on my hair. As far as he knew, I had been wearing it like this for years. Maybe he thought this was why my job interviews weren't going well.

"You look like a cross-stitch sampler."

It was the orange gauze. You could see the stitchwork in it. Honestly, the whole effect made me look like a demented Rag-gedy Ann doll. I wasn't going to admit my discomfort in front of the Fontbonners though. "Embroidery is a luxury," I said. "And I'm nothing if not luxurious."

"Embroidery *in childhood* is a luxury," said Stephen. "Of Idleness." Stephen had a schoolmarmish tone in his voice, as though he were correcting me.

"Are you quoting from something?"

"Yes," said Stephen. "Benjamin Britten. I wrote my senior thesis on Benjamin Britten. I thought you were sucking up to me by quoting him."

"Is that an opera singer?"

"He's a composer," said Stephen with a sigh. "It's from *Peter Grimes.*"

"Is he an opera singer?"

Basically all I could remember about Stephen's senior year was that he talked a lot about opera singers.

"*Peter Grimes* is an opera. There was a local production of it like two weeks ago."

"Sure," I said. I had learned long ago to switch to monosyllabic responses when Stephen started talking about opera. Any additional responses could send him into full-fledged lecture mode.

"I was *in* the production. I've been posting about it on Facebook for weeks. How can you not know this?"

I gave Stephen my best *aw, shucks* smile. "I missed you too."

And he was off. Maybe the Fontbonne boys were serendipitous for me too, because clearly I had some extra sucking up to do. Why had I written everyone off? Was it because I was just embarrassed? Depressed?

Seeking clarity for those kinds of questions can haunt you, and I was being haunted with enough already. I wasn't going to invest mind space in whatever the hell had been wrong with me months earlier. Because what did it matter, really? And Stephen was, well, still Stephen. Apparently less caffeinated now, but behind his crusty layer of tut-tutting, he was still happy to see me. I thought, possibly, that we were still friends, even. He gave me a harp, which had to stand for something.

There wasn't time to worry. I had things to do.

My transformation into crazy woman was complete when I awoke at three AM with a burning idea. I should speak to Aishwarya Patel. She was a real person, Emily had mentioned. Just not a person at the address provided. So my question—the question that woke me up in the middle of the night—was: Why the address change? And why fake having received a copy of the spear? Was Aishwarya on the move for some reason? Did she have something to hide?

There I was, pink-haired in the moonlight, googling Aishwarya's whereabouts. You might think that Aishwarya Patel is very particular name—Ophelia Odom revisited—but this is a decidedly American perspective. There were scads of Aishwarya Patels, most of them in India. The first name was slightly unusual, but the last name was common. The English equivalent would be googling "Ruby Jones."

The truth is that I couldn't rule out the Indian Aishwaryas. All I really knew about her is that she didn't know anyone in Saint Louis, which is probably true of a plurality of people in the Western Hemisphere. If she did live in India her –ping would be high, which I suppose would have been a useful thing to check if I had thought about it earlier. Which I hadn't.

It was 3:07 in the morning, however, and this was a time to simply play the odds. Let's assume that Aishwarya lived in the United States. That narrowed it down to five people. If you took out the folks who seemed too old, I was left with two ladies. One of them had an open Facebook page, and I could see that she was studying at Duke. She was pretty, with long black hair, and she was improbably wearing an old-time country-western outfit. It was pretty silly—pink suede with a cowboy hat and actual rope for fringe. Probably a Halloween costume, but who knew?

The other Aishwarya was on Twitter. No picture (of herself) but she was a different person because she lived in San Antonio, which was a helluva commute to Duke. She tweeted a lot, but only about Shonda Rhimes. I sent a private Facebook message to Dukewarya and tweeted directly at Shonda/warya, in full view of anyone following me.

"Do you play Zoth? Pls respond. I am a private detective investigating a murder and this is improbably important."

I probably shouldn't have done that. In addition to potentially tipping off the spear thief, there was a distinct chance that Grandma Moss was going to spot that tweet and query me about it later. Six years earlier, Grandma found the online detritus of an aborted booty call, and I'd been getting grief about it ever since.

But I'd risk Grandma's wrath for this. I wanted answers.

CHAPTER TWENTY

I managed to get through the rest of the night without messing up my apostrophe hair too badly, and Syd had given me extremely explicit instructions on the care and management of it. There were manuals for Microsoft products that were less detailed. So, I'm saying I looked pretty good.

I dressed for the airport of course, which meant that I was business-professional. I felt that security was going to be looking at me askance, given my hair, so it was best to compensate with the rest of my clothing. The result was confusing. Was I an extremely conservative and homely-faced supermodel? A successful businesswoman for a company that sold E? I tried to carry off confidence and normalcy as well as I could, but this was certainly made more difficult by Charice, who was in full Griselda garb, minus the neon lights and wings. Even without the wings, she was disturbing and harpy-like. She had fangs, which is never what you want to see next to you on a passenger plane.

And you have never lived until you have gone through airport security with pink hair and a traveling companion wearing fangs. My greatest fear, however, was that Detective Shuler was going to show up yet again, and I would have to explain

236

(1) why I was not only spending time with Jonah's friends but doing so extravagantly and at great personal expense and (2) what was going on with my hair.

Probably I should have listed those things in the opposite order.

It was strange that I should have been quite so excited on the plane to Phoenix, but there was a palpable sense of something growing in me. Anticipation? Fun? Whatever it was, it made me nervous and excited and simultaneously embarrassed and proud of my pink hair. I both was amused and mortified by the looks we were getting from our fellow passengers. It was fun to be an oddball. And it was even more fun to be an oddball on a mission.

This was more than just a convention I was going to. This was a showdown—the thief would be here, Chtusk would be here, possibly Orchardary would be here—and I would have two days to piece everyone's lies together. Plus there would be a costume parade. I could handle this.

There were a series of steps from the plane to the Games Summit, and each step made a little clearer why I was excited. On the plane, we were utterly out of place. Two clownishly dressed people in a world of business travelers. At the Phoenix airport, we were almost entirely out of place—but not quite. A careful eye would notice things. A *Zoth* T-shirt. Someone with ridiculous hair. A man with a papier-mâché shield. By the hotel we were not out of place anymore. We were a contingency. Fully a third of the people here were like us—twentysomethings with elaborate costumes and geeky T-shirts. One third of the people at the hotel were people in African garb, and someone in a kitenge asked me what all the crazy costumes were for, and I told her a computer-game convention. I asked her what all the kitenges were about and she told me a Swahili ESL convention. It's exchanges like these that make me love America.

By the time we got on the hotel bus, the inmates had taken over the asylum. There were still some folks in plain clothes, but the looks we got were not of shock or concern. Instead we were given cool nods of recognition or outright smiles or thumbs-ups.

Charice had put on her full regalia for the bus, even though the wings were terribly impractical, and no one complained. Rather, people moved out of her way and gratefully gave her as much space as she needed. "Oh, excuse me, Auctioneer Griselda!," "I'm glad to see you here, Auctioneer Griselda!," and "Have you seen my lamb, Auctioneer Griselda?," the last of which was some *Zoth* in-joke that I never did quite understand. It was suddenly as if I was traveling with the queen of England.

I am not a *Zoth* player. Truthfully, I wasn't. RedRasish was only level two, and I did not understand half the references that were on people's T-shirts, and yet. *Zoth* had dominated my life a little bit, with the spear and even before that with Erik's obsessive raiding. Maybe it was Stockholm syndrome, but I was happy to be here. It was enough to just be among their number. Maybe I wasn't a queen or demigod of Zoth, but I was at least a citizen. And for once, I was just happy to be on the pilgrimage.

While I'm sure there are nicer convention centers—and nicer halls somewhere—at the particular moment in time that I entered the Games Summit, I couldn't imagine one. An enormous black dragon battled with a phoenix in the main lobby, and even though they were just enormous balloons, really, it somehow filled you with a sense of scale. Charice, whose last-minute cosplay really was turning a lot of heads, instinctively knew that she did not want to tour the main floor with me and quickly ditched me with an only half-interested "good luck with your case."

This was perhaps fair, because I had all but pretended to not know her at airport security, but too soon, Charice, too soon.

I texted Clemency shortly after I left. "RedRasish is in the building" was the message, which should give you some sense of the giddy rush I was feeling. After a few exchanges where we tried (unsuccessfully) to figure out where we were relative to each other, we managed to meet up at a snack bar.

"What's happened to your hair?" she said when she saw me, not even bothering to mask her surprise.

Clemency was not dressed up at all. Well, she was wearing a white dress that could be said to be slightly fancy, but she was certainly not dressed up in healer garb, with a gnarled staff and a headdress. Frankly, I was a little disappointed. I was also disappointed that Threadwork wasn't around. It wasn't until I saw Clemency without him that I realized how much I had imagined them as a sort of old married couple. But no matter.

"I had my hair styled like RedRasish," I told her.

"Ah." I had expected a little more warmth from Clem, but although she clearly registered an opinion of dismay regarding my new pink coif, she quickly returned to form and hugged me anyway.

"I'm glad you came," she told me. "I always wanted to come to this event, but now that I'm here, I'm a little sad. It's a little like a second funeral for Jonah."

"It'd be his third funeral," I told her. "Although it's not going to be as grim as all that. It's a party. Jonah would have wanted a party."

I didn't ever know Jonah terribly well, but from what I had

put together about him, I think I was on the right track. Certainly Clemency seemed to think so, because her face brightened right up at the idea.

"There'll be food, at least."

I needed to ask Clemency about the business with Jonah's parents. I didn't want to, and every pore in my body was telling me that, truthfully, it wasn't relevant. But I had to ask. So I did.

"Why did you see the Longs the night before the funeral? You told Threadwork you were going to the grocery store."

Clemency gasped audibly at the question, which I had asked without any kind of preamble. I suppose it's these sorts of gasps that the Sam Spades and Inspector Alleyns live for, but I found it embarrassing. Sure, I wanted to catch Clemency unaware— not give her a chance to create a cover-up story if she were hiding something. But that's just it—if she wasn't hiding something, then I was kind of just being a jackass. A lot of detective work involves being a jackass, actually, which is maybe why it plays to my strengths.

"I know Mrs. Long. And Jonah, years ago. I used to be his babysitter, many thousands of years ago, back when they lived in New Hampshire."

"Why didn't you tell Threadwork? Or me?"

"Jonah had invited me to be in the guild, you know. He'd always sort of kept in touch with me, like I was his older sister. But at the same time, he was also embarrassed about it. He never introduced me to anyone as his former babysitter. Actually, he sort of pretended to not know me."

"That's it? I don't see why you couldn't tell Threadwork about it."

"It's not that I couldn't tell Threadwork about it. It's that I didn't. I just didn't feel like it was my secret to tell. Jonah was cool about it while he was alive, so I didn't feel right to make a big deal about it the day before he was going to be buried."

"Sylvia was glad to see you?"

"Sylvia adores me. I think she always had some scheme that I was going to fall in love with Jonah and start a family, which seemed really bizarre to me when I was younger but has started making more sense to me lately."

"You're getting the motherhood thing?"

"Don't even start with me, Dahlia."

"And that was the entire extent of your relationship with Jonah."

I could tell that Clemency was holding something back—I hadn't the slightest idea what it was, but I knew it was there. When you confess, you relax, or at least slump with embarrassment. I knew from what I was speaking. Three months earlier I had run into an ex-roommate at a greasy spoon, where I had been applying for a job. I had an entire lunch with her at that damned diner, the job application hidden under the place mat the whole time. When I got home, my back was so stiff I had to take a muscle relaxant.

Clemency was still tense and nervous and looked like she hoped a waitress might come and bring the check. There was still something under her place mat.

"You're a horrible person, Dahlia Moss."

This was undoubtedly true, but I was at least a horrible person who was going to get to the truth.

"Go on," I told her.

"I think I was Jonah's first kiss. He was fourteen, I was eighteen. Which is probably illegal somewhere, somehow. But it's not I like planned anything. He just came out and kissed me out of nowhere!"

"You didn't date him after."

"No. Honestly, it was a pretty poor kiss. I'm embarrassed I'm talking about it now."

And thus concluded my digging into innocent people's lives. Oh sure, I could have dug deeper—checked times and dates to see if the story checked out. I could have interviewed Jonah's high school friends for mention of a hot babysitter, and God knows what else, but I let it go. Clemency didn't look nervous anymore; she looked freed.

"Let's go downstairs," I told her. "And enjoy the floor."

———————◆———————

I won't go into the details of the floor at the Gamers Summit. There were vendors selling geeky T-shirts, some of which I understood, some of which I didn't. There were voice actors, there were design artists. There were giant videos of PvP tournaments.

Truthfully, I didn't understand most of it. I got the gist, but not the details. But sometimes, enough enthusiasm for something becomes infectious. And you don't need to understand it; you can just enjoy it. It is for this reason, I believe, that soccer is popular anywhere.

As Clemency and I were waiting in line to have a painting of hers signed by a gaunt-faced man (he's the voice of Jaelin Thorn, Clemency explained in an absurdly reverential tone) we were texted by Oatcake:

"Horizons, time to converge. North End, Level 2. By the beanbags. With smiles on please, gents, this is a funeral."

Through a combination of haste and the good fortune of being close to the North End, we were able to get there before anyone else. Oatcake was someone who I had imagined looking a little more imperious than the fellow before me. He had a small face with short hair and delicate features. He also wasn't wearing any sort of geek T-shirt, which marked him a little in the crowd, opting instead for a plaid overshirt that was entirely too hot for Phoenix in the summer.

And true to form, he had brought food for everyone. He handed a cupcake to Clemency when she arrived, whom he seemed to recognize.

"Are you Dahlia?" he asked me with concern in his voice.

"Yes," I said, suddenly wondering if I wasn't welcome here. I was not, after all, a Horizon.

"I didn't make you a cupcake," he said. "I'm afraid you'll have to go without."

This did not concern me. And I had suspicions that Chtusk and Orchardary weren't going to show anyway, which would leave me two cupcakes to eat. I told Oatcake not to worry about it.

The next person to show up was Wayne, who was a lot more handsome than I had imagined, with wavy blond hair and quarterback good looks. Plus he was wearing a fancy gray suit, and I'm a sucker for that sort of thing. But then he spoke with that awful Southern accent of his, and the spell was broken.

"Dahlia Moss? Is that you? Jesus, you didn't change your hair to look like your level-two character, did you?"

"No," I told him, "my hair looked like this all along. It's just one of life's funny coincidences."

There was chortling, not so much at my joke as at my hair. My hair was going to be the source of amusement for many of the Horizons, but I just took it in stride. Somewhere, sometime, my hair would have been considered wonderful.

Ophelia and Kurt arrived together, and it struck me that they were conspicuously trying to not act like a couple. They walked apart, they didn't touch, but if you left your eyes on them for any length of time it was impossible to miss the little looks, the shared smiles. Well, good for them. Kurt was wearing that same devil hoodie I'd spotted him in the other day, and Ophelia—who had dressed in full battle regalia for Jonah's online funeral—now wore a funereal dress to his after-party. Or maybe it was how she always dressed—I recalled the picture of her in the *Globe* in a similarly subdued outfit.

I also noticed that she was wearing a costume jewelry bracelet—with a gem missing from its inset. That explained that.

"How's the viola?" I asked her.

"How's your hairdresser?" she asked me. "Still vomiting up pink hearts?"

There was something about Ophelia's crabbiness in the face of aggression that I admired, so I just tipped my lovely pink head at her.

There was a gap of time before our next Horizon arrived, and we all awkwardly stood around and talked about how nice the cupcakes were. Except for me, having no cupcake. I also learned that the cupcakes were some sort of inside joke that I did not understand, despite it being explained to me by three people consecutively.

No one mentioned Clemency's baby bump, for reasons that weren't clear to me, aside from a guess that if everyone ignored it, it might go away.

The next to arrive was Threadwork, who I could still not quite get used to seeing outside of Clemency's company. The reason he was late was clear—he was rolling over in his wheelchair, talking to a dark-skinned woman in African garb also rolling over in her own wheelchair. The old dog had picked up a groupie.

"What's up, everyone? This is Frances—she's my ladyfriend."

Frances laughed and said, "I can't believe you just used the word 'ladyfriend.'"

"That's how I roll," said Threadwork.

Threadwork was emphatically not using his "Threadwork" voice and, in fact, introduced himself as Garrett. While no one else seemed impressed by this, I was having the same reaction I had had the first time I had met him, only now in reverse. I had gotten so used to that tepid Alec Guinness voice of his that now that he spoke in an American accent, it seemed utterly wrong.

But from the looks of it, everyone else was taken aback not by his voice but by Frances.

"You're not in our guild, are you?" asked Oatcake, with less certainty than I had heard from him to date.

"Oh, no," said Frances. "In fact, I don't completely understand what any of this is."

"Typing All-Stars?" asked Kurt.

"I don't know what that is," said Frances agreeably. "All these people in amazing costumes. I just met Garrett at my hotel, and one thing led to another." She trailed off, leaving us to connect the dots ourselves.

"Well," said Wayne, amused with himself, "the hookers here in Phoenix certainly are specifically tailored!"

Which earned him a hard punch in the arm from Tambras. Ophelia, rather. Although I do consider her more Tambras-like while she's punching someone.

"I'm kidding," whelped Wayne, who certainly took a punch like an elf. I shouldn't be too smug, though, because I thought his joke was pretty funny, and I had to stifle a smile to avoid getting smacked in round two.

Frances did not seem to mind, however. She seemed, well,

happy. "Forget it. It's just that Garrett and I have so much in common, it feels wrong to at least not spend the day together."

"Or the whole weekend," said Threadwork.

From the anticipatory look on Frances's face, I had the awful feeling that this was going to spiral into some sickly sweet new lovers annoying everyone with their treacly nonsense soon, and so I said, realizing it only as I said it:

"You're here for the convention on teaching Swahili!"

"*Ndiyo*," said Francis, which I assumed was Swahili for "yes."

"You're ditching the conference for this?"

"Well," considered Frances, "a bit, yes. But I'm teaching Garrett Swahili, so I figure that mitigates it a little. He's very good at mimicry."

I thought about the veering inconsistency of Threadwork's accent and said, "Not that good."

At which point Tambras socked me. The woman was a walking beatstick. Probably years of playing second fiddle (ho!) to violinists. I was amused enough at this joke that I considered saying it aloud, but I decided that it would only get me socked again.

Instead, Garrett said. "Are those cupcakes? How lovely!"

And his Threadwork voice was there again, just around the edges. He can move fast for a guy in a wheelchair, and before anyone could object, he and Frances were each eating cupcakes. Well, damn.

Oraova, the drunken fire mage, arrived in a Megadeth T-shirt that was so lame that I assumed it had to be ironic, and apologized to everyone, explaining that he was extremely hungover. This looked to be true. He looked exactly like I had imagined him looking—lean and mean and with very badly cut hair.

At this point, we were all here except for Chtusk and Orchardary. And Jonah, obviously, but no one was much expecting him to show. I was eyeing that last cupcake, which really did look pretty good, but the damned bug showed up.

Chtusk was a plain-looking girl, with long, straight, almost waist-length hair that managed to be both very simple and yet somehow very badly cared for. She was wearing a green heather T-shirt, which hung over her limply. Kate Moss thin, this girl, like a ghost. But not in the way that guys find alluring. She seemed like your classic wallflower.

It took me a double take to put it together, but this was the girl from the fish-eye lens.

"Hello, everyone," she said, even meeker than I had expected. "I suppose you're all wondering why I've gathered you here."

We all looked at her blankly.

"That was a joke," she explained. "Are those cupcakes?"

I nearly knocked the cupcake out of her hand, but what could I do? Scarbati ruin everything.

"You ditched me the other night," I told her, quietly enough not to embarrass her in front of everyone but forcefully enough to let her know that I wasn't past having Tambras punch her by request. "And you abandoned me at my own doorstep. What's your story, lady?"

"I did," she said quietly. "You and I should talk after this."

Which appeased me for the moment. We waited around for what felt like forever for Orchardary to show up, but it never happened.

CHAPTER TWENTY-ONE

I'm proposing," said Oatcake, "that now that we've buffed ourselves up on cupcakes, we now all go out to the bar and drink a beer in the honor of the man who brought us here."

"It's ten o'clock in the morning," said Threadwork.

"And a beer costs eight dollars," said Wayne, who, nice suit or not, had a budget.

"This is my proposal," repeated Oatcake, saying it in such a way that it sounded less like a proposal and more like a vague threat. This was how guild leadership worked.

I quickly sent a text to Charice, signaling that this was the time. It would take a moment for her to get in place, and so in the meantime I would need to stall a little bit.

"Before everyone runs off, I have something important I want to say."

The eyes of the Horizons turned toward me, and it was not pleasant. Let's face it, I was a stranger keeping them away from midmorning beer. It was especially intimidating because I didn't have anything important to say. I was just bullshitting until Charice was ready.

I led off with flattery.

"I didn't know Jonah as you did, but this whole trip has meant more to me than I can say. The immense kindnesses you've shown me over the past week—arranging Jonah's funeral, sharing stories about him with me, and of course welcoming me as one of your own—has been an amazing experience."

"Who is this person again?" I heard Oraova discreetly ask. I looked up to the balcony, and no, Charice was still not there.

"Thank you, Dahlia," said Clemency, and with this the crowd began immediately to disperse.

"I'm sorry, just one more thing. Two more things." Where the hell was Charice? "Jonah's parents wanted me to quote a few lines in his honor."

This worked. Everyone stood obediently. I just didn't have any lines to quote. My head went blank. It was as if I was in the second-grade talent show all over again.

After an expectant stare, I quoted the first thing that popped into my head.

" 'This, Children, is the famed Mongoose. He has an appetite abstruse.' "

Heads nodded respectfully, if a little confused.

" 'Strange to relate, this creature takes a curious joy in eating snakes. All kinds, though, it must be confessed. He likes the poisonous ones the best.' "

More nods.

" 'From him we learn how very small a thing can bring about a Fall.' "

I was getting squints now, but they at least they were still.

" 'O Mongoose, where were you that day, when mistress Eve was led astray?' " I quoted, noting that, thank God, Charice was waving at me now from the balcony above.

"'If you'd but seen the serpent first, our parents would not have been cursed. And so there would be no excuse for Milton, but for you, Mongoose.'"

There was a golf clap from Threadwork.

"It was one of Jonah's favorite poems, or so I was told."

"Who told you that?" asked Tambras.

I ignored this entirely reasonable question. "I do have one last bit of news about the spear." And this piqued them. I paused for a moment, savoring the complete command I suddenly had over the Horizons. "I have been in contact with Left Field Games and they have verified that the spear...was taken by a gold farmer—in this case, Hungarian. It is presently posted at an off-site auction house. The current bid is nine hundred dollars—if you're interested, I can give you information on how to bid. I'm sorry."

Charice was taking pictures of the group from above as I scanned their faces for a reaction. Everyone should be shrugging their shoulders, given that this is exactly what everyone had expected. Everyone except for the thief, whom I hoped would have some sort of visual reaction to my stealing the spear for myself. And everyone was nonchalant. Mostly they seemed happy that I wasn't quoting nonsense poetry.

Except for Tambras aka Ophelia the violist.

———◆———

Charice had filmed the thing from above so I could study the faces more closely. But I didn't need it.

I pulled Ophelia aside as the Horizons ambled down to the nearest bar, which was conveniently still in the convention center.

"You were expecting me to say something else, Ophelia?"

I wish I could include some witty repartee here, some amazing bit of deduction where I wheedled out of Ophelia that she had stolen the spear—while she, all the while, continued to weave a bewildering web of lies that my deductions slowly broke through. But none of this happened. She just socked me in the arm.

"You jackass," she said.

I liked Ophelia. I really did. I didn't quite understand why she was interested in Kurt, or why she had stolen the spear, and as it was socially acceptable to ask only the latter of these two questions, that was what I did.

"I was trying to smoke you out," I told her.

Ophelia grimaced at me. "How did you know it was me?"

"You came to visit Saint Louis two weeks ago to visit Kurt. You went to go see the Saint Louis Opera Theater's production of *Peter Grimes*. The spear went missing when you were in town."

Ophelia just looked at me, impressed.

"Why did you come in secret?" I asked. "Jonah never knew that you were involved with Kurt."

"It's embarrassing," said Ophelia. "Starting a romantic relationship with a guild mate who lives across the country. That was the first time I had ever actually met Kurt, so it could have been a disaster."

"I see. You also lost this," I told her, handing her the gem. "It was in Kurt's...place." I was not about to explain that I had found it in Kurt's car.

"Oh, gods," said Ophelia. "Kurt made this for me with a BeDazzler. I thought it was just good, clean, ironic fun, but he seems to think I should wear it. Keep the gem. Every gem that falls off of it is a gem closer to me throwing it away."

"Why did you do it?" I asked.

"Oh, I don't wear it most of the time. But I figure it's a small thing that would make Kurt happy, and it's not like people aren't wearing tackier things here."

"Forget the BeDazzler, Ophelia. Why did you steal the spear?"

"That's pretty obvious, I should think. I stole it because Jonah was being a jerk to roll for it in the first place. It should never have gone to him. It was infuriating."

"So Kurt logged you in to his account when you came out to visit?"

"Oh, Kurt had nothing to do with it. We just came by the apartment one day while Jonah was at work. Kurt was taking a shower, and Jonah had left himself logged in to the game. I wasn't planning it. It was just one awful impulse. I wished I hadn't done it almost immediately."

"You did take the time to write that nasty note, though. 'What comes around goes around.'"

Ophelia blinked at me.

"What?"

" 'What comes around goes around.' It was a note that Jonah was sent immediately after the spear was stolen."

"I didn't send a note."

"Someone sent a note," I told her. I wasn't exactly accusing her, but I was a little confused. It wouldn't make any sense for her to cop to the theft and deny sending a note afterward. But if not Ophelia, then who?

"I don't know," said Ophelia. "Not my problem. Anyway, I probably would have eventually given it back to Jonah, but then he died, and there was all that nicety and free tickets from beyond the grave. Which I still kind of think is bullshit, somehow. But even so, what else could I do?"

There was a pause, and I had expected Ophelia to ask whether I was going to tell everyone that she had taken it. But she didn't, and I could tell from her body language that she didn't much care about the issue. She looked happy and relieved, glad to have gotten the story off her chest.

I chatted with her for a few minutes more and left her to return to the Horizons, where she could finish drinking with her friends. Even with all these folks around, I was drinking alone. I was at journey's end. I had recovered the spear, found the culprit, and earned every bit of my money. So, why did I feel so sad about it—or so I felt the bartender should have asked me. There was no denying that there was something anticlimactic about Ophelia's tossed-off confession. Although the truth was, I think I would have found anything dismaying, even if Ophelia had wrestled me to the ground all the while screaming, "I'm innocent, you wench! I'm innocent!"

CHAPTER TWENTY-TWO

It was in this doldrums that Chtusk found me. I was only drinking water—four-dollar water, mind you—but I was sitting alone at the bar with a facial expression that suggested that it was vodka.

"I'm sorry I keep running from you. It's really not very like me at all."

Chtusk was stammering and embarrassed. She wasn't very buglike at all, I realized. More like a rabbit. And running did seem like her. She looked like she wanted to run now.

But I was suddenly tired and didn't feel like talking to her. "What do we need to talk about?"

She was probably too self-absorbed to tell, but my heart was not remotely in the question. I had the spear, I had the thief—what did I care about what Bug Girl had to say to me?

"I'm Lurleen."

I blinked at her.

"That's why I wanted to avoid you. I'm Lurleen. The Lurleen." She looked down at the floor.

I knew two people in this life named Lurleen. One was a former governor of Alabama, who ran for office with the slo-gan "Vote for Lurleen, but Let George Do It!" George being her husband, who had been governor for so long that he had run into term limits. The other was Lurleen Rice, the dental hygienist that Erik, my ex, had cheated on me with for at least eight months. I should have guessed something was going on from his biweekly cleanings.

Truth be told, I wasn't fond of either Lurleen, but at least Lurleen Wallace was a product of her time. Lurleen Rice was just a whore.

I think her next line was something about wanting to come clean and make amends. I don't completely know because I couldn't hear her over the sudden rage that was overpowering me. Flames on the side of my face, as Madeline Kahn said. I also kept looking at her, my detective's eye suddenly coming out when I would have preferred it to sit this round out, and it asked, "Erik left you for *her*?"

Not that I'm that great shakes. I could stand to lose a few pounds, and mostly in my face. But Lurleen. She was older than me. And she was so plain-looking. With that oversized T-shirt hanging off her thin, shapeless body, she looked like she could be wearing the uniform of a particularly unimaginative cult. I had imagined "the hygienist"—as I preferred to call her—as a shapely blonde, with oversized boobs and maybe a sexy gap in her middle teeth, like Lauren Hutton. Somehow that was better.

"I got dumped for *this*?" I thought—or I thought I thought. Apparently, I said it aloud. Again, flames, nostrils, heaving.

"I don't want to focus on the past," said Lurleen. "I just feel really badly for the way Erik and I took advantage of you. I just want to make sure you're okay."

If Chtusk had kept talking, I swear to God that there might have been a catfight. Possibly with actual cats. If one had been nearby, I certainly would have thrown it at her. Check to make sure that I'm okay? I was an inch away from yelling for Tambras and punching her in the gut, but suddenly my detective bits just started taking over. I was asking questions that I hadn't really even intended to ask.

"Everyone else got spears," I told her. "Orchardary's was sent back, because she is not a real person. Or at least, not the person she claimed. But you got none at all."

This question disarmed her a little. "What? That's not really important," she said. "The important thing is that I give you the apology that you deserve. I behaved abominably."

"Why did Jonah not give you a spear? Because you were too new? Did that make you angry?" *Angry enough to kill?* I wondered, then instantly put the question out of my head. Lurleen was a wallflower obsessed with getting my forgiveness. Whatever she was, she wasn't Jonah's murderer.

"It's not like that at all," said Lurleen.

"What was it like, then?" I asked. "Why did Jonah send a spear to everyone else in the guild but you?"

"Because I told him not to," said Lurleen, who was visibly deflated by the question. "I was his dental hygienist—that's where he had talked me into joining the Horizons in the first place, and the last time he came in was right after he had won the spear. He felt guilty about rolling for it and told me about his plan to buy one for everyone in the guild. I told him that I thought it was a good idea but that I didn't want a two-thousand-dollar spear." Chtusk looked really embarrassed now. "I suggested that he give my two thousand dollars to charity."

I wasn't a perfect judge of character—by now I'm sure that's perfectly clear to you—but it was obvious that Lurleen was hiding something from me, so I pressed. "And what charity was that?"

Lurleen sighed. "You. I had him hire you as a detective."

———————◆———————

My initial response to this was to be too overwhelmed to actually be upset. "What the hell are you saying?"

In retrospect, I found myself wondering if Lurleen had been enjoying all of this—pretending to be a naive and helpful little waif while she twisted the dagger into my heart—but looking back, nope. The girl is just that naive. She's perfect for Erik, really.

"I told him that I didn't want a two-thousand-dollar spear lying around my apartment. He came up with the idea right there during the dental cleaning, and I couldn't put him off of it. I seriously didn't want one, though, and so he insisted that I name a charity. And I thought about the ASPCA, but then I settled on you."

Yup, Lurleen was the kind of gal who would not realize that a comparison to the ASPCA, especially one that in the mold of "I found you more in need of charity than the ASPCA," could, in certain lights, seem an awful lot like an insult. By now, though, my mortification had rendered me mute, and so I just stared at her while she kept talking.

"Erik was so worried about you, and truthfully, I was too. You had just gone so long without a job that you were starting to seem like a different person. And I felt badly about stealing your boyfriend, which is the kind of thing that should only happen in eighth grade. And so Jonah and I put together this plan. We'd hire you with my spear money to investigate the spear theft. And when Jonah heard about the dire straits you'd been having with work and your love life, he thought he'd try to set you up with Kurt."

I remembered now that the outfit I had been sent to see Kurt in was quite specifically requested by Jonah. It looked like the sort of thing that, well, like the sort of thing that Ophelia was wearing today. Starchy funereal garb with just a hint of dominatrix.

The whole thing—my entire detective career—was the dumb setup for a blind date. And even that failed; Kurt hadn't given me a second glance.

"And you sent me those notes about gaming addiction," I said, practically choking on the idea.

"What?" said Lurleen.

"You were worried about me spending too much time in *Zoth*."

"What?" repeated Lurleen. "I didn't do that. I think *Zoth* has been good for you. I'm sorry I've been so evasive. I didn't know what to say, and I didn't think I could make it through you asking me questions about the spear without laughing a little. I mean, I know you're not a real detective."

At this point, I was surprised that tears were not welling up in my eyes. I'd been floating over all of this awfulness that I had been purposefully ignoring for the past half year. Erik, joblessness, and the increasing certainty that I was somehow destined for failure. And this *Zoth* business had distracted me very effectively from it. Maybe that was why people played. But now there was Lurleen, and suddenly I was back where I had started, drowning in my successive failures.

But not quite exactly. My little detective brain was spinning just as quickly as my heart was despooling.

"And neither you nor Jonah realized that Kurt and Ophelia were already dating."

"Kurt and Ophelia? No, I didn't realize."

"I wouldn't have expected you to, no. The relationship was a secret. But it's still surprising that Jonah didn't know."

"I suppose," said Lurleen, who didn't seem to know what to talk about when she wasn't on her script about apologizing to me.

"It's ironic, though, because even though Jonah was just trying to fob me off on his wingman, it ended up leading to the stolen spear anyway. Ophelia took it, and I found Ophelia from Kurt."

"Ophelia wouldn't take the spear," said Lurleen, somewhat uncertain. "Jonah said a Chinese gold farmer took it. You said that too, just now."

If Jonah thought it was a Chinese gold farmer, then that meant that he must have written the "What comes around goes around" note himself. It was just plot thickener, all along.

"Nope," I told her. "It was Ophelia."

"Are you going to get it back from her?"

"I already have. I did that days ago."

Lurleen still didn't have a bit of malice in her. She just kept looking me, and I could tell that she was trying to think, which was perhaps not her strongest suit. But when she got out her question, it was pretty fair.

"Then why are you here?"

That horrible "heart and soul" part of me just started silently burbling with awful responses—I'm trying to forget, I'm trying to bury my problems in an imaginary world, I'm spending money on imaginary hair because my own is so dreadful—but before those parts could put things together enough to actually speak something aloud, the detective part of me was answering the question.

"I'm here to catch Jonah's murderer."

And although I hadn't planned on saying it, and although I had never admitted to myself that this was the game I was after, the moment it came out of my lips I realized that it was true.

Lurleen was almost in a whisper now.

"Do you know who it is?"

"I'm getting closer," I told her.

"Are we good, then?"

"About the murder? You're not a suspect, even if you do have the means."

"No, about Erik."

I thought about Erik. I had liked Erik. Loved, perhaps not. But liked an awful lot. But my relationship with him had been like my *New Yorker* subscription. I liked it in the abstract, but I never seemed to care enough to make the time for it, and issues kept piling up in the bedroom. Charice was right. It was time to forget about Erik. And if I couldn't be with him, then he may as well go with someone who will ensure that he has clean teeth.

"We're good," I told Lurleen. "And don't mention that bit about Ophelia to anyone just yet."

I was feeling frayed now. Jonah had played me for a chump. I can just remember his face, smug, sitting there drinking my alcohol while he hired me. Well, technically it was Charice's alcohol, but my point is the same.

I desperately wanted to speak to Charice, but I couldn't figure out where on earth she had run off to. I even ran up to an Auctioneer Griselda and started bawling at her before I realized that this was a different Auctioneer Griselda and that Charice was elsewhere. Some detective I was.

I tried calling Nathan. I even tried calling Masako. No dice. I don't know how to describe how I was feeling at the moment—I'll go for the word "deflated." I felt I was just disappearing, and not just in an emotional sense. I needed to sit down; I didn't think there was enough air left in me to stay upright.

My cheeks were flushed and my eyes were stinging, and the whole world seemed to playing by me in some awful blur. Like wearing the One Ring in the Lord of the Rings movies, only much weepier. But I managed to make it to the glass wall that overlooked the floor show, and as there were no open chairs nearby, I just collapsed on the floor. It was a good thing to do—just sit and watch all of the people in their colorful costumes go by. I found myself looking at them and wondering about the lives of the people underneath the outfits. Was the enormous djinn with the floating cloud an unhappy mother of three? Was the lanky redhead in the peeling mummy costume secretly lonely? I admit this exercise might have veered toward the morbid. But there are times in your life where you just want to imagine that there are people sadder than you.

After a few minutes of this, I started to pick myself up a little and began thinking about the case again. Someone murdered Jonah Long. Maybe I was a fraud of a detective, but that didn't make the murderer any less real. Who was the culprit? Was it someone here? It had to be. I needed it to be.

Detective Shuler had gone out of his way to give me a warning: Be careful around Jonah's friends. He'd said that, presumably, because I was spending time with—or about to spend time with—someone that he thought was dangerous. Shuler surely would never have guessed I'd fly out to Phoenix in a fairy costume, so that meant that all of these extra Horizons. Oro-ava, Oatcake, Lurleen—they were all out of the picture. Not that I had ever considered them much in the way of suspects, but it was nice to have that confirmed.

Who had I met? Kurt, Clemency, and Threadwork.

One of these three people had to have been Jonah's murderer. Kurt had the motivation, certainly, as well as the means. Plus I had been hanging around him before Shuler made his warning to me. On paper, he seemed like the most obvious candidate. On the negative side of the column was...what? The fact that he looked a little bit like Snorlax? Fine, he wasn't pinging my murderer spider senses, but what did I know?

Clemency was almost impossible to imagine as the murderer. She had such a fundamental niceness to her—but then there was that strange backstory between her and Jonah and his parents, a backstory that I still wasn't sure that I believed in its entirety. I didn't think that Clemency had lied to me, but I was willing to bet there were bits she was leaving out.

Finally there was Threadwork, if that was his real name. It seemed frankly impossible for him to have committed the crime, at least without help. He lived in Baltimore, seemed to loathe travel (and rightfully so—wheelchair accessibility is terrible), and short of him having faked paralysis could not possibly have done it.

Still, of the three, I somehow picked Threadwork. It's hard to trust someone who is so committed to talking in a fake voice all the time.

I was pulled out of this theorizing by my iPhone, which was ringing. Someone with an unfamiliar number was calling me. On FaceTime. I would have no qualms with answering an unknown caller; what's the worst that could happen? But FaceTime, I maintain, is an app that was designed by extremely photogenic people. I did not like chatting face-to-face on my phone with strangers. I didn't like it with family or friends. For one, it meant that I had to look at myself, which I generally avoid. And besides which, if I looked anything like what I felt like, I would have been a veritable pity magnet.

But I answered; I was apparently lonely enough that I could put up with looking at a one-inch reflection of my face if it meant human contact.

It was Masako, who looked as wild and frantic as I'd ever seen her.

"Dahlia," she said in what I would later regard as a stage whisper. "Thank God you're there. I've just discovered something vital about your case."

I should have said "What case?" But as gullible as ever, I said, "Yes?"

"It's Nathan! He's—he's—"

And after a slightly awkward pause I heard Nathan's booming voice from outside the frame.

"Silence! My secrets are tantamount! Tantamount!"

And then I watched a pink pool noodle whack Masako in the head. Repeatedly.

"Aarrgggh! I'm being murdered!" said Masako, who, it had to be said, was a terrible actress, gesticulating her death wildly. "Despite the relative softness of this flotational device, I am somehow being bludgeoned to death."

Blood, or rather fake blood, was now running down Masako's head in gory rivulets. When Nathan held the bat still enough—which was rare, he really seemed to be into the spirit of the thing—you could see that he had duct-taped packets of fake blood to it.

This was the man who was becoming my next boyfriend.

After a rustling and awkward pause that suggested Masako

had missed a cue, she suddenly closed her eyes and plopped her head on the table, all but screaming her final words: "Pool Noodle'd!" I later—much, much later—concluded that this was her Strong Bad impression, which, given its gross inadequacy, was the scariest thing on display yet.

Nathan came into frame, moving the camera so that Masako's obviously still-breathing corpse could not be seen. He looked about as happy as I had ever seen him.

"Oh, hello there!" he said, preening. "Why, I didn't know that you were around! How is your trip coming?"

I don't think that there is a word for wanting to simultaneously hug someone while you whack them to death with their own pool noodle, but if there was, I would employ it here now. If you are aware of such a word, please feel free to write it in the margin and underline it. Thrice.

"It's been a horrible trip," I told him.

"Could you not figure out who stole the spear?"

Well, I had done that. "No," I told Nathan. "That wasn't actually that big a deal."

"Well then, victory!" Then Nathan looked at me, with those adorable little eyes of his, and he could see that I was not joining his celebration.

"I'm a fraud," I told him. "It's official. Everyone will find out eventually."

"You're not a fraud."

"Jonah hired me because I was not a detective, and he dressed me in a sexy outfit to go interview a sad sack."

"How much do you charge to wear this sexy outfit?"

"This is no time for flattery, Nathan."

When someone tells you that there is no time for flattery, what they generally mean is that there is a little time for flattery, but you should do it quickly. Nathan, literal fellow that he is, dispensed with the flattery altogether.

"Listen, it's like that bit in *Breakfast at Tiffany's*—they were trying to hire a fake, and they accidentally got a fake that's real."

"Have you even seen *Breakfast at Tiffany's*?"

"I've seen parts of it."

And I would have argued with Nathan, then and there, over the merits of dispensing advice from movies you have not seen—and this quite possibly would have cheered me up—but I was distracted by the sight of a treant on the convention floor below me. A treant with mismatched earrings.

CHAPTER TWENTY-THREE

Oh my God," I said to Nathan. "Jennifer Ebel is in the building."

"I didn't realize that she played *Zoth*," said Nathan. "That's a little strange, I suppose."

Strange? It was beyond strange. But then again, this was coming from the man who faked the death of his ex-girlfriend on Skype with a pool noodle. I suppose that I should bow to him as the master purveyor of strangeness. But it isn't the word I would have used. Fishy, perhaps? Suspicious? Concerning? Jennifer had told me outright that she did not play *Zoth*. And now, here she was in a tree costume that must have taken weeks to build.

Between the fake murder and Lurleen's emotional takedown on me, I had clearly lost my mind, because I had a plan. A terrible, terrible plan.

"I don't want her to get away," I told Nathan. "I'm going to track her."

"Like a park ranger?"

"No, I'm going to sneak up to her and plant my iPhone on her. It's light enough that I think I can squeeze it into her costume without her noticing."

From the blank look I was getting from Nathan on FaceTime, it was clear that he did not see the value of my scheme.

"She's dressed as a giant tree, right? How hard can it be to lose her?"

"It shouldn't be hard while she's here." Although when I considered it, there were four floors, which meant that I shouldn't be too cavalier about tailing her. "But what do I do if she leaves? If she hops in a cab, it's game over."

"Why would she do that?"

"Maybe she gets spooked. Or maybe she just gets tired of the costume and wants to go to her hotel to change," I said while scratching at my orange gauze.

"I think if she leaves that you should get into the subsequent cab and say, 'Driver, follow that birch!'"

"That probably sounds a lot more fun than it would work out to be in real life," I told Nathan, who regarded this idea with a lot of skepticism. "I need you to go to my apartment and get my iPad. I want you to use the 'Find My iPhone' app, and we can keep nice and close tabs on Jennifer. You can call Charice and give us updates on her whereabouts if she bolts."

"Isn't your place locked? Don't I need a password for your iPad? What's Charice's phone number?"

I gave Nathan instructions to get a key, explained that Charice's phone number is visible from her public Facebook page, because she is insane, and told him my password, which I was embarrassed to explain was "NathanWilling<3<3<3." He, of course, had follow-up questions only for the last bit.

"What was that password?"

I repeated the password for him.

"With three hearts?"

I told him with three hearts.

"Any exclamation points?" he asked.

"Go," I told him. "While I still like you."

Looking back, I suppose it's important to note that I didn't actually *know* that the treant was Jennifer. I couldn't see her face, which was obscured underneath layers of bark and lichen. But there was something about the cosplay—not just the earrings— that made me think it was her. She had enormous apples all over her, and she had positioned two of them so that they functioned as kind of arboreal earrings. One yellow and unripe, the other bloodred. Maybe it was optimism on my part, but damn if she didn't look like Orchardary and Jennifer both.

It was a reasonable guess—although one that could have cost me a $400 iPhone if I had been wrong, but desperate times call for desperate measures.

The nice thing about tracking a treant is that they are a giant fucking tree. The treant costume was seven feet tall, and it was as wide as a truck. I might have been a lousy private eye, but even in a crowded show floor with people dressed in glittering costumes of genies and harpies and elves, you're not going to lose a giant tree.

I came down the escalator and tried to track Jennifer, while keeping a respectful distance. I wasn't sure if the iPhone plan was going to work, despite my confidence on the phone with Nathan earlier. It would have been much easier if she had been carrying a bag that I could have just dropped the phone in. It was crazy that she wasn't—everyone here was carrying bags; they came free with your ticket. But not the tree. Perhaps she had felt that it would distract from her costume.

She was waiting in line to get something signed by a shaggy-haired voice actor, and I took a spot a few people behind her. Looking at it up close, I could see that I had a problem. The costume looked to be entirely made of wood—or maybe some sort of polyurethane that was made to look like wood. It was astonishingly detailed—there were even little sprouts growing out of the legs in places. But I was less impressed than flum-moxed. There were no pockets, no crevasses, nowhere obvious to squeeze an iPhone.

Of course, I could only see the costume from the back. I was wary of getting much closer, because I did not want to be seen, and I wasn't entirely sure where the eyeholes were on that thing. Still, there were some flyers you could take on a red table nearby, and so I zipped out of line, and pretended to be very interested in them. It was apparently a design document for a zone called "The Hive," and I looked at it intently despite the fact that I could not imagine a zone less interesting. I was in front of the treant now, and I had this awful feeling that Jenni-fer was boring eyes in my back. Paranoia, surely. When I turned around, I would be able to get a good glimpse of the front of the costume, possibly being able to confirm my suspicion that it was indeed Jennifer Ebel, and maybe—maybe—plant my extremely expensive bug on her?

Having stared at the Hive flyer well beyond any credible length, I decided to take my chance. The front of the costume gave me no clues to its inhabitant, but there on the treant's shoulder was my opportunity. She had carved a knoll into her shoulder, and a terrifyingly realistic squirrel peered out. But there was no realistic way that I could shove my phone down the burrow of a tree in front of everyone. Besides which, it would surely rattle around when she walked, giving up the game.

I needed to prep.

What follows is the most pissant episode of *MacGyver* you

have ever seen. I acquired, on the floor of the Left Field Games Summit, a cheap paper Princess Penelope mask, a gray "Visit the Sundered Lands" T-shirt—which cost thirty dollars—and three packs of chewing gum, which was another nine dollars. This bug was getting more and more expensive. I chewed the gum, wrapped my phone inside the T-shirt, and tried to affix as much chewy gum to the outside of the shirt as possible. The effort was barely passable. Laughable, maybe, but passable. If I could find the right moment, I could probably shove the squirrel out of the way and wedge the sticky T-shirt down her hallow. The right moment would be something like an earthquake, but there you have it.

I put on the cheap mask and I tailed the tree for another few minutes. Clearly, I had gone insane. This was what it was like to lose your mind. Probably what was going to happen was that I would going to molest this tree with my sticky gum and discover that it was not Jennifer Ebel at all but an angry Hells Angels biker. That was undoubtedly it.

A moment came. Music swelled over the loudspeaker and someone announced that designers of the spider goddess Zxlyphxix would be answering questions on level two. I don't even know what this meant, but there was actually an "Ooh!" that went over the crowd, and I took my chance. My heart was racing, my palms were sweating. But I did it. I scampered up to the side of the tree—all fairy-like—and pushed the ruined T-shirt down into her crevice. I tried frolicking away—difficult when you are on the verge of a heart attack—and saw a slightly tubby mummy staring at me, clearly having watched the whole exchange. I lifted my mask and winked at him and tried to make a silent hand gesture that suggested this was good clean fairy fun. The mummy sighed at me but shuffled away.

I couldn't bring myself to look back at the tree. I just picked an arbitrary direction and kept walking toward it. Fifteen seconds later, I looked back and the treant was gone.

———————————◆———————————

I was frayed at this point, seriously frayed. I waited in line nervously at a hamburger place—thirteen dollars!—and tried to calm my nerves with food. Maybe it was just the butterflies in my stomach, but the sandwich I got seemed more than worth every penny. I really wanted to speak to Charice now, but of course I couldn't call her. Hopefully she would respond to my text soon—I wasn't sure why she hadn't shown up already. This was exactly the kind of thing that would draw her out.

I retreated to the safety of the women's restroom. I'm embarrassed to say that I didn't need to actually pee. I sort of thought I might sneak into a stall and cry for just a bit—but when I got in there, I suddenly found that I wasn't stressed or even sad anymore. I felt amazing. This could be my moment; I could catch the killer, return the spear, make peace with my ex-boyfriend, and in one stroke make right everything that had gone wrong in the past two years. That looks a little melodramatic when I type it out now, but I told you already that I had lost my mind.

I left the stall, washed my hands, and stepped out of the restroom to find an enormous tree waiting patiently for me.

"I noticed you've been following me," said the tree in a thick Indian American accent. "Do I know you?"

I wasn't wearing that stupid cardboard mask anymore, and I would have killed to have had it on right then. There was nothing to do but lay my cards on the table.

"Oh, yes," I said, shooting for casual friendliness. "I'm sorry.

271

You look like a friend of mine in-game. Your name isn't, by any chance, Orchardary, is it?"

As the tree's eyes were unmoving lumps of wood, it was hard to read the face for a reaction, but if I had to guess by her voice, I would have said that she was as nervous as a cat.

"No," said the tree. "Although I think I know the person you mean. People keep mistaking me for her."

"Oh, I'm sorry," I said amiably. "I suppose I could see why. Two female treants with Indian accents."

"What are the odds?" said the treant.

And that was my chance to leave, safely and without incident. She didn't seem to know about the iPhone, as far as I could tell, so I could have just walked away and kept tabs on her from a distance. But I just couldn't resist pressing my luck.

"I love your accent," I told her. "What province of India are you from?"

There was a pause that was just one beat too long.

"The Marhashi province. You probably haven't heard of it."

I had not heard of it, no, although to be fair I couldn't name a single province of India. I wasn't even 100 percent sure that India had provinces—maybe they had states or counties or something? But I had googled my line days ago, and I tried it now.

" मुझे माफ करना, लेकिन आप हम क्या शहर में हैं क्या जानते हो?"

Jennifer might have sensibly responded with confusion. Or laughed at my terrible accent. I was speaking from a memorized version of a speech learned from Google Translate, so even if my pronunciation was close (and I can assure you that it was not), there was no telling if the construction was correct.

Instead Jennifer took an intuitive leap of her own—a brilliant one, a leap that could have secured her own success in her deceit, had it only been right. When Jennifer went in, she went all in. What's the one phrase that everyone learns to say in a language?

"I believe," said Jennifer, with false certainty, "the bathroom is right behind you."

But as soon as she said it, she knew the gig was up. My face is entirely too expressive for detective work. I was thrilled to catch her out, and I must have lit up like a candle. So much for bluffing.

CHAPTER TWENTY-FOUR

Jennifer sighed.

"Anyway, I like your costume," she told me, dropping the accent. "Especially the hair."

Of course she did. The one incongruous element. This was her modus operandi.

"Jennifer Ebel," I said to her, trying to make it not sound like an accusation but like a pleasant surprise. "What are you doing here?"

"Oh, you know, I'm a big fan of *Zoth*. Like you, I guess."

My mouth could not be stopped, nor even quieted. "Is that so? You told me that you didn't play the game when I interviewed you."

"I've only just started," said Jennifer with the same fake tossed-off enthusiasm that I had tried using on her. This line might have been plausible if she weren't wearing an elaborate tree costume that must have taken months to build.

"You are Orchardary," I told her.

"You caught me," said Jennifer. Then she shifted into her Indian accent, which now sounded incredibly fake, but perhaps this was only because I knew it was coming out of a decidedly occidental tree. As if to confirm her identity, Jennifer brushed away the moss beard of her treant, revealing her own face beneath the costume. "Was it my voice that tipped you off? You'd think that more people would see through it, although no one does."

"You also didn't know what city we are in when I asked you in Hindi."

"Yes, well, this wasn't a charade that was worth learning a second language for."

There was an air of practiced innocence about Jennifer now, as if this were all just a delightful misunderstanding, or kooky coincidence, but I just wasn't having it. I had come this far, and I wanted answers.

"Why did you lie to me?"

Jennifer was looking at me with a catlike thoughtfulness that was a little alarming. She was trying to piece together what I had figured out. At the same time I was looking at her and trying to determine if she had any inkling that she was wearing my iPhone.

"I was embarrassed," she said. "I'm a very serious person"—a line that seemed terrifyingly true, even as it was being delivered from an elaborate tree costume—"and I feel like people would respect me less if word got out that I was this into *Zoth*."

"You didn't tell me that you had been dating Jonah when I first interviewed you."

"It was more of a one-night stand. And he was alive at the time, so I didn't think it was any of your business."

Jennifer had answers for everything. But if she had been concerned about her privacy, why had she sought me out in the women's bathroom in the first place? She needed to know how much I knew. The trouble was that I needed to know the same thing. Some part of me was crying out that Jennifer was implicated in this deep—as deep as it gets. But I couldn't prove any of it, or even tell you why I felt so strongly. But my mind was churning around everything I knew. Jennifer was Orchardary. It was like working a cryptogram—the extra information I had from this had to reveal another clue.

"Did Jonah know your secret identity as a tree?"

Jennifer thought about her answer, scrunching up her face as though she were considering a verbal trap. "No. I didn't want him to know. Jonah allowed himself a frivolity that he would have certainly mocked in me."

"He invited you in the game without knowing who you were?"

"Oatcake invited me into the guild. When I realized that Jonah was in the guild, I decided to fake an identity."

"Aishwarya Patel? You think quick on your feet."

"She was an old college roommate of mine, and I did a decent impression of her. I never imagined I'd be doing it for so long. I wonder if that's how it went for Threadwork's silly voice."

I couldn't resist showing off how much I knew.

"Duke University, right? Likes country music?"

Jennifer stared at me incredulously.

"When you started dating him," I told her, "you tried telling him." It wasn't a question.

"No," Jennifer said flatly.

"You gave him the 'Walk to Wachusett' idea."

Jennifer seemed suddenly alarmed. This was a revelation, however small, that she hadn't been prepared for. I explained.

"An obscure reference to Henry David Thoreau? I didn't know Jonah well, but I'm guessing that nineteenth-century philosophers did not occupy a lot of his reading. But you're a philosophy person," I told her. "Your workstation in the graduate office was lined with tracts. And you were the only person that caught Jonah's reference in the invitation. 'This level life too has its summit.' It was your idea all along, and you couldn't stand that we wouldn't get the reference."

There was an almost audible click in Jennifer's thoughts.

"I had thrown him some clues," said Jennifer. "I had hoped that he would piece it together himself. I had this silly idea that he would be deliriously happy when he discovered that I was already in his guild. But he never figured it out. Jonah was many things, but he was not intellectually curious."

Why was I not walking away? Why did I keep peppering Jennifer with questions?

"How did you know what the spear looked like? The replica, I mean?"

Jennifer's response came instantly—the words coming out faster than she could actually lay down the track for the thoughts. "Well, I mean, of course I was just bluffing about having seen it. And I knew what the spear looked like in-game. And other people had described it and I just piggybacked off their responses. I did a pretty good job, didn't I?"

But I had been there for that conversation. No one described the spear at any length but Jennifer. And no one had actually wielded it in the game—she shouldn't have known what it looked like at all. Because unlike everyone else in the guild, she had not received a copy, her copy going to Aishwarya Patel and returned to sender.

"You even said that it was heavy. How would you know that?"

Typing up this account now, I have no idea why I would say that out loud. My best analogy is that you're like the nerd in algebra class who, despite their nerdy reputation, nonetheless is completely baffled by algebra. And in one shining moment, the clouds part and you suddenly get it. And so you shout out the answer to every question, even though it's going to get you seriously ostracized after class. Because you're right and you can't help it.

That analogy, you might guess, is closer to home than I would like.

"Right," said Jennifer. She didn't look angry or maddened, or even particularly remorseful. "I guess that's where we are, then."

"You sent me those job-fair flyers. You didn't want me to come here. You were afraid I'd recognize you."

"You couldn't just go to a fucking job fair, Dahlia? It was a good idea."

"And you killed Jonah Long," I told her, still beaming with accomplishment. Then once the moment passed, I was suddenly confused again. "Why?"

Jennifer sighed. "I guess you'd say it was a crime of passion."

She was digging around in a fanny pack that she had on the inside of her bark. I should have been alarmed by this in retrospect, but my thinking at the time was *What dangerous thing could possibly come out of a fanny pack?* And besides which, she was still talking. I suppose my expectation was that she was getting a tissue.

"We'd had a romantic interlude the weekend before. I'm sure you heard about that. I was coming by to break up with him, and he, of course, beat me to the punch."

"But why did you do it?" I asked her.

"He was an asshole."

That was probably true. But if I went around killing every guy who was a jerk, America would have a population problem. "That's not much of a reason," I told Jennifer.

"You're asking me why I snapped?"

Yes. That's what I was asking. Jennifer was, clearly, a very tightly wound woman. But it wasn't as if she had gone on routine killing sprees to let off steam. Something put her over the edge.

And I was curious too because I remembered what it was like when I found out that Erik had been cheating on me for months. I remembered that white-hot rage. I had directed it inward. There had been no danger that I was going to kill Erik—even in my craziest fantasies. But look at what it had done to me. I had become completely deflated. No friends, no job. I was like some horrible shadow of myself. Maybe murder wasn't *such* a terrible option—for all her faults, Jennifer could at least be said to have vigor.

"It was Orchardary that killed him."

I pondered this. Was Jen crazy enough to have multiple personality disorder between her and a tree? I thought, *Crazy, but probably not that crazy.* But Jennifer caught my confused expression.

"No, not like that," she said. "I killed him—not some imaginary tree. But it was the tree that caused it."

I didn't comment. With something so oblique the explanation had to be coming,

"You ever read one of those romances where the heroine and the hero hate each other at the beginning? And then it turns out that behind all that hate is passion?"

I never read books like that, but I lied. "I've skimmed a few."

"It started out like that. Or I thought it did. Jonah joined our program and infuriated me. Everything came so easily to him—the science, money, relationships. I had gotten where I was by working harder than anyone I knew—and then he just shows up, waltzing around like he's enchanted. But I couldn't take my eyes off him. He was so . . . magnetic."

I had never thought that Jonah was magnetic. He was good-looking, sure, but I could take my eyes off him easily. I can take my eyes off car crashes. Just let them rest on a point in the distance. But that's chemistry for you.

Jennifer went on with her story. "Then Oatcake invited me to join the Horizons, and there he was again. At the time it had felt like this weird kismet. But I didn't want him to know it was me, because I was sure he would make fun of me doing something so frivolous. So I made up a disguise. A false-face to wear when he was around—like at a masquerade ball."

It suddenly struck me that Jennifer had read a good many more Harlequins than I would have put her down for at first glance.

"You were hoping that he would fall in love with you online?"

"Not really. It was just fun to spend time with him in a different environment, in a different way. We weren't competing, and I didn't have to be perfect Jennifer Ebel. It's just, the longer I did it, the more Orchardary became sort of a prison."

"You couldn't just give it up?"

"When you've been speaking in a fake Indian accent for close to a year, it becomes hard to figure out how to suddenly change. The disguise had gotten so elaborate—I had a name, a job, a sister. A whole double life."

Goddamned Wilfrid Laurier. But his Canadian insights from beyond the grave weren't going to help me now. And I wanted the rest of the story, regardless.

"Then Jonah found out," I added, as Jennifer looked a little faraway.

"No," said Jennifer, instantly back from wherever she had been. "I wish he had. No, what happened was that we went on, playing the game together with me as his girl Friday online, and being cordial rivals in the real world. Until Freddie Garrison's party."

I didn't know who Freddie Garrison was, but I decided to try leaving him out of the exchange altogether.

"Nathan told me that you and Jonah had gotten together."

"You spoke to Nathan? Yegads."

I had done more than speak to Nathan, but this was not the time to detail my sexual conquests. I nodded.

"At Freddie's party. But it was the next day that had been so wonderful. It was just a perfect day. Like in a novel. Well, aside from the hangover. Jonah made me breakfast, spent the morning with me, and then he made me a picnic lunch at Forrest Park. And we talked—really talked. It wasn't even like a romantic surge or anything, it was just sort of as if we had always been a couple. It was like being given this wonderful present that I hadn't known I wanted. It went on like that for a couple of days, and he started getting weird and distant. I thought—oh, we've been moving too fast."

"And he still didn't know that you were Orchardary."

"No—and there were like seven or eight times that I had thought about telling him."

"So what made you snap?"

Jennifer sighed. "I was online. Orchardary was doing a little gardening, as she does, and Jonah showed up. He wanted to talk. Not to Jennifer. To Aishwarya. He wanted to talk to the fake me about the real me."

"Oof," I said, thinking that this could not possibly be good.

"At first I thought that he was playing some sort of romantic game with me—that he had known all along that Orchardary and I were one and the same." Jennifer's voice grew dark. "But that was not it."

"What did he say?"

"He was looking, from me, on advice on how to break up with me. Which I could have handled. But his descriptions of me were just so cruel and unfair and…I don't know. I don't even want to talk about the details of it."

"So you went over there to his place to murder him?" I tried asking that neutrally, but I couldn't keep the incredulousness out of my voice.

"I went over to his place," said Jennifer, her voice raising suddenly—and then, just as quickly dropping back down to a whisper, "to break up with him. Things just took a hard turn. We started arguing and he called me selfish, without a hint of self-awareness—while this enormous fifty-pound, jewel-studded replica of the theft he had made only days before just sat there on his expensive Oriental rug. How selfish is that? He stole from his own guild mates and then spent thousands of dollars to make a trophy out of it. And dared to call me selfish? After I picked it up, I even started speaking to him in my Orchardary voice, and he still didn't put it together. Jonah was book smart, but he really wasn't very clever. I mean, he shouldn't have made the thing so sharp in the first place. But of course, it was done exactly as it was in the game. Jonah just didn't ever think ahead."

I was listening to her little soliloquy somewhat spellbound. Jennifer hadn't known that the spear was a test model for the ones that would be sent out to the guild later. That the final model would not be quite so sharp. She murdered Jonah Long with his own apology.

"You don't think that much ahead either, do you, dear?" asked Jennifer, her voice even more manic than before.

And I realized that what had emerged from her fanny pack was a gun.

CHAPTER TWENTY-FIVE

I am pointing a gun at you," said Jennifer evenly. "I don't want
to fire it, because it would make a terrible scene and could also
send bits of your face flying everywhere. Important bits. The
bits that you like."

To be perfectly honest with you, I don't like many bits on my
face. At best I have a relationship of ambivalence with them.
But I told Jennifer that I agreed with her premise.

"Good," she said, tucking the gun behind her moss beard.
"What I would like for you to do is walk with me. A nice walk,
with no incidents. As easy as that. A pleasant stroll, in which
nothing bad will happen."

I did not like the way she was repeating the same idea with
different words. A cheerful jaunt, in which you will not be murdered. An idyllic promenade, in which your face will not be
blown off. Anyway, I must have looked skeptical, because Jennifer was all reassurances.

"Look, Dahlia," said Jennifer, using that fake friendly voice
of hers, "I've got no hard feelings here. I don't want to kill you. I
just can't trust you to not tell the police. You understand?"

I did understand. I knew too much.

"See, I'm not going to kill you, unless you make me. We're

going to go somewhere nice and secluded, and we're going to drug you. Then I will get out of town. Maybe I'll go to Canada. They need botanists in Canada."

It was hard to tell whether Jennifer was extremely bonkers or extremely sane. I felt as though her factoid about the botanical job market of the great white north lent itself to the bonkers camp, but what did I know about it? She spoke in a dementedly ingratiating voice; the kind you would use to speak to some family dog—a frilly one, like a Pomeranian.

"Don't worry," she told me. "Nothing bad is going to happen."

When people who are pointing guns at you inform you that nothing bad is going to happen, it's generally wise to take it with a grain of salt. It seemed that not only was something bad going to happen, it was happening right now. That said, what was there to do? Marching to undisclosed locations with a gun-wielding treant was clearly a dunderheaded move, but the alternative was worse. I walked.

And walked, and walked. Jennifer lumbered along behind me every so often, saying something ominous like, "I'd hate to see you get shot" and "Don't forget I'm pointing a loaded gun at you." Jennifer apparently believed that without these reminders my mind would wander and that I might momentarily forget that I was being marched at gunpoint. Without her help I would start lingering at a merch booth to buy a T-shirt, or get a *Zoth* sound track signed. She needed to wave the gun periodically so I would recall—"Oh, right! The *death march*. You know, I just don't know where my head is lately."

I was alarmed as well, because if Jennifer wanted to make a quick egress from the Games Summit, I would expect her to move downstairs. Toward an exit. Instead we went up—all the way to the secluded top floor of the convention center. There was not much on the top floor, and as we reached the top of the stairwell, I had an uncomfortable feeling that Jennifer was weighing the merits of killing me on the spot. It was about as secluded as we were going to get.

But thankfully, we reached the top floor. Jennifer hustled me down a wide hallway, and gestured for me to sit down on a wooden bench next to a planter.

"That was easy, wasn't it?"

I had not found it terribly easy. I had found it deeply stressful. They say that your life is supposed to flash before your eyes in situations like these, but I kept thinking of odd little details. I had library books that were due in a week. If I were killed here, there was no way in hell that Charice would return those. It was just going to cost the Saint Louis Public Library a lot of money, and I did not feel that they were an institution that could afford to take the hit.

Jennifer was eyeing the crowd up here. It was not empty, but it was very sparse. Imagine mall walking—at a lousy mall—on a Tuesday morning. That should give you the idea. There were people about, but they seemed to be on the way to something else, and not interested in a fairy and treant resting on a bench.

Jennifer reached back into her fanny pack of doom and pulled out a syringe. A motherfucking syringe. Who the hell travels with a syringe?

Jennifer gave me the syringe and an unmarked vial. It looked like it might hold insulin—there was something clear in it.

"You must think I'm out of my mind. But I did allow for this contingency. I tend to worry, you know. I even had this with me at Jonah's funeral, just in case. It's just a nice sedative."

There was something markedly false about Jennifer's voice when she said "nice sedative" that gave me reason to believe that it was less a nice sedative and more a death-inducing poison. But then, a bullet to the head was pretty death-inducing as well.

"I'm going to stand over here," said Jennifer, "and continue to point this gun at you. Just because you can't see it behind the lichen doesn't mean that it's not pointed at your head."

Jennifer was loving that gun.

"I'd like for you to stick the syringe into the vial and fill the vial to the fifty. Not any less, not any more."

I filled the vial to the fifty.

"Now," said Jennifer amiably. "I need you to inject the vial into your skin. If you want to lift your shirt, you could put it in your belly."

"I'm kind of squeamish about needles," I told her.

"How are you with bullets?"

"What if someone comes over?" I asked hopefully.

"They will not. But if they do, you can explain that you are a diabetic."

I lifted my shirt a little. It felt like there had to be a point at which I could divert this path; knock Jennifer from this plan that she had apparently perfectly envisioned. I thought about throwing the syringe at her face, ninja-style, but it's the kind of flourish you can imagine much more readily than you can do. It was obvious that it wouldn't stop her. There was nothing to do.

"Please do it so I can see it."

I did it where she could see it. The syringe stung quite a bit more than I felt it should. What can I tell you? My skill in at-gunpoint, self-induced phlebotomy could use some work. Jennifer, at least, seemed happy by the sight of blood.

"Now slide the syringe back to me."

I did. Jennifer packed it back up into her fanny pack of horrors and then smiled at me.

"No cotton ball?" I asked her.

"Use your shirt," she told me, smiling brightly.

Were this scene ever to be re-created on film or stage, the next bit would most definitely have to be excised. What followed was twenty minutes of Jennifer silently pointing a hidden gun at me as whatever drug she had injected me with gradually began to take hold. I was feeling tingling in my extremities now, and I felt reasonably confident that I was going to die. Internally, I suppose things were in a bit of a turmoil, but if you were to have been watching us for that twenty minutes, it could have passed for an early experimental film of Andy Warhol.

That is to say: Nothing happened.

I thought about Nathan, and Erik and Lurleen. I think perhaps that I had made a muddle of things with all of them. And I was angry at myself—not about the fact that I had stupidly gotten myself killed. But angry at myself for being so self-involved that I had spent the past two years of my life not having any fun at all. Stephen was right. Why hadn't I seen him? Why had I talked myself into seclusion? I had been unemployed and had maybe had the wrong boyfriend for a couple of years. So what? I was young, not horrible-looking, and...

And people were coming up to us. I was feeling clearly drugged now, but I was together enough that I enjoyed the look of alarm on Jennifer's painted-green face peeking out from behind that beard.

"Don't move," she hissed at me.

"You are just beautiful," said the man, who himself was dressed as a surprisingly scantily clad elf. There was a second female elf, even closer to clotheslessness, who also came up to

Jennifer, who was equally, if not more, enamored of Jennifer. They were all over her costume.

"I love this," said the elf. "I always want to wear a more elaborate costume, but my husband always steers me toward outfits with visible boobs."

The man laughed awkwardly. "My wife is kidding."

Jennifer was momentarily dumbstruck by the nigh-upon-naked couple, who were actually fondling her bark and saying things like: "Is this real wood?"

There was a moment—just a moment—where one of elves crossed the path between Jennifer and me. The whole thing happened fast enough that I had been as surprised as Jennifer. But drugged or not, I was operating on hairline reflexes, whereas Jennifer was wearing a tree costume and being pawed at by naked people.

I threw the harp at her. I had been gripping it tightly for a while. I'm guessing she had thought it was costume harp—light, made of balsa wood or something. It was, of course, made of metal, and it made a terrific cracking noise followed by a strum as it hit her face.

"Eat harp!" I yelled, running as fast as I could down the hall.

Blood was dripping down Jennifer's face when I glanced back, still running.

"It's a lyre, you uncultured clod!" she boomed at me, the elves staring agape at us both. She pulled out her gun, scaring the bejeezus out of the near-naked elves, and I supposed meant to end me as I turned the corner. What happened next was the most improbable thing ever. Jennifer's aim was the slightest bit distracted by the "Flight of the Valkyries" ringtone that suddenly emanated from inside her knoll.

I have three ringtones—one for my family ("A Hard Rain's

A-Gonna Fall"), one for strangers and friends ("Who Could It Be Now?"), and one for job callbacks.

This was a job callback. Boo. Yah.

"Is that a ringtone?" she asked to the elves.

The elves said nothing because it's the sort of question that is rhetorical even before you factor guns into the equation. But the moment the Wagner ringtone sounded meant that when Jennifer pointed her firearm at my head and shot—the bullets missed me and went through my fairy wings and into a plate glass window.

I'm not in amazing shape, but it's surprisingly easy to outrun a woman in a tree costume, even drugged.

I zipped down the hall with a fairy's quickness but also with the mental capacity of a cloudy bowl of soup.

"You're only spreading the poison through your bloodstream," coughed out Jennifer, who sounded impossibly far away. To be fair, she was far away, but it was clear that the syringe was doing something to me. I felt loopy and lightheaded as I ran down the hall with no particular idea where I was going. The stairs were behind me, and there was not another way down unless I made it all the way to the south side of the building, which seemed to be towns away.

I did my best to keep running. I turned the corner and saw, in an alcove far over the main floor, what I believed was my salvation. It was Auctioneer Griselda, with her enormous black wings spread, peering over to look at the chaos on the main floor. The neon-blue letters of her name were backward, of course, since she wasn't facing me—but I'd recognize that "adlesirG" anywhere. It was Charice, who was going to somehow save me from this madwoman.

I didn't actually manage to stop before I reached Charice; rather I collided into her, pushing us both dangerously against the rail that protected us from falling to our deaths.

When I spoke, I realized that my tongue and lips had gone numb, which could not possibly be a good sign. "Tharith! Thenither Abuh muthud Donah Lonth and thees a thwee anth ith thasingth me and poisoned me with themon!"

The above line is a very charitable rendering of what I said, which was probably about half as intelligible. I did feel I did a good job with the "poisoned me" bit, however, which in many ways seemed like the most pressing part.

Apparently Jennifer was not so far off after all, because she came lumbering up toward the two of us. She made a pass at seeming friendly and sweet, but the effect was somewhat dimmed by her still holding a smoking gun.

"Oh, Dahlia!" said Jennifer. "You're not having another one of your panic attacks, are you? It's okay. Come and sit here under my branches, and I'll take care of you."

"Tharitwith! Pwothec me!"

And it was at roughly that moment that I realized that I wasn't clinging to Charice at all. The Auctioneer Griselda I was holding on to for dear life had black, pupil-less eyes, and much scarier makeup, and there was actually blood coming from her mouth. Her actual name, I would learn later, was Linda Yoon, and she was a paralegal who worked in Santa Monica whose hobbies included cosplay, *Zoth*, and windsurfing. But I'm not embarrassed to admit that at the time, I actually thought that this woman was Auctioneer Griselda and that all of this *Zoth* paraphernalia had brought her in the world and made her manifest. She spoke in this terrible withered rice paper voice—as if her words were not spoken but somehow darkly effervesced. This may have been the drugs.

"Why have you come to Griselda, treant?"

Jennifer was not interested in cosplay.

"Stay away, harpy. This fairy is meeting her end."

"She claims you have poisoned her. You dare attack someone under the protection of Griselda?"

At the time, I was thinking that Griselda did not know what a gun was, since she had never seen them in her world. Yes, it was definitely the drugs. My plan was to warn Griselda about the danger of firearms, but my lips had swollen to the size of Chinese sausages. And what did it matter, because Jennifer was going to fire her handgun regardless. I don't know why the presence of it had surprised me so greatly. There was, of course, no metal detector at the convention center. Because this was Arizona. At the Phoenix airport white people are offered complimentary handguns after passing through baggage claim, as way of saying thank you and welcome to the Grand Canyon State.

"So much for doing this the quiet, easy way," growled Jennifer.

I don't know the precise order of things that happened. Jennifer shot at us, I took a bullet through my arm, and Griselda leaped over the edge of the rail with me, to what I assumed was my certain death. But she apparently managed to grab a line attached to a banner reading 11 YEARS OF ZOTH, which had been strung across the main floor. Suddenly there I was, in the arms of a harpy with black wings spread, swooping Douglas Fairbanks–style, in a graceful arc toward crowds of astonished, terrified, and amazed onlookers.

Bullets were flying at me, the ground was coming toward

me, and blood was spraying out of my arm and into the crowd below. It was, impossibly, at this point that I knew everything would be all right. I was shouting—I suppose I wanted to get out some last words before I died—"I never thought my life would end this way."

But I didn't say that. I said, "I never thought my life would be this way." (Or: I nwevah thwoth my wifth thwod be thith thway.) It was the old Moss family line, the overwrought one that my dad would use for undersalted pastas or the post office taking an extra two minutes before they opened after lunch. The one that I had once used, back before my life had been become a horrible landslide of ex-boyfriends and failed job interviews. Again: It may have been the drugs, but the suddenly serendipity of the family line pouring out of me made me unspeakably happy. It was like going to your high school reunion—and having, against all expectations—a really good time. I was being shot at by a crazy woman in a tree costume and I thought it was, well, a little humorous. A small victory for Dahlia Moss.

As we arced toward the ground, we of course managed to fly directly into the enormous inflatable phoenix in the middle of the room, because why not? The phoenix was totally destroyed, hemorrhaging helium and flame-y bits of orange fabric. Although insurance agents later determined that this was the result of gunfire, not harpy impact.

There are a lot of competing theories as to what was actually yelled as we flew off the balcony and into the phoenix. The prevailing one is that Griselda yelled, "Death to the Boar Runners of the Third Age!" This should give you some idea of the psychological makeup of the people below. Another is that Griselda was announcing the name of next year's expansion to the game. What can I say? Even with the gunfire and the spray of blood, there was a general sense that this was all somehow part of the show. Or there was, until Jennifer—still intent on somehow completing the kill—attempted the same trick and leaped onto another banner, which promptly broke and sent her crashing to the ground.

She was fine. Not fine in the way of a horror-movie monster that was going to get up and start pursuing us again, but fine in the way of having only two broken legs and no serious head trauma. And also being a complete psychopath. Also that.

CHAPTER TWENTY-SIX

So I was wrong about the poison. You might have surmised that already, given that I survived to write this account. It's a bit strange—I feel like I owe Jennifer Ebel an apology for not taking her at her word about it? And yet she did try to shoot me, which would generally suggest that she owes me an apology. Let's say we're even?

I can't speak much to the immediate aftermath at the Games Summit, other than to say that, Usune bless them, they actually went on with the thing. Jennifer was taken into custody, and I went to the ER and had my stomach pumped. Because they thought I was drunk.

The thing that kills me is that none of the Horizons actually came to see me. I mean: really. I had had these sorts of experiences with gamer folk before—I drove my damned self to the ER when I broke my toe once, while Erik was raiding in the other room and shouting out unhelpful advice like "Put some ice on it!" But this was really a bridge too far. I was the freaking hero; I caught a murderer. I had been reading detective novels since Jonah hired me, and there were rules for how this is supposed to go down. The detective catches the killer, and everyone is supposed to be amazed. There are occasionally drinks. There is generally a sunset and someone walks into it. Occasionally, lovers snog. But never is the successful detective taken to the hospital to have her stomach pumped while everyone else goes to a panel about the upcoming plague of the spider demon.

That sort of thing is not supposed to happen.

I recognize now that you may have some questions of your own here, and I will try to anticipate them now. Where was Charice? I'm sure you are asking. Yes, where was Charice? Where indeed? The answer was certainly not at my bedside. She participated in a costume parade and won fifth prize—which was an unspeakably tacky bronze medallion that she continues to wear around the apartment. Afterward, she went out drinking. I am not shitting you. She does claim, in her pitiful defense, that she made phone calls to make sure that I was okay, but come on. Oh—shit!

Hello, darlings.

This is Charice. Dahlia has been reading this part aloud to me, because she is a tyrant. She tells me that this is the part of the book where she will "wreak terrible vengeance upon those who have wronged her." Dahlia says things like that, as I'm sure you know by now. I'll give her back to you in just a second, but I want to clear up a few things before she drones on any more.

1) I did not know anything about her being poisoned. Which she wasn't. I thought she had just fallen into an inflatable phoenix. Isn't that enough? Yes, I was worried about her in the moment, but I had a long conversation with very dashing paramedic who assured me that she was fine.

2) Her speech was slurred, but I assumed that she was drunk. You've read this far, so you know that's not out of character.

3) Dahlia herself told me that I should march in the parade. She also told me to not go to the hospital and that I had beautiful hair. It was things like that made me think: drunk.

4) I visited later but she was asleep.

That is all. Now return to the rantings of this otherwise delightful madwoman!

Hugs,
Charice

———————◆———

Hmph, as Ophelia would say. I reluctantly concede to some of Charice's points, but honestly, it was very disquieting. That hospital room was lonely, and I didn't have even my iPhone to entertain me. The other question you might have had (she said, moving awkwardly away from Charice's requisition of my narrative) is what happened to Clemency? Surely kindhearted Clemency would visit you?

The answer is no. But she gets a pass. Amid all the gunfire, Clemency started experiencing some hard-core contractions. She was rushed to the hospital on her own—the same hospital, different ambulance, and—after what was described to me as six hours of hell—gave birth to freaking twins. Apparently the whole experience was a nightmare, because twins Prudence Zxlyphxix and Justus Threadwork were born very, very premature. And yes, she gave one of her daughters a middle name based on an imaginary spider demon. But the twins are fine, aside from the silly names. I think Clem and her husband did not experience the first month of parenthood the way they had dreamed it, with the first month of their children's lives spent under a heating table. But what happens the way that you imagined?

I did get one visitor. I woke from sleep to find a mummy staring at me. Remember, the one who watched me palm my iPhone into Jennifer's knoll? At first I thought I was being stared at by some disoriented burn victim, but I remembered the way the bandages were falling off around his belly.

"You're the tubby mummy," I said dreamily. "Are you really here?"

"You did not just call me tubby," said the mummy, whose voice sounded eerily familiar. "Dahlia Moss, you are the worst."

I sat up in bed, suddenly. I knew what voice. It was Anson Shuler.

"What the hell?" I said. "Are you just standing in here with a mask on? What kind of creeper are you?" Although I was glad to see him. Honestly, I was glad to see anyone. I was glad to be alive.

"I was going to surprise you," said Shuler.

I was trying not to look too critically at Shuler's belly, which was peeking at me through torn bandages. The trouble with mummy costumes is that wear and tear on them eventually leaves you naked. "Tubby" was maybe too harsh a word; Shuler wasn't really fat so much as puffy around the middle, like a man made of dough. My tastes in fellas generally ran toward the emaciated, but I felt like squeezing him now, regardless.

"Are you naked under that costume, Detective Shuler?"

"Everyone is naked under their costumes, Dahlia. And call me Anson—I'm not on duty."

That wasn't at all what I meant, and the question largely answered itself, as I could clearly see Detective Shuler's underwear, which was a vivid shade of blue. Royal blue is a poor color selection for undies when one is dressing in white bandages. Shuler was going to be a real fixer-upper.

"So you're not here to protect me?"

"Nope," said Detective Shuler. (I could never get the hang of calling him Anson.) "This is another example of why you are the worst, Dahlia."

"The worst at what?"

"I told you to be careful around Jonah's friends!"

"I was careful," I said. I'd squeezed out some whoppers in the past couple days—and I was getting better at them as I went—but that line was too incredible to get out in an even voice.

"You got shot in the arm. You were drugged! You jumped off a balcony!"

"I was pushed," I corrected him.

"By a woman I told you to avoid," said Anson.

"You didn't tell me to avoid that woman particularly. You offered me a vague description of people to avoid, which happened to include her."

"You. Are. The. Worst."

I think I felt a little like Charice—I was being reprimanded, but I was glowing with happiness at the same time. "Worst" is a *kind* of superlative, after all. And there was a half-dressed mummy in my room who was happy I was alive. Not so bad, really.

I took a second to bask, as Charice would have, and then asked: "So why were you at the convention?"

"I'm on vacation," said Shuler.

"You play *Zoth*?"

"I'm just getting started," said Shuler, which was almost certainly a lie.

"You certainly seemed to have jumped into it with a lot of drive."

"Well," said Shuler, "and I thought it couldn't hurt to keep an eye on Jennifer Ebel."

"So you were chasing after her while she was shooting at me?"

Shuler looked unhappy to have walked into this. "I was actually over at a merch table when that happened."

I gave him a look, and he tossed a T-shirt to me; it was bright blue (like his underwear) and said: "I Survived the Gamers Summit."

"That's the real reason I came by," said Shuler. "You earned it more than me."

Charice and I flew back on the same plane, and it was a lot like coming back from a good spring vacation. I was exhausted and maybe a little sad that the case was over. But a good sad, a satisfied sad. You can probably guess the first phone call I made (on Charice's phone, since my own was evidence).

"Stephen?"

"Who is this?"

"It's Dahlia Moss. How's my favorite music librarian?"

"How's my lyre?"

I always felt that Stephen was wasted on librarianship. He could ask questions in this angry Morpheus voice that seemed better suited to law, or perhaps thaumaturgy. I was hoping that we could have done introductions before we got to death questions. I gave him my best Sydney Greenstreet impression, which I hoped would lighten the mood. "Here's to plain speaking and clear understanding," I told him. "By all means, let's talk about the black bird."

"Bad impressions will not help you now," said Stephen flatly. "Do you have my lyre?"

"Well," I said. "Some police have your lyre."

Stephen sighed. "I suppose you're going to tell me the story of how that happened."

"I was thinking I would. Should I tell you now, or should I tell you over lunch?"

"Do you think that you'll be safer in a crowd?"

"Oh, come on," I told him. "I'll tell you my adventures, and you can tell me who you've been catting around with lately. We'll have mixed drinks with umbrellas and ridiculous names. It will be like old times."

And he bit. I knew he would. I had him at drinks with umbrellas.

———————————◆———————————

My next phone call was to Nathan. The path had been cleared, and now I could date with impunity. If that's what I wanted.

"Hello there, Nathan."

"Dahlia, you minx. How was your plane flight?"

I wasn't sure why Nathan was calling me a minx, but I couldn't believe that after the cliff-hanger I'd left him on, his first question was about the plane flight. "The flight? That's what we're leading with?"

"What would you prefer I ask you about?"

"My adventure? Whether or not I was killed? What happened to me in the hospital?"

"Clearly, you have not been killed. Besides, I've already spoken to you about that."

"What?!"

"You were very drugged at the time."

"Oh dear," I told Nathan. "What did I say?"

"You wanted me to ***** ****** your *****, while ******** *******. On a *******."

"I said that?"

"Repeatedly. I'm just a guy who likes to ****** and *****, so I didn't know what to make of it."

I wanted to steer the conversation away from this, so I tried veering things back to the case.

"What did I tell you about my adventure?"

"Just the bare bones. Mostly it was just ****** ****** in the *******. And ****** ******."

"That doesn't sound like me at all," I said. Although it sounded entirely like me. Honestly, looking over these paragraphs, I'm worried that I haven't redacted enough.

"I thought you might say that," said Nathan. "Which is why I made a recording of you. I've even Auto-Tuned it. I was thinking of using it as a ringtone. Listen!"

I listened. The ringtone literally was a booty call. I had to meet with Nathan now, if for no other purpose than to destroy that ringtone. It was probably about to start ringing at me from under the floorboards of our apartment, like in "The Tell-Tale Heart," only much smuttier.

"Do you want to have lunch with me? We're going to have a little party. And be sure to bring that phone with you."

My final call was to Beth, of all people. Remember Beth?

"I can't believe you hired me!"

"Who is this?" Beth's tone was naturally one of suspicion. She probably interviews lots of people, and so a phone call that opens with this sort of thing could potentially be dangerous.

"It's Dahlia Moss. The insane detective. Although, speaking of insane, are you out of your fucking mind?"

And Beth's tone brightened when she heard it was me. I can't tell you how much that cheered me. "I'm not insane. Just desperate. All the other applicants turned down the position."

"What strange new economy is this?"

"I know, right? So, do you want in? Accounts payable for a tractor manufacturer?"

"I do not want in, no. Amazingly, no. I think I have a job."

"Did you find your spear?"

"I found the spear, caught the woman who murdered my client, took a bullet to my arm, and—I know you're going to think I am making this part up—jumped off a three-story balcony while being held by a woman dressed as a harpy."

"So I'll put you down as no, then? I should say that this position comes with three days' vacation annually."

"A respectful no. Very respectful, in fact. You can tell the employers that the job offer may have saved my life."

"Are we speaking metaphorically?"

"No. You called to offer me the position at the very moment that I was being shot at."

"That was helpful?"

"It was, given that I had planted my phone in a knoll on the murderesss. But listen, that's not actually why I'm calling."

"You're not calling to thank me for saving your life or to turn down this very fine job offer?" You had to admire Beth's powerful skills at restatement.

"I'm calling to ask you to lunch. With friends. How do you feel about cheap sushi?"

"I don't like sushi."

"But this is cheap sushi. It's really not even that similar. And there will be silly mixed drinks."

"When?"

———————◆———————

I don't know what the waiters at I Love Mr. Sushi thought of our party. I don't even know what I thought of our party. But we must have made a pretty picture. Jesus was there, too, appropriately enough in the middle of the table, but without his wig and robe, he just looked charming and roguish and did not give the effect of the Last Supper. Charice sat to his left and kept trying to order unusual dishes they did not have. Quail egg sushi! Monkfish liver sushi! Sponge! Beth was next to her, initially skeptical at the whole thing, but was soon won over by the ordering, which quickly became a kind of Mad Lib of unusual sea creatures.

Stephen not only told me who he was catting around with, he actually brought the cat and proceeded to paw him at our table. Very unlike Stephen, but then, I hadn't been keeping up with him as of late. His boyfriend was utterly improbable—this tall ginger guy named Osric Whiteleaf, which I feel is the sort of name that belongs on a level-seven druid and not a computer programmer in madras pants. But Osric was cool; I liked him. A little hipster-y, maybe, but who am I to judge? He also kept the topic off lyres, so yay. Masako was good for that too, alternatively frowning at food and smiling at everyone else. I don't know what I was thinking before—she had a great smile, on those occasions that she wheeled it out. Nathan and Shuler were both dressed to the nines, in their own respective ways, and were geeking out to each other about prog rock, of all things.

And I was there, wearing the shirt that Shuler had given me. "I Survived the Gamers Summit." I was feeling pretty damned epic.

Nothing important happened. Stephen and Osric told me

how they met, Masako talked about a play she had attended, Jesus (whose name was actually Daniel) told great stories about failed auditions, which Beth had a keen ear for. Nathan and I played verbal games. Shuler recounted another episode of *Interrupted Cop*.

And at some point I looked around the table at these clowns and thought: *Yeah. This is pretty good right here.* Maybe I hadn't imagined my life would go this way, with a madwoman ordering quail eggs and police detectives commenting on my capriciously colored pixie hair. But what does it matter how you want your life to go, anyway? What matters is that it goes. And things were purring along nicely.

ACKNOWLEDGMENTS

Confession time: I've never actually read an acknowledgments section before. Occasionally I'll assay one, but they always begin with something like "To my darling wife, Colleen, and our faithful Irish Setter, Swampy," and I suddenly decide that I am done reading. Are you done reading? I wouldn't blame you. Unless you're Colleen or Swampy, what's in it for you?

How about this? To things spice up, I have included secret instructions on where my FORTUNE has been hidden. They're very subtle, but read these acknowledgments closely, friend, and you may discover the riches of a lifetime.

First off, much thanks must be made to my husband, Clay "Begin at Harvard Square" Wirestone, who has put up with a lot of nonsense from me over the years. The sink is filled with unwashed dishes even now. Secondly, I must thank my unerring agent Caitlin "Face East" Blasdell, who helped shape the book immeasurably. Of no less importance is Devi "Fifty Paces" Pillai, whose insightful editing of this book has made it nearly readable.

Behind every writer is an even stronger critique group, and I bow down before the superior writers of the QK Cabal, a group whose motto—"Look for the Man with the Dolphin

Tattoo"—inspires me every day. I'm also indebted to my readers Caitlin "He Will Point the Way" McCuistion, Alex "Bring a Shovel" D'Souza, Carol "That's Not a Leaf Pile" Ayer, Cale "Dig Until You Find a Gold Key" Dietrich, and N. K. Traver, whose forthcoming book, *Now, To Baltimore!*, is bound to be a real hit.

Naturally, I have to thank my mother, Jane, who taught me from a very early age that I should visit First Regional Bank. And my father, Eddie, who told me that if I said in a firm and confident voice that my name was Carlotta Cho and that I have come for my lockbox, the bank tellers would hand it over, even if I did get some weird looks. A wise man, my father.

Finally, reader, I should thank you, even though you're probably pawing through my fortune right now. Oh, and I promised to thank Amanda from the Bon Ton. There's no clue there; I just needed to thank her. Seriously, that's not a clue or anything.